HOW TO DATE A DOUCHEBAG SERIES BOOK FOUR

HOW TO DATE A DOUCHEBAG

THE COACHING HOURS

SARA NEY

Copyright © 2018 by Sara Ney

First Edition: January 2018
Library of Congress Cataloging-in-Publication Data
How to Date a Douchebag: The Coaching Hours – 1st ed
ISBN-13: 978-0-9990253-9-0

Thank you, Internet, for providing the inspiration for the dating quotes at the beginning of each chapter. They're all based on *real* conversations, pick-up lines, come-ons, and texts between actual people.

For more information about Sara Ney and her books, visit:
http://www.authorsaraney.com

Stacy.
Well. Is it?

Eric Johnson
University of Iowa Wrestler

We've all heard whispers about her, but we never knew if they were true:

Coach has a daughter.

Some kid he didn't raise but has been living with him now—a transfer student from a smaller school out east. How do I know this? A few guys overheard him yammering on and on about her to some of the coaching support staff on a night they forgot the walls have ears.

"She's a chip off the old block."

"We're finally getting to spend time with her after all these years of her living with her mother."

"She must get her looks from his ex-wife."

Yeah, thank God for that last one; Coach is one rough-looking motherfucker. Short and angry and prematurely gray, I like to compare him to a wrinkled old troll who lives under a bridge, one who's seen better days. A pissed off, miserable old sonofabitch, I don't think I've ever seen the old man smile—not *once*.

Certainly not in *my* direction anyway.

I squat a few more times, beads of perspiration dripping down the indent of my spine, knees buckling under the three hundred and twenty-five-pound weights stacked on either side of the bar. I'm pushing myself harder than I've pushed since arriving to the Iowa wrestling program, the pressure to perform greater now that the new guy, Rhett Rabideaux, is threatening everyone's spot on the team.

With the team's two stars gone, I want every opportunity to steal a spot on Coach's good side, to replace those winningest few as the new golden boy and rise to the top.

They made us all look bad.

Like lazy fucks.

I do three more squats before I'm interrupted by Rex Gunderson, my roommate and the wrestling team's manager. The towel he's holding is accompanied by a water bottle with my name on it, written in Sharpie but wearing off.

"Wrap it up." He snaps me in the ass with the towel. "Team pow wow in five."

I press the weights again.

Bend.

Stand.

Squat. Drop the barb to the ground, stepping back when it bounces on the weight room floor with a satisfying thud.

"What's it about?" I snatch the white towel out of his hands before he can snap me a second time.

Gunderson shrugs beneath his black Iowa wrestling polo, looking like a complete fuckstick in his lame khakis.

"I don't know, they don't tell me shit anymore."

I don't point out that they don't tell him anything anymore because they no longer trust him; he can't keep his damn mouth shut, and he's always pulling pranks on people.

He babbles on, shrugging his bony shoulders. "Probably information about Clemson this weekend."

Probably, although there's nothing special about the Clemson University meet that would warrant an emergency assembly. Nevertheless, I peel off my sweat-soaked t-shirt and wipe down my chest, my neck. Give my blond hair a tussle.

I'm sweating like a whore in church, and it feels fucking great.

It takes three minutes to amble into the locker room, take a bench by my cube. Gunderson is standing in the doorway with a clipboard, taking attendance, making sure we're all accounted for, all assembled to hear whatever it is Coach has to say.

Must be important—I've only seen him take attendance twice in the entire two years I've been on this team.

3

"Ladies, listen up." Without preamble, Coach wastes no time. "I want your asses on the bus at nine sharp tomorrow—we're heading out early. Masters, I want you in the gym first light working on that form—you look like shit. You've been slacking lately." Donnelly leans against the metal desk at the front of the locker room, crossing his meaty arms. His weathered skin has seen its fair share of hard work.

He rubs his chin, the beard he's been cultivating gray and trimmed short.

"There is one more thing I want to mention before I let you leave tonight, gentlemen. One thing I want to make clear: my daughter—who I've thus far managed to keep far, far away from you ingrates—is going to become a student here." This earns some curious glances from the other members of the team, brows raised.

Coach continues. "When school starts, you will no doubt see her in and out of my office from time to time. She will be using the facilities to get her workouts in. I am telling you now, stay away from her. If I catch any of you sniffing around, I will hand you your ass so fast, when you wake up, your clothes will be out of style."

A few guys laugh.

Gray, tired eyes narrow. "I don't want you befriending her. I don't want you offering to play tour guide. I don't want you dating her."

I watch as Gunderson raises the clipboard to cover his mouth; the moron is probably smiling behind it.

"Be civil. Be gentlemen. Leave her alone. Are we clear?"

The room is silent.

"I said, are we clear?" Coach bellows when only a few guys nod. A few grumble.

"Yes Coach," we chorus like good boy scouts.

He grabs a spiral notebook off the desk and stands. "Get dressed and get the hell out of here. Check in tonight at eleven—I expect you all to be home."

I shuck my shorts, wrapping a towel around my waist. Hit the shower, the cool water sluicing down my hard body. Lather up, washing away the daily grime. I'm not the tallest member of the team, not the most fit or the best looking, but I do all right for myself.

Honestly, my record isn't the greatest either, but I don't suck, and at least I continue making the team—which is more than I can say for my roommate, who slinks to my side when I return to my locker.

Gunderson's bony shoulder hits the cube where I store all my shit, his beady eyes alive with a mischievous glint.

"Are you thinking what *I'm* thinking?" Rex starts in as I'm drying my thighs and chest, pulling on a clean pair of shorts.

"I have no idea what you're thinking."

Don't know if I want to know.

"About Coach's daughter."

"You mean the one he told us to stay the fuck away from?" I yank my bag out, dropping it on the ground. Toss in my sneakers. "*That* coach's daughter?"

"Yeah." He gets into my personal space, a little too close for comfort. "I bet you don't have the balls to bang her."

I pause, turning to face him for the first time since he walked over. "Are you out of your fucking mind?"

Why does he do this shit?

Why do we let him talk? I should tell him to shut the fuck up, put an end to this entire conversation, but resistance has never been my strong suit. If there was a big red button on the wall that said *DO NOT PRESS*…I would press it.

"The last time you had an idea, you got us into trouble."

The last time he had an idea, we plastered our ex-roommate's ugly mug on campus to help get the poor bastard laid. It worked—a little too well, because he promptly moved out and in with his smoking hot girlfriend, leaving us with his portion of the rent and a big empty bedroom we can't fill.

Not to mention, Coach is still riding our asses about all the pranks we pulled on him. The coaching staff kept calling it hazing—I mean, if you want to get technical about it, sure, maybe it was, but no one got hurt, or died, or had to pull their pants down in public.

The shitty part about it? Gunderson and I have had to keep our heads down, noses to the ground to stay out of trouble since they're watching us. I've had to bust my balls in the practice gym and on the mats just to prove all over again that I'm worthy of being on the team, of them keeping me on the roster.

Gunderson gets closer. "You can't tell me your mind didn't immediately go there when he mentioned her."

"No, I *can* tell you that." I grab a clean shirt out of my locker. "My mind didn't go there."

But now that it has...

"Why not?" he prods, breathing down my neck, lowering his voice. "You don't think you could fuck Coach's daughter?"

My head whips around and I make sure no one is listening. "Jesus Christ, could you not talk about that shit here? If anyone hears you, we're both fucked."

He backs up a pace, slugging my bicep. "Think about it, man. You banging Coach's daughter—bragging rights for *months*."

My shirt comes down over my head. "We don't even know what she looks like. She could be a brown bagger."

Brown bagger = someone you'd only fuck if their face was covered. Coyote ugly.

"Maybe she is, maybe she isn't—there's only one way to find out."

I ball up my towel and shoot for the cart in the corner of the room, aiming high and lobbing it dead center. It falls in easily.

"You need to stop with this bullshit before they kick you off the team."

"I'm not on the team," he stipulates. "I'm just the team manager. No chicks ever want to screw me."

That's true; in the food chain of life, as the team manager, Gunderson is on the bottom rung after girls feast on the endless banquet of athletes and other student body elite. They'd rather fuck a hundred of us than one of him.

He's a glorified water boy.

"Plus," he continues, grasping at straws, "you're way better-looking than I am."

Also true.

"Give me a reason why I should keep listening to your bullshit. Why I would jeopardize my spot on the team to do something so idiotic?"

Even if it would feel really fucking good if I could get her to go out with and screw me—whoever she is.

"You can't turn down a bet?"

Another good point: I never can turn down a bet.

I grab the hoodie out of my locker and slam the door shut. Spin the combination lock. "What stakes are we talking about?"

What the fuck am I saying?

Gunderson leans in, hand braced against the wall. "Let's make it interesting."

My laugh is hollow. "It would have to be *real* fucking interesting to get me to do it."

"First one of us to bang this chick—"

"Oh, you want in now too?" *What is that shit all about?*

"I had a few minutes to give it some more thought while you were resisting the idea."

Right, as if he has *any* thoughts going through that thick skull of his.

I laugh.

He frowns. "Don't think I can do it?"

I laugh again, hefting my duffel bag. "I know you can't."

He trails behind me like a lost puppy dog. "Winner gets the big bedroom—the one Rhett just moved out of."

7

I halt in my tracks. I've been dying to move into that fucking bedroom, but Gunderson and I both agreed when Rabideaux moved out that we could charge more rent for it since it's the largest of the three, and we need money more than either of us need a bigger bedroom.

"The big room?"

Cherry on top? It has its own bathroom.

He nods. Affirmative. "The big one."

Well *shit.*

The whole stupid fucking idea gives me pause.

Has me turning toward him, shit-eating grin spreading across my face, matching his.

Has me holding out my hand.

Gunderson holds out his.

I want that bedroom.

"Deal."

1
#DOUCHEBAG

"I want him to
remember me forever
as the vagina
that got away."

Anabelle

*A*nabelle.

My parents couldn't have chosen a more feminine name for me, but here's the thing, they didn't choose it because it was pretty or ladylike.

No.

They chose it because of *wrestling*.

Everything was always about wrestling.

Before I was born, the masculine part of my father wished for a son, as men often do, someone to carry on the family name.

The Donnelly family tradition: wrestling.

As far back as I can remember, the sport flows in the Donnelly family blood. It's my father's livelihood.

My Irish grandfather wrestled.

My father wrestled.

Instead of a son, he ended up with me, an Anabelle instead of an Anthony. Ana instead of Abe.

A little girl scared of her own shadow who, instead of taking an interest in her father's hobbies, clung to his leg. A little girl who carried around dolls and cried for her mother on the rare occasions he took pity on her and tried to teach her a few self-defense moves.

Back in college, when Dad was a novice wrestler at a junior college in Mississippi, he had a best friend on the team named Lucien Belletonio. Belle, they called him, though he was the very antithesis of such a feminine nickname—dark and broody and destined to be something big.

A champion.

My father's best friend.

The year before I was born, just five months after my parents met, Belle and my father were tapped for greater things.

Coaching.

Life was good and only getting better—Belle a rising star on and off the mats, my father with a new wife and a baby on the way—but then fate got in the way, along with five tons of steel, ending Belle's life and taking my father's best friend along with it.

Belle.

Ana*belle*.

Feminine and smart and strong.

My father never wanted to forget Lucien Belletonio, and now he never will, because he has me.

Mom didn't exactly make it *easy* to see or visit him after they got divorced, always citing one ridiculous reason or another. Your father is too busy with his career to have you stay with him. It's wrestling season. It's *almost* wresting season. He cares more about those boys than he cares about you.

I used to believe her.

Until I grew up and realized what she really meant was he cared more about those boys than he ever cared about *her*.

Me? I never felt abandoned by my dad, never felt left behind.

I grew older and wiser, started seeing Dad on television, on ESPN. Knew he was an important man with an important job, and I respected that.

It was my mother who didn't.

As a young woman with a small child, she wasn't willing to make the sacrifices many coaches' wives have to make, moving in the fall when coaching staff changes. Pay cuts. Pay increases. Promotions followed by demotions. Moving across the country, going where the jobs are.

The thought makes me cringe.

My feet move at a brisk pace on the treadmill, thoughts of my parents' divorce propelling me forward, the machine I'm on at a steep incline. Pushing me to my limits. Making me sweat. Making my legs climb and climb and run faster, pounding the rubber in time to the music, my entire workout a metaphor for my life.

It's time to move, Anabelle. It's time to move. My feet tap out the rhythm of the words.

It's time for a change. My legs burn out the chant.

It's time to—

"Hey, you almost done with this machine?" The question is followed by a tap on my upper arm, and I glance over, curious about the person with the gall to interrupt my workout.

I don't bother pulling out my earbuds as I shake my head, ponytail swaying. "Fifteen more minutes." My eyes assess the room, the empty row of treadmills. "You can use one of those machines."

I try to be polite as possible, but he's just standing there, watching me. His lips move, but with my ears plugged, I can barely make out what he's saying.

They continue moving.

I yank out an ear bud, holding it near my head. *"What?"*

"This is my lucky treadmill." He gives me a wide grin I'm sure he thinks will have me hopping off in a snap.

It doesn't. "Your lucky treadmill? You don't say."

I mean seriously, who's heard of such a thing? So dumb.

"Yup. Lucky number seven."

I do a quick scan, counting the machines from right to left. He's correct; I am on the seventh treadmill.

"Okay, well, give me another thirteen minutes, and it's all yours."

His arms cross. "I can wait."

"Can you, um, wait over there?"

His closeness is a tad invasive, unnecessary, and weirding me out.

Determined to ignore him, I pop the music back in my ears, cranking the volume to drown him out. His mouth moves again.

I point to my ears. "Music is too loud, I can't hear you."

His mouth curves into a smirk, a knowing little smile—and if I didn't know any better, I'd think his lips were saying, "Thank God you don't look anything like your dad."

That can't be what he said, can it? This guy doesn't even know me.

Doesn't know my dad is Coach Donnelly, the winningest coach in college wrestling history. Doesn't know I'm here to live with him and my stepmom until I can get my own place off campus, as soon as freaking possible because Dad's hovering is about to drive me nuts.

I understand his need to watch over me, I really do.

The man hasn't seen me in over a year, and I haven't lived within a thousand miles of him since I was eight, since my mom packed our bags and moved us to the east coast.

But I'm not a little kid anymore.

Dad can't know where and what I'm doing all hours of the day. He's been making my lunch like I'm in elementary school, leaving the lights on in the hall at night like you'd do for a child afraid of the dark. His wife—my stepmom, Linda—has been great, preparing the guest bedroom for my arrival, outfitting me with everything I need.

Or would have needed—for the dorms, or for when I was twelve.

Everything is pink.

The problem is—and this is a big one—I'm not a freshman anymore. I *don't* want to live with my parents, and I sure as hell don't want to live in the damn dorms.

I want a house or an apartment. I want to come home and sit on the couch in my underwear, eat pizza out of the box, and watch TV until two in the morning without having my father walk into the room to shut it off.

I want what I had *before* I transferred.

An apartment. A roommate.

Friends.

I love my family, but the college experience just isn't the same if you're living at home.

Sighing, I finally hit the twenty-minute mark with one mile under my belt for the morning. Not too shabby.

Tap the cool-down button on the controls, letting the treadmill slow on its own. Slow my gate from a run…to a light jog…to a walk. Look over and see the guy with the blond hair and cocky grin leaning against the wall, watching me. I study him right back.

The cutoff tee.

The biceps. The perspiration under his armpits, staining his shirt. His damp hair.

The wrestling logo on his shirt.

My lips purse.

I'm not judging the guy, I just don't want him knowing who I am. Not yet.

Not if he's a wrestler.

There's only one way to find out.

Four minutes left.

Two and a half.

I lower the speed, pressing until the machine hits a sloped two-point-six. Lazy, tired paces.

Blondie meanders over, headphones draped around his neck. "Done?"

I nod. "Done."

His hands rest on his hips—lean hips that are obviously in shape. He offers me a patronizing smile. "Thanks for understanding."

I fight the urge to roll my eyes. "*Right.*"

"You come here often?" he asks, approaching with a sanitizing wipe, beginning with the handles of the treadmill before I've even stepped off it.

"No. I'm new here."

"Junior?"

"Yup. Second semester transfer."

"From where?"

He's just full of questions, isn't he?

"A small school out east."

A real small Catholic college, if you want to get technical. The college where my mom went, in the town where she met my dad, back when times were good and he was beginning his coaching career. They were young and excited and hardly fought about all the time he was gone, leaving her alone.

Newly graduated and full of ambition, his first job was as an assistant conditioning coach at Holy Immaculate of Massachusetts College. He bumped into my mother coming around the corner near the gym, almost knocked her off her feet, and when he moved to help her up—well, the rest was history.

Until it wasn't.

I don't know why Mom pushed and pushed so hard for me to enroll there. She *hates* my dad with the passion of a thousand blazing suns, blames him for the breakdown in their marriage. Blames the college recruiting process, his driven nature to always want more, to be more, to *have* more.

To win.

I was young when they separated, but I can still remember them fighting every time he got a new opportunity at a new college or university, doing his best to advance on the coaching path. The next best school. The next level.

Until he landed Iowa.

Holy Immaculate must have held enough good memories for her because she pleaded with me to give it a shot, to give it at least one year until I transferred.

I gave her two and a half.

"What was your small school called?" the guy prods, done wiping down the handles, rubbing the wipe back and forth against the control panel.

Lost in thought, I've forgotten our conversation. "Huh?"

"Your last university—what was it called?"

Right. "Oh, you've never heard of it, trust me."

"Try me." He's so cocky it's almost unbelievable.

This time, I do roll my eyes. "Holy Immaculate of Massachusetts College."

His eyes widen. "Yup, definitely never heard of it."

I laugh at him; he's kind of goofy, if a bit relentless. I can't decide if it's annoying or refreshing—probably a bit of both.

I take his measure. Average, he has the look of a wrestler, no doubt about it: wide forehead, ears a tad bent, intense brown gaze directed at me.

I smooth a nervous hand down the front of my tight athletic pants, conscious of my appearance. Of my tight tank top, the sweat dripping between my boobs. The skin on my back squishing out of my sports bra. My mass of long, out of control, chestnut hair.

"Are you like—*holy*?" he enquires.

"Am I holy?" I play dumb. "What does that mean?"

He waves a hand in the air. "You know, are you saving yourself for marriage and shit?"

My nose goes in the air. "That's personal—I don't even know you."

His smirk is cocky, like he has me—and the universe—figured out. "So you *are* saving yourself."

I sigh. "Holy Immaculate is where my mom went. That's where she wanted me to go, so I…went."

"How did you end up here?"

I grab the towel hanging off the handrail, patting at the perspiration dampening my chest, the wet hairs at the nape of my neck. "Family."

My dad.

His discount as a member of the staff.

Iowa's stellar law program.

"What family?"

I shoot him a look. "Why are you so nosy?"

"Why aren't you answering me?"

"I don't know you."

"My name is Eric. You can *get* to know me."

"Maybe I don't want to." I laugh. "You seem like a total…" *Pain in the ass. Too pushy for my taste.* "You're a complete stranger."

"I'm not a sixty-five-year-old pervert, I can tell you that."

"Not yet, but you will be someday." It slips out before I can stop it and I cover my mouth, laughing. "Oops, did I say that out loud?"

He looks surprised. "Am I weirding you out?"

"You're coming on a little strong," I answer honestly.

"Coming on? What does that mean?"

My eyes narrow as I gather my things. "Look around you, pal. You cannot tell me you have to run on this same treadmill every day and if you don't, you'll have bad luck. That's such a load of crap."

Eric studies me, lip twitching. "Fair enough. Maybe I did want to come over here to meet you—do you blame me?"

"Making up a string of lies isn't a great way to start a friendship with someone."

"So we're friends now?"

I shrug.

He pauses, considering this information, looking into my eyes. Dark chocolate gaze slides down my nose to my mouth. Up again, to my hairline. "You look familiar."

"Maybe I look like someone you know."

"You know, you're right. You do."

"Who?"

I have a feeling I already know the answer, but I wait for him to fill in the blanks. He looks like a semi-smart fellow.

"I heard a rumor that one of the coaches here had a daughter."

I nod knowingly. "Ah, so you *are* a wrestler." God, I love it when I'm right.

"So what if I am?"

Ha! Yes! I knew it. "My father is the coach."

"You look nothing like him." He continues watching me. "Well, you kind of do, but you're much better-looking."

Obviously, I'm much better-looking. I mean, my dad is a *man*. Plus, he hasn't aged well. The stress of his job has definitely taken its toll, and he looks nothing like the man my mother fell head-over-heels in love with twenty years ago.

Whoever this wrestler is, he came over here knowing who I was.

I step onto the carpeted floor. "Eric, what's your last name?"

"Johnson."

I bank that away in my mind for a rainy day, just in case I need to shake down my father for intel on the kid.

"Well Eric Johnson, it's been swell, but I'm pretty sure my dad warned the entire team off me, and you've just lied to me twice. So, you're either hard of hearing or looking for trouble. Which one is it?"

"You don't think this meeting was purely coincidental?"

I squint at him, unable to read his blank expression. The guy has an amazing poker face.

Shooting me another friendly smile, the mischievous glint is telling me he's definitely interested in whatever he thinks I have to offer, or he wants to get on my dad's good side.

He's also kind of dopey but in a cute way.

Hmm.

Still, I decide not to give him the time of day. I have things to do, and his level of persistence can only lead to trouble, I'm sure of it.

"What's *your* name?" he calls out as I weave through the exercise machines, heading toward the locker room.

Jeez, why is he so loud?

Halting, I retreat, not wanting to yell back across the gym, not in a room full of athletes I've never met—*hot*, perspiring athletes. Did I mention hot?

"Would you keep your voice down?"

He does a mini shrug. "It's loud in here."

"Not so loud you have to shout."

"Sorry?"

"My name is Anabelle."

Eric Johnson, my new acquaintance—one my father will *not* be pleased about—sticks out his hand, offering it up for a shake. I hesitate to take it at first, certain my palms are sweaty and gross.

"Nice to meet you, Anabelle."

I can't say the same, but nonetheless, my hand slides into his, pumps his arm up and down, gripping his hand firmly. "Eric, it's been interesting."

"See you around?"

"Sure." Then I add, "Why not?"

"Hey Dad, is this a bad time?" My knuckles give a soft rap on the window to his office, located at the entrance of the wrestling locker room. He sits at his desk, head bent over a sheaf of papers, bright yellow sticky notes on his computer, walls.

His head lifts, happy to see me standing in the doorway. "Hey Ana Banana."

I used to hate when he called me that—he's been doing it since I was five—but now I'm so used to it, the nickname actually brings a silly grin to my face.

"Got a free minute?"

"Anything for my baby girl."

Oh brother.

I dial down my nervous energy and shuffle to one of the chairs in his office, a blue-painted cinderblock room with only a bank of windows separating it from the changing area, the showers.

A veritable fishbowl.

"I'm not going to accidentally see any naked wrestlers, am I?" Not that I'd be mad about it, but it might be embarrassing if my father was sitting beside me when it happened.

"Nope. No one should be getting here until"—he checks the ancient watch circling his wrist—"four."

I dump my backpack on the concrete floor, which at one time was painted beige but has now faded, and plop down in an uncomfortable metal chair. No luxuries for my old man.

He leans forward, already interested in whatever it is I'm about to say. "How are classes?"

"Good." *Real* good actually. "I was just on my way to grab a bite to eat. I'm starving. You want anything?"

I steal a peppermint from the bowl on his desk—the same brand he's eaten since I was young—and peel it open, pop it in my mouth. Toss the green wrapper into the nearby wastebasket.

"Why don't you just run home and grab something to eat?"

"Because I'm already on campus. I'll just grab a sub in the union shop."

"You don't have to eat in the cafeteria you know—the food here is utter shit."

There it is—my opening for the conversation I've been wanting to have.

"Actually Dad, that's why I'm here." I clear my throat, garnering my courage. "You know I *love* living with you and Linda, it's just...I think it's time to find my own place. It's been a month," I add hurriedly. "I think I've adjusted really well and there's no need for me to, you know, stay with you guys anymore."

Ugh, do I sound ungrateful? I feel terrible even bringing it up, but I really do need and want my own place.

Dad shifts in his seat, tipping it back until it squeaks, steepling his fingers in a move I've learned is his signature when he's thinking of what to say next.

"Have you started looking?"

"Not really. I'm not sure where to start. I thought maybe you could help me."

This puffs him up a bit, and he sits up straighter. Crying teenage girls, he knew nothing about. Scared little girls who missed their mother during a routine weekend visit, not a clue. Periods? Hormones? Boy troubles? No, no, and heck no. Those were all things he could never understand or help me with.

Finding a place to live?

That he knows a little something about.

I pat myself on the back for asking him. I hate that he feels like he failed me when my mother divorced him, hate that he missed so much of my life because of it—because he was busy chasing the dream while my mother only became bitter.

I can only wonder and imagine what it would have been like had they stayed together, tried to make it work. If my mother hadn't minded moving every December when he took a new job for the spring. I wonder if it would have felt like an adventure not staying in the same town my whole life.

My hands fiddle with the hem of my sweatshirt, the only warm thing I've unpacked since I got to his place, knowing—hoping—it was temporary.

"I don't want you living with strangers, Annie."

"Everyone here is a stranger, Daddy. I'm still meeting people."

"Then maybe now is not the right time to move into your own place."

"Well." I fold my hands on his desk. "Maybe that's the solution. Maybe I should get my *own* place—maybe I shouldn't do the roommate thing anymore. I'm a junior. I'll be twenty-two in no time at all."

His head lolls from side to side and he stares up at the ceiling. "Don't remind me. It only makes me feel old," he teases. Sits up again and directs his steely green gaze in my direction. "You really want to live alone?"

"Not *really*, but I don't want to wait. It might take me forever to find people to live with." I take a deep breath. "I love you Dad, and I love Linda. I just, you know, need my own space. It feels weird wanting to have my own guests."

"Sure you can!"

"Dad, come on," I deadpan. "By people, I mean guys."

If I ever manage to meet someone.

I ramble on as if his face hasn't just contorted into a horrified expression. "Can you imagine me sneaking someone into the house at night while you're asleep? I snuck friends in when I lived at Mom's. Man, she used to get so mad."

"Why would you have to sneak people in?"

"Uh, because she was strict, never really wanted me to have people over. It's not a big deal."

Dad's entire face changes and I feel guilty for bringing her up. "Anabelle, you know we will let you have people over. You don't even have to ask." He pauses. "Maybe not guys, but other people—girl kind of people."

I'm still laughing when a door opens inside the locker room and we both look, watch as a dark, broody figure stalks across the tile floor.

"Who's *that*?" My voice is breathy though I try to disguise it.

He cranes his head to look. "Zeke Daniels. He graduated but helps out from time to time."

My lips part and I feel my head tilt as I study him. I let out a little puff of, "*Whoa*."

"He has a girlfriend—and even if he didn't, I wouldn't want you anywhere near him."

My shoulders fall because *damn* he's good-looking.

"Which reminds me—you might meet him at a dinner Linda and I are taking you to. Probably his girlfriend, too."

I peel my eyes away...barely. "What dinner?"

"It's the Big Brothers program I've had a hand in sponsoring the last few years. Daniels is a mentor for one of the boys, along with a few of my other wrestlers. Anyway, there's an annual fundraising dinner at the end of February. Dinner, dancing, a silent auction. Linda and I enjoy it, make it a date night."

"Date night?"

Dad does that thing where he narrows his eyes ever so slightly to gauge a person's reaction—and no matter how much I school my expression, I know he sees the excitement in my eyes at the mention of a date.

"I told you, you're not allowed to date any of these assholes."

"Which assholes? You've warned me off practically everyone."

"The wrestlers. It just doesn't cotton." Dad's southern roots are showing. "I don't need you tangled up with anyone on the team. It won't end well."

"Won't end well for who?"

"Them." He picks at a yellow sticky pad, scribbles something on it, and slaps the square of paper onto his computer monitor. "Besides, you know I've already told each and every damn one of them to stay away from you."

"Some of them aren't the best listeners," I quip under my breath with a laugh.

My father doesn't find it the least bit funny, unflinching in his chair. "Who?"

A tiny shake of my head. "No one."

"Has one of them already come on to you?"

"No Dad. I was just making a joke."

"Anabelle Juliet."

"Oh brother, here we go with the middle name."

"I'm not shitting around here Annie. Half them boys wouldn't know their ass from a hole in the ground."

I smirk. "What about the other half?" *Those* are the ones I care about.

He levels me with an unamused stare. "Were you this much of a smartass with your mother?"

23

"Yes, kind of." It's one of the reasons Mom and I fought when I was a teenager. She couldn't stand my mouth or my sense of humor, said I reminded her too much of my dad. *Since when is that a bad thing?* I'd always smart back.

"The other half don't have time for dating, Anabelle. The other half are *winning* national championships and don't need the distractions."

Ahhh, there it is. "So *you're* the one who doesn't want the guys dating."

He scoffs. "Anabelle, not a single coach in the history of the NCAA wants their athletes dating."

I laugh, tipping my head back because he says it so matter-of-factly, like it should be obvious. "I get that Dad, but you can't control everything they do."

"No, but I can stop them from dating my daughter."

"What if I end up liking one of them?"

"That's not going to happen." His tone dares me to argue with him.

So I do.

"Seriously Dad, what if I meet one and they are just so hot and funny and captivating I couldn't possibly resist him?"

His fingers steeple again. "Lucky for me, *those* boys are already off the market. Is that what you kids call it? The meat market?"

"Worst metaphor, but sure." I shrug. "We'll go with meat market."

"I'm not kidding about this."

"I know that, Dad."

"Good." He makes a show of shuffling some papers to let me know we're done with this conversation. "Besides, I don't know why you'd want to date a wrestler to begin with—their ears are all funny."

"Are you making a joke?"

"Yes. Was that not funny?"

"Not really, because I think those funny ears are kind of cute sometimes." I'm giving him a hard time and he knows it. I rise from my seat and reach over, giving his earlobes a little wiggle. "Look at my daddy's cute little ears."

He swats at me, grouchy. "Stop it, people are looking."

I give him an eye roll worthy of my teenage self. "No one is looking."

Not if you don't count the wrestler shuffling around the locker room. Zeke Daniels catches my eye and scowls, immediately presenting me with his broad back as he changes into a gym shirt. The entire expanse of it is covered with a black tattoo that looks like a rising phoenix. Stark against his skin, hard lines with a dark mood.

Mysterious and hard and angry, just as he appears to be.

"Is he always broody like that? Or is it just me?"

"Daniels?" My dad cranes his neck again, peering through the glass. Grunts dismissively. "He's always like that."

"Why?"

"Suspect it has something to do with his upbringing. He doesn't get along with his parents."

"Ahh."

Neither of us speak after that, and I wonder if he's thinking the same thing I am. That a person's parents shape the person they become, whether they want them to or not. I mean, look at me—I have two perfectly normal parents who happen to be divorced, and in a way, it kind of did a number on me.

I moved halfway across the country to seek my dad's approval, to atone for my mother leaving him. I've taken enough high school psych classes to know this behavior stems from my past and has everything to do with my family dynamic.

"You wouldn't believe it," Dad is saying, "but he's really come a long way. He was such a goddamn prick last year, I almost had to suspend him."

I study Zeke through the glass, gaze roaming up and down his body, ogling. *Really Anabelle, in front of your father?*

Ugh.

"Suspend him? Why?"

"Piss-poor attitude—pardon my French."

"He doesn't look all that terrible."

Dad *hmphs.* "Looks can be deceiving, and I suspect his girlfriend has a lot to do with it."

"Have you met her?"

I watch as Zeke sits on the bench, back to us, lacing up a pair of black wrestling shoes and sliding a tank top over his head. Such *a pity*, covering his broad back.

"Once, at the Big Brothers fundraiser. I'm guessing by now, that blonde has him wrapped around her little finger."

Blonde? Typical.

Guys like that always go for the blondes.

ʼ   "Tiny slip of a thing, not much to her. Has a stutter."

Say what? "A stutter?"

"You know, a speech impediment."

"I know what a stutter is, Dad." My brows go up, curious. "*That* guy is dating a girl with a speech impediment?"

"He is."

I can't peel my eyes off him now, curiosity getting the best of me as I second-guess my initial valuation of him.

"What's she like?"

"Who, Violet?"

"Is that her name?"

"Yes." Dad steeples his fingers once again. "She volunteers a lot. Babysits. Small and quiet, I guess. I wouldn't have paired the two of them together in a million years, but I guess we can't choose who we fall in love with."

I can't decide if that's a dig at Zeke or at Violet's choice in romantic partners.

"Anyway, I have to hand it to the boy—he works his ass off for the team."

I would say so—he's an hour and a half early for practice, already wrapping his wrists. Tilting his head from side to side, head-gear dangling from around his wrist.

"Enough about him. We need to get your living situation squared away."

I breathe a sigh, relieved he's ready to talk about it. "Yes. Thank you, Dad."

"If you want to live on your own, I have nothing to say against it, but I don't want you in a shithole."

"They're all shitholes," I say, feeling the need to point out this unfortunate fact.

"True." He stands, coming around his desk. "Find a few options and we'll have a look. In the meantime, do your old man a favor and try to find a roommate, preferably one who studies a lot and likes to stay home, one who hates partying and boys."

"Haha." I rise too, wrapping my hands around his shoulders and squeezing. Give him a kiss on his weathered cheek. "I'll see what I can do."

"Love you, Annie." When he ruffles my hair, I let him.

I roll my eyes at the childhood nickname. "Love you too, Dad."

I've found the perfect little spot on campus to study.

Climbing the steps all the way to the top floor of the university's library, I weave through the peaceful space, past the archaic volumes of books, newspaper archives, and outdated, old-school periodical machines—you know, the ones where you search for articles from before we had the internet.

There are several study rooms on this level, but I choose a table instead. It's in the corner, tucked away, hidden behind a bookshelf almost five feet high.

No one would be able to see me if they came up here.

No one will bother me since I haven't seen a single soul the four times I've studied up here. It's peaceful, the perfect environment for getting homework done.

Five floors down, there are *way* too many young people. It's a place for students to socialize, yet another breeding ground for procrastination and flirting.

The damn library is like a nightclub.

I crack open my laptop and log into the school's social media site. Click through, searching the classifieds. *Roommates wanted* and *apartments for rent.*

Too expensive.

Too far from campus.

Six roommates in a four-bedroom house? No thanks.

I scroll on by, passing over anything old and outdated. The houses that look dilapidated and falling apart. The ads with no photos.

The rentals with pets? Pass—I'm allergic to cats.

Furnished would be fantastic; the last thing I want after moving out is to burden Dad and Linda with the task of scavenging for furniture with me. I can't imagine what that would cost.

Plus, Dad's in the middle of wrestling season; he doesn't have time to orchestrate an entire move, so if I could find something even partially furnished, I'd be winning at life.

Frustrated, I close out the website and open the document I started earlier for my ethics class, determined to pound out the required word count, resolute to ace this assignment.

School doesn't come easy for me; I have to work at it. Sometimes I'll be reading and by the end of the first paragraph or page, I have to go back and read it again. Memorization is not my forte.

The sixth floor remains silent and empty, except for me, and I wonder why it's not utilized. It's the perfect place for studying, and...other things.

You hear stories at other universities about the top floor of the library, stories about couples having sex in the aisles of books. The long, dusty rows are dark and secluded and unsupervised by employees.

I've never heard any such stories about the top floor of this one.

Bummer.

I push my earbuds in deeper, sliding the button for noise cancellation to on.

Drop my head and get to work.

"I was so lonely last night,
instead of actually watching porn,
I read the comments posted
below all the videos."

Elliot

The sixth floor.
                Empty. Secluded. Quiet.
                Just as I like it.

The lights are dull here on the top level of the library, almost as if it's the forgotten floor. Row after row of dusty books, some of them long outdated but never replaced, keep its few study tables company.

I move toward the same table I always occupy, in the corner to the right and all the way back. There's a window there, too, but it's nearly dark out, so there's not much to see outside but the glowing lights of the campus commons below and a few students hustling by hurriedly.

Rounding a corner rack of journals, I stop in my tracks when I see my table is already taken. A young woman sitting in my seat. Books set where *I* study. Feet propped where *I* prop my feet.

Shit, I hardly know what to do with myself.

No one ever sits there.

No one ever comes up here.

Pausing, I shove my glasses up the bridge of my nose, eyeing her up, only getting glimpses at the crown of her bent brunette head. She's hunched over an open book, one hand stroking a yellow highlighter along its pages, the other tapping the acrylic tabletop, nails clicking the surface.

Black long-sleeved T-shirt. Hair down over one shoulder.

She doesn't see me.

Doesn't look up when I grunt out my displeasure. Doesn't look up when I shuffle along, irritated, moving to find a different table.

I gaze at my options critically, not wanting to sit in a repressive study room for the next few hours while I kill time before my soccer game in the park.

Also not wanting a table out in the open in case someone else comes up and decides to get chatty, which has been known to happen occasionally.

Near the east-facing window, I settle on a desk with two chairs. Its location is a little too bright for my liking, but beggars can't be choosers, and until that girl packs up her shit and leaves, this desk will have to do.

Sullen, I get settled, using the second chair to rest my legs on. It's way too fucking small for my frame, and I gripe to myself as I set down my bag, laying out all my crap. Laptop. Water bottle.

None of it fits on the desk the way it fits on my normal table, and it's throwing off my groove. How am I supposed to study this way if I can't spread out?

I power up all my electronics and click open the paper I started writing yesterday. It's required to be a minimum of twenty-five ungodly pages long.

It's due in two days.

Neuroplasticity. Neural connections.

Fuck.

I'm *never* going to learn this shit in the course of one semester.

Cursing myself for declaring kinesiology as a major as the workload continues to pile on, I open the search engine on my computer. Find a diagram of nerve cells in the human body.

In the brain.

Begin jotting notes and set an alarm so I don't lose track of time and miss running with a soccer teammate. The minutes tick by and I stare at my laptop, overwhelmed by the assignment. I do everything but write my paper: message a few friends who have already graduated. Scroll through Instagram. Chug some water.

I take a quick break to piss, making my way back from the bathroom located in the far left corner, catching a side view of the girl—the squatter—glowing streetlamps outside hitting her in a way that has a halo circling the top of her head, long hair shining.

She's pretty.

She stole my table.

"Relationship status:
slept in the pile of laundry
I was too lazy to fold last night."

Anabelle

There are no available seats in the middle of the lecture hall, so I take two steps at a time, making my way up the center aisle, eyes scanning the back row for a chair. It takes a few moments, but I manage to locate one in the very last row, against the wall—the very last place I'd purposely choose.

I'm more of a front-row-center kind of girl, and the last row is usually reserved for those who want to rest their head against the wall and sleep during class.

Not me.

I've always found it difficult to budget my time between studying the occasional part-time job, and extracurricular activities. I wouldn't call myself unorganized, but...

I'm unorganized. That said, I try to do my best as much as I can.

I trudge up the stairs, my bag slung over my shoulder, heading straight for the seat sandwiched between a girl with green braids and a guy who *clearly* just rolled out of bed—mussed brown hair, unkempt, disheveled, as if he went to bed too late and woke a little too early, throwing on whatever he could find before blindly stumbling out the door.

He's wearing khakis, but they're as wrinkled as his gray, untucked polo shirt. With a little effort—and a shower—I bet he'd really be kind of adorable.

I give him a friendly smile when I park my rear beside him, setting my aqua backpack near my feet.

Instead of typing my notes on the computer, I get out a notebook and pen, intending to write them longhand. Later I'll go back and transcribe them into a document, hopeful the repetition will help me with memorizing all the terminology our professor is about to throw at us.

Pen poised above my blue spiral notebook, I give the guy beside me a sidelong glance. He seems okay. Friendly.

"Hi." He smiles, a charming grin with one slightly crooked bottom tooth, delivering a cheesy pick-up line. "Come here often?"

I give a tortured groan. "Actually, yeah. This is my second time taking a contract law class," I confess. "I should be teaching this course by now."

I don't know why I'm telling him this.

He scoffs. "Don't sweat it. If you need a study group, they have a sign-up sheet by the door. I've been to a few of them already."

"You think it's helping?"

He laughs, sliding down in his chair, feet spreading sluggishly. "Let me put it to you this way: my grade can't get any worse."

"Same, but I have high hopes this semester." I set down my pen and introduce myself. "I'm Anabelle."

"Gunderson. Rex."

"Gunderson Rex? That's kind of a fun name."

He laughs, knobby Adam's apple bobbing in his throat. "First name is Rex, last name Gunderson."

"It's still fun, however you say it."

"You think?"

I nod. "Sure! Is Rex short for something?"

"Yes, but I'm not telling you."

"Why not?"

"Because that's what you'll start calling me—everyone always does."

I laugh. "No, I won't. I'm not a complete asshole, promise."

Rex rolls his brown eyes. "That's what everyone says."

I nudge him, already taken with his casual demeanor and playful attitude. He's fun, non-threatening, and not at all aggressive—unlike a few other guys I've met on campus.

"Come on, just tell me."

"Fine." He lets out a groan. "It's short for Reginald."

"Reginald?" I don't think I've ever met a person under the age of eighty named Reginald.

"It's terrible, I know."

"Nah, it's kind of cute."

"Cute?" Rex rolls his eyes. "You're a shitty liar, but I do appreciate the effort."

"Thanks. I really had my game face on."

We pause when a student tries to slide by us, making their way to the end of the row, to the only other open chair in our section.

"So what's your story, Anabelle?"

My shoulders lift up in a casual shrug and I list my quick stats: Junior. Transfer from a small school in Massachusetts. Still trying to meet new people and make friends. Not acing this class.

"A transfer, eh? What's that like?"

"It's not what I thought it would be, honestly. This school is—phew—way bigger. By thousands." I laugh. "Still getting used to the giant campus, still finding out where everything is, where the best places are to hang out." Another shrug. "That sort of thing."

"Been to any parties?"

"Not yet. I wouldn't know which way to walk from campus."

Rex's arm shoots out, hand pointed toward the dry-erase board at the front of the room. "You walk that way until you hear loud music and see drunk people!"

I pretend to scratch my chin in thought. "Now why didn't I think of that?"

"You like parties?"

"Doesn't everyone?"

Down toward the front of the lecture hall, the teacher's assistant begins scribbling notes on the board with a black marker, glancing down at the sheet of paper in her hands before writing them, outlining today's lecture.

Class is about to begin.

"I'll write down an address—there's a party tonight if you're interested. Lots of chicks going. Maybe you'll meet some new people."

Chicks?

I try my hand at flirting. "Are *you* going to be there, Rex?"

And fail.

He shakes his head. "Negative, Ghost Rider, can't. I only go out once a week, and tonight's *not* the night."

"Why is that?" I wonder if he's on a sports team because I know most of them have curfews during the week, and most certainly the nights before games.

"I'm team manager. We have rules to adhere to." His chest puffs out a little, much like a peacock posturing. "It's my job to make sure the players follow those rules, so, you know, I have to set a good example. I'm pretty important."

"I see. Bet that's a huge pain in the rear."

"It can be, but with a position like mine comes a lot of responsibility. I'm part team manager, part social director."

My smile is wry; I find Rex amusing. Though he's not normally my type, his rumpled appearance and ridiculous conversation are charming.

"Social director? Is that an official position or one you made up?"

"I'd say it's just a well-known fact." He winks.

A projector gets clicked on by the professor, who saunters to the center of the room, remote in her hand. Nods to her assistant, who cuts the lights.

"All right everyone." Her voice booms out, slicing through the noise like a knife. "Let's cut the chatter!"

And just like that, class has begun.

Elliot

I don't know why I keep hanging around these goons; I swear, the more time I spend with them, the dumber I get.

But they were my old roommate's friends and for some reason, they keep coming around. So when they join me for lunch, I scoot over to make room at my table.

"Long time no see, man, how's it been going?" asks a big black dude named Pat Pitwell as he slides into the spot across from me. He's larger than life—huge—regarding me earnestly, like he actually gives a shit about my answer, unlike the other three morons.

"Good." I shove my sandwich into my mouth, tearing off a hunk of bread with my teeth. "Quiet."

"Living alone now?"

"Yup."

"Haven't seen you out at all lately."

"Nope."

Brian Tenneson—a guy I cannot fucking stand—leans closer.

"You're not living in Osborne and Daniels' shadows anymore—don't you think it's time to let loose and have a little fun?"

I glance at him sharply. "When was I living in their shadows?"

"Uh, only the last two years?"

I shrug. "Whatever man, you're dreaming. We're friends—it's fucking weird you'd see it as competitive, but whatever."

"I didn't mean anything by it, just meant it must be nice that they're gone, not there to steal your thunder."

"Dude, I don't have any thunder."

Everyone laughs.

"And there was never any competition between us."

I might not have played sports for the university like they did, but my roommates and I did everything together. Worked out when we could. Conditioned. Ran. Did homework at the library.

Sebastian helped me write a term paper or three, and Daniels bought and paid for my share of the groceries more than once.

So, *no*, I never felt I was living in their shadows, and we were never competitive with one another. Tenneson is just a little fucker with too much free time and way too much drama surrounding him.

"Don't you have anything more to add to this conversation? You always have something to say." I shoulder Rex Gunderson in the arm. "You've clammed up all of a sudden."

"Shit, hold that thought." His hand goes up, silencing us. "I see someone from one of my classes—I'm gonna go say hi."

"Suit yourself."

That "someone" from his class must be a girl, or he wouldn't give a shit about leaving to say hello. I don't know what it is about Gunderson, but he always manages to smooth-talk the ladies, always manages to have them eating out of the palm of his hands.

It hardly matters that he's the biggest dipshit of God's creation; girls fucking love him.

Gunderson pushes away from the table, standing, skimming his hands down the front of his pants to iron out the wrinkles. Finger-combs his messy hair.

"Dude, are you primping?" Pitwell deadpans. "No amount of grooming is gonna help you. You're hopeless."

There's a raucous chorus of laughter as Rex grabs his backpack in a huff. Turns toward the table before walking off. "Shut the fuck up you guys, and keep it down—I don't need you embarrassing me."

"You don't want us to embarrass you?" I crow, gesturing around the table, waving my sandwich in the air. "Are you hearing this, boys? He doesn't want *us* to embarrass *him*."

The guys are dying, falling all over themselves, loud and rowdy.

"Don't worry, bro. We won't embarrass you—you'll take care of that all on your own."

"If I dated you for less
than two months,
you're not allowed to call
yourself my ex-boyfriend.
You were only an experiment,
and your dick was small."

Anabelle

"**L**et's get real here—the only reason he wants to fuck her is because she's Coach's daughter. I heard she's not even hot."

At the word *Coach*, my interest is instantly piqued—naturally. I strain my ears, slowing down the elliptical machine I'm on to make it easier to hear. Resist the urge to turn my head and stare down the two guys talking, trying to figure out what they're discussing.

Maybe it's another coach's daughter?

One of them snorts. Grunts as he deadlifts a barbell. "Where'd you hear that?"

"Basketball player. Conrad was in here one night when she came in to talk to Donnelly."

Oh shit. It is me.

My stomach drops, and I instantly feel ill.

I can hear the skepticism in the other guy's voice when he says, "I don't know, man, Gunderson says she's locked up tighter than a vault."

Gunderson.

Rex Gunderson? That guy from my contract law class? I never in a million years would have thought he'd do something like this; he looks so unassuming.

Looks can be deceiving, and I just learned the hard way.

"Cute? He says that about anyone willing to bang him."

"Maybe." His breathing is labored, breaths coming hard. "The idiot says he's one more smooth-talk away from getting her into bed."

One smooth-talk away?

One.

He thinks I'm that easy? That I'd sleep with him after a few contract law classes—because he makes me laugh? That all he has to do is be nice and funny—and I'll *sleep* with him?

We've only attended a few classes together! He's never even asked me on a date!

What a dickhead!

"That's impossible," the guy is saying. "No way would any chick with half a brain purposely fuck that loser. He's a parasite."

The big guy shifts on the balls of his feet, the weight in his hands pumping up and down as his biceps flex.

"All I know is, Eric says somehow Gunderson became friends with her. You know how it is with him—for some fucking reason, girls love him."

"That's because he doesn't look threatening."

"Because he's so skinny. My sister could take that guy down."

The other sets his barbell down momentarily to laugh. "What does his weight have to do with anything?"

"Dude, my sister's always preaching about how she won't date any guy who weighs less than she does, and Gunderson is skinnier than everyone we know, including most chicks."

My cheeks flush; they're right—I immediately trusted him because he looks unassuming and nerdy and too thin to be any harm, like the dorky sidekick from a bad television sitcom everyone is annoyed by but still finds endearing.

"Little do they know what a friggin' moron he is. Bitches be learnin' the hard way."

What he says next is devastating.

"You know if Coach finds out those two were making bets about who could sleep with his daughter first, they'll be gone in a heartbeat."

My stomach finishes dropping to my feet; Rex was making bets about being able to sleep with me? I want to puke, toss my cookies all over my shoes and the elliptical machine.

"Donnelly would go through the fucking roof if he knew."

He lets out a huff of breath. "Do you think we should tell him?"

"I don't know, maybe. Maybe I'll ask my girlfriend tonight—she has the answers to everything."

"Yeah, ask her. The whole thing just doesn't sit well with me."

"I can't believe I'm even saying this, but me either."

I don't stand around waiting for the rest of the conversation. I've heard enough. I shut down the treadmill and hop off, grabbing my towel before fleeing to the locker room and grab my things from the locker before I burst into tears, not bothering to shower or change into clean clothes.

I make my way to the one spot on campus I know I can be alone before I have a panic attack.

The library.

"The best thing about
being single is sleeping around.
You can sleep all over
that bed of yours.
Middle, left side, right side.
Wherever."

Elliot

Fiddling with my headphones, I pull one of the earbuds out to adjust the tiny piece of plastic, hesitating to put it back in when I hear a soft whimper.

Then a cry, and it's coming from my usual spot in the corner, which was once again occupied when I arrived.

I tap my pencil, staring in the direction of the back.

Curious, but also...

Concerned.

Rising to my full height, I slowly make my way toward the sound.

Yup, someone is definitely crying, and it sounds like a girl.

Weak. Low. Barely perceptible sobs.

A hiccup.

I move closer, feet shuffling against the carpet, hoping to make just a little noise so I won't spook her.

"Hey." My voice is gravelly, gentle.

Her head comes up at my words, face splotchy from tears, red marring her skin, chest, cheeks.

Lips parting, she brushes the hair out of her eyes, the long brown strands glossy under the neon light.

She swipes a hand across her face, batting at the tears, dabbing them away. Dries them on the leg of her jeans, all without lifting her gaze to face me.

I advance a couple paces, stopping a few feet away.

"Are you okay?"

Another hiccup and she's dipping her head deeper into her black Iowa hoodie. "I'm fine."

She doesn't *look* fine, certainly doesn't sound fine, not even close. Those aren't happy tears.

"W-Was I bothering you? I'm so s-sorry, I..." She can't keep the crying out of her voice as she swipes at her rosy cheeks again, doing her best to hide it. "I'll try to stop."

Hiccup.

"Do you want to talk about it?"

"No." She pauses, voice muffled. "But thank you."

She looks up at me then, and I can see that her eyes are blue—a brilliant blue from the weeping, set ablaze by the redness of her blush-stained skin.

Dark brows.

Chin trembling, she offers me a wane smile, and I realize I know her; it's the same girl who was here earlier in the week, the one who stole my study spot.

"You're sure?" I have two sisters, so I'm kind of an expert on when girls are bluffing; this one is trying to get rid of me.

"I'm sure."

I pull down the brim of my ball cap, tipping it in her direction.

"Well, I'm just across the way if you need anything, at the desk in the corner. Paper, pencils, body chalk for the corpse if you need an accomplice." I give her a wide smile.

She tucks the hair behind her ears. "Thank you. That's very kind."

"All right, well, I'll just be..." I point over my shoulder. "Give a holler."

"Thanks."

I meander back to my desk slowly, listening for the telltale sign of sniffles. Weeping. Sobbing.

Anything.

Despite hearing none, I have a hard time getting back to work, unable to focus, straining for noise on the other side of the room, and before I know it, I've wasted an entire forty-five minutes doing jack shit.

Deciding there's no hope for it, I start packing up my crap.

"Hey." A small voice practically whispers, interrupting.

Backpack slung over one shoulder, long hair now pulled back into a sleek ponytail, the girl bashfully approaches my table, face still red, eyes tired.

But friendly.

I bet when she's not ugly-crying all over the library study tables, she's actually kind of cute. Pretty.

"I'm heading out, but…I just wanted to say thanks for coming over to check on me, and, you know, being a concerned citizen and all."

She musters up a weak smile.

"Don't worry about it, I have sisters—I've been down this path a time or two." Or a hundred, usually under duress.

When I was younger—ganglier—my sister Veronica used to sit on my chest to hold me down while she spilled her guts so she'd have someone to talk to. I had to hear all about her drama—drama with my parents, with boys, with her friends.

Her teen years were my worst nightmare.

"So are you feeling better?"

Her smile is wobbly. "I am. *Much* better."

I shift on the balls of my feet, hands stuffed in the pockets of my jeans. "That's good."

"I'm…" she considers her words. "I'm new here this year and it's been…a challenge meeting new people. Everyone has their friends."

The backpack I've hoisted over my shoulder gets set down on the study desk.

"Yeah?" I want to ask her *how* it's been challenging, but don't want to pry. Still, it seems like she needs someone to talk to, and I have a little time to kill, so I sit back down in my chair. "How?"

She shifts, worrying her bottom lip, and I can tell she's holding back, unsure about invading my space and taking up more of my time.

"Want to sit?" I grab a nearby chair, dragging it over as a gesture of encouragement.

"Uh…sure." Tentatively, she closes the space between us, pulling the chair out the rest of the way. Sets her bag next to mine. "But only if it's not a bother?"

"Nah, I have a few minutes."

"All right." Pause. "Is this weird? I'm so sorry my crying interrupted you before—I'm really embarrassed about that."

"You were crying? I thought that was a herd of dying cats,"

I joke, failing to mention that her crying was less irritating than her hogging my favorite study spot.

"Haha, very funny." She laughs, sniffling. "But also true."

"We've all had our shitty days—this one was yours, I guess."

"Yeah." She's quiet for a few beats. "So what was it I interrupted? What are you working on?"

"Human anatomy paper. Tedious."

"That sounds…" her voice trails off.

"Boring? It is."

"Boring is *not* at all what I was going to say! What's your major?"

"Kinesiology." I grab the water bottle out of my bag and take a long pull, trying to stay hydrated. "What's yours?"

"Pre-law."

My brows go up. "What's your focus?"

"I'm thinking family law."

I smile. "My dad is a lawyer."

This news perks her up. "Really? What kind."

"Real estate. Mergers and acquisitions."

"Whoa, fancy."

It kind of is. "He loves it." I rack my brain for something new to say, blurting out, "So do you want to tell me what's wrong?"

Her shoulders sag. "Not really. It's kind of embarrassing."

"Why, did you do something stupid?"

"Maybe. I don't know—I guess time will tell."

"Time will tell?" I ask slowly, treading lightly.

"As in, nine months from now?"

"What?" She looks horrified, the implication turning her face an unflattering shade of red. "No! No, that's not even remotely close. God no."

"You know what, forget I asked."

"Is it weird that I kind of want to talk to you even though I don't know you?"

"No, it's not weird, because you don't know me and I'm not going to judge you. Plus, I live alone and wouldn't have anyone to tell when I get home, haha."

Her lean fingers toy with my notebook, bending back the edges nervously.

"So there are these guys," she starts.

There always are.

I nod. "Uh huh."

"Why does this have to be so embarrassing?" Her hands cover her face self-consciously and she shakes her head. "Phew, here goes nothing!" She takes a deep breath. "Okay, so, you know how some guys are complete assholes, and occasionally you hear about, like, fraternity guys or whatever betting that they can sleep with a girl?"

"Yeah. Happens all the time."

"Well it happened to me."

I'm ramrod straight, unmoving as she blushes bright red, silently waiting for her to continue.

"They, um..." Her tongue darts out, licking her lips. "They had a bet to see who could sleep with me, and I overheard some guys talking about it in the gym."

"Were they laughing about it?"

"No, not these guys. They seemed upset about it—actually, they were discussing whether or not to rat out their friends."

"Do you know who the guys are?"

"Yes."

"Did you end up actually…" my sentence trails off and I can't bring myself to ask her if she actually slept with the guy. Man this is awkward.

Her head gives a shake. "God, no, I'm not desperate. Or stupid. What is wrong with someone that they'd make a bet like that? What assholes."

"Who were they?"

"Some guys who know my dad."

"How do they know your dad?"

"He's…" her voice stalls. "He works here."

"Staffer?"

"Coach."

I sit back in my seat, eyes glued to her face. "Are they players?"

Slight nod.

I let out a low whistle. "Holy *shit*." Talk about shitting where you eat. "Does your dad know?"

"No, and I'm not going to tell him—not yet anyway. I have to give it more thought."

I don't point out that she won't have to; these things have a way of being discovered all on their own. Her dad will find out soon enough.

Snitches, snitches *every*where.

"Do you mind me asking what sport he coaches?" Curiosity gets the best of me. "I won't say anything, promise."

Her response is a long, weighted pause as she considers whether or not to tell me.

Her lips move, the low mutter barely audible.

"Say again?"

"Wrestling."

Wrestling. Coach Donnelly.

I've never met the man personally, but last roommates were wrestlers and have shared plenty of stories over the last few years.

From what I've gleaned, the man is sharp, shrewd, and tolerates *zero* bullshit.

"I might have heard rumors that they've had problems with some people on the team."

"Rumors?"

"Yeah. Last year a few guys were busted for hazing a new member on the wrestling team. Half of them faced suspension."

"Really? Wow, I didn't know that—I'm surprised my dad never said anything." She tilts her head curiously.

"He never railed about it in front of you? He had to have been pissed."

"I actually didn't live with him until this semester, and our phone conversations were always about me." Her shoulders slouch. "Man that sounds selfish."

"No, it sounds like you didn't have tons of time to sit on the phone talking about his job. He wanted to hear about you, not complain."

She bites back a smile. "Tell me more about the hazing. Do you know anything about it?"

I'm quiet, racking my brain for specific details.

"So I only know this information because my roommates were wrestlers and they would come home and bitch about it. Last year, when a new guy joined the roster, they gave him shit. Stuck him with a restaurant tab, ditched him at some cabin in the woods, shit like that. It probably seemed like harmless fun, but it wasn't. I'd tell you to ask your dad about it, but he probably won't discuss it if he hasn't already."

"Why?"

"Confidentiality."

Her, "Oh," is small.

"Have you considered telling him about these dickwads?"

"No. Well, yes, but he would totally lose his mind. This is our fresh start and it would, I don't know, make him *so* mad. He'd freak, and I don't want to ruin the semester." Her sigh is loud. "Why do guys do stuff like that?"

"*Stuff?* You mean act like fucking idiots? I have no freaking idea since I generally try not to act like one."

"I can tell."

"How?"

"I don't know—you have a way about you. You're more mature, and you're not... you're just different."

Anabelle

This guy is kind of awesome.

He's gazing at me insightfully, waiting for me to say something, to tell him what happened that had me so upset I was ugly crying in the back corner of the library.

So upset that I interrupted his studying.

Ugh.

As if that wasn't embarrassing enough, the guy is really cute, and it's never fun making an ass of yourself in front of a complete stranger you find attractive. Like, shoot me now.

He waits me out with a neutral expression schooled on his face, dark brows dipped into a worried line. They're darker than his hair, a rich brown, expressive, arching and bending with each word I utter.

I noticed his height when he first approached my table, tall and toned with a gray T-shirt stretched across a set of broad shoulders. Tapered waist. Eyes I can see are green now that I'm up close.

A tiny cleft in his chin I'm finally forced to peel my eyes off of.

"As I mentioned, I, uh..." *Could he not study me so intently? He's listening so hard it's making me nervous.* "I overheard some guys in the weight room talking about me."

"What did they say?"

I lower my voice into a false baritone. "Let's get real here—the only reason he wants to fuck her is because she's Coach's daughter. I heard she's not even hot." I pause. "In a nutshell."

"Not hot?" The guy laughs, tipping his head back. "Well we know *that's* bullshit, and I can say this because I'm not trying to hit on you. You are definitely *not* a brown bagger."

That's his take-home factoid from all that? "Uh...thanks?"

"The good news is, now that other people know about it, it won't be a bet for long. It *will* get back to your dad, trust me."

"Yeah." My voice is small and I hate it. "I bet it will."

"Was that a joke?"

"Not on purpose."

"I'm not trying to tell you what to do or anything, but maybe you should stay out of the weight room for a while, just until you figure out what you're going to do, until the whispers die down."

"Maybe, but I still have to exercise. If I see either of those guys, it'll make me want to…"

"Cry?" he supplies when I don't finish my sentence.

"No, punch them in their faces."

He draws back with another laugh, his whole face changing.

Jesus, that dent in his chin—so freaking *ugh*!

"I doubt anyone would blame you if you planted them a facer, and Donnelly wouldn't either."

I sigh into my hands. "Yeah, my dad's been known to support a good, swift kick to the groin."

"That would level them to the ground, for sure."

"That doesn't solve my problem though—I have class with one of these guys."

"Right." His voice is smooth and steady like a rich whiskey. "What are you going to do?"

"Besides avoid him like the plague? I don't know, I'll have to think about it, maybe Google voodoo magic and revenge spells."

"Well, I'm here all the time if you want to run any ideas past me." He chuckles low and deep.

And that's my cue to leave.

"I should get going." I rise, collecting my things. "See you around maybe?" I glance at him over my shoulder, silky hair swaying.

He lifts his hand in a wave. Smiles. "Take care. I'll see you around."

"Thanks for, you know, listening."

"No problem. Good luck."

I saunter away slowly, checking my phone, shooting him another glance over my shoulder. He's watching me, that handsome smile plastered on his classically handsome face.

What a nice freaking guy, unlike those assholes on the wrestling team.

I feel so much better after getting everything off my chest, but my mind still reels, not quite ready to let Eric Johnson or Rex Gunderson off the hook.

Those douchebags need to learn a lesson.

And I'm just the girl to teach them.

"Someday you'll meet someone amazing. And they won't text you back, either."

Anabelle

"**W**e have to stop meeting like this."

Without even looking, I know it's Eric Johnson—that fucker—standing next to the treadmill, lurking.

It takes every ounce of self-control I have not to turn on him. Scream. Knee him in the nuts. "Meeting like what?"

"At our special spot."

My legs continue moving to the rhythm of the music beating through my headphones, the thumping bass a lively melody I was enjoying until a moment ago, praying I wouldn't run into him.

Seems God wasn't taking requests this morning.

"This is not our special spot, but nice try. This is you interrupting while I'm trying to get my workout in."

"It could be our special spot if you let it."

I remove my earbuds, an exasperated sigh building in my throat. I force it back down. "You're pushy, aren't you?"

"Is that a bad thing?"

"I'm just trying to figure out if it's a jock thing or an asshole thing."

He clutches his chest in mock pain. "Ouch! So angry today."

I laugh because I can't help myself; the look on his face is priceless. So dramatic. "Well? Which is it, jock or asshole?"

"Honestly? A bit of both."

I hit the speed button on the machine, dropping it from a light jog to a walk, slowing so I can get a better look at this guy, the one who made a disgusting bet with Rex Gunderson, who has the gall to think I'd be interested in sleeping with him.

"Can I be honest with *you*? You drive me nuts."

"Nuts in a good way or a bad way, because I photocopied mine once."

"You photocopied your nuts? Why?" I hold my hand out to stop him because I don't actually want him to answer. "Never mind, I don't want to know. I meant it in a bad way."

I grab the towel hanging off the treadmill, tossing it around my neck, intent on heading to the locker room, hoping he won't trail behind me.

He does, because he's dense, quickening his pace to keep in step. "What's your name?"

I halt.

"I've told you before, *Eric Johnson*." I throw out his name to rub in the fact that he forgot mine so quickly. "We've already exchanged names."

"Sorry. I meet a lot of people." He doesn't look the least bit apologetic.

"I just bumped into you a few days ago."

"Can we start over?"

I keep walking, waving him off. "Nah, we're good."

"Lilah, wait up."

I roll my eyes. Stop in my tracks. Spin on my heel to glare at him. "It's Anabelle—Lilah isn't even close."

Eric Johnson grins. "I *knew* you'd tell me your name."

"Oh my God, you're—you're such a…" *Douchebag.*

His stupidity has rendered me speechless, and I wonder what my dad would say about all this, what he'd say if he knew Eric was making bets and stalking me around the gym.

"I seem to have that effect on all the ladies."

"You're not having an effect on me."

"I'm not?"

When I laugh, it's a little too loud, turning a few heads in our direction. *Oops.* "No, you're not."

"What's it going to take to get a girl like you to go out with a guy like me?"

A girl like me? That's weird, I thought he said I wasn't hot, which in guy speak essentially means *unfuckable*. Curious, I face

60

him, giving him the smallest fraction of my time. "What do you mean, a girl like me?"

"You're obviously out of my league, but I want to take you out anyway."

"I can't believe you're basing this all on my looks—I haven't exactly been pleasant."

"That's because you're gorgeous. I don't expect you to be nice—hot chicks usually aren't."

Oh boy. Now he's laying it on a little thick. I'm not completely unfortunate, but I'm also not winning any beauty pageants either.

"Just let me take you out once. If you can't stand me, I promise you can tell me to fuck off."

I gape at him incredulously. What would have made him think I'd want to go out with him?

He tries again. "What if I meet you somewhere—you don't even have to tell me where you live."

An idea takes root, burrowing deep in my imagination, picturing Eric Johnson arriving at my father's house to pick me up for a date.

My dad would kill him.

And Eric Johnson would be in for one hell of a surprise.

A rather unpleasant one.

The look on the kid's face alone might be worth whatever drama it would cause, just to see his reaction when my dad yanks open the door of the house.

The thought has me positively giddy.

"Tell you what, Eric, I'll give you one…let's not call it a date. Let's call it hanging out. I'll hang out with you once. If you drive me nuts, I'm calling time-out and you're taking me home. Do we have a deal?"

He nods enthusiastically. "Deal."

"I'm not going to text you my address—I don't need you knowing my phone number—but I will write it down for you."

"I'm picking you up?"

"Sure, why not." I write down my address, giving him an evil grin beneath my lashes. "See you at seven. If you can get past my doorman, you have yourself a buddy for the night."

"What, do you have a guard dog or something?"

Another grin. "Something like that."

"Dad, can you get the door?"

It's Friday night on one of the only weekends Dad's been home at a reasonable hour, and I watch from the top of the stairs as he hauls himself up out of his old recliner, hobbling with a slight limp, knees crooked, toward the foyer.

He's still in his typical uniform, the one he wears to wrestling practice every day: black Adidas track pants, black Iowa wrestling T-shirt, and track jacket to match, zipped to the neck.

Baseball cap.

Cantankerous set of his mouth.

Along with my dad hobbling to the door, the normal sounds of the house can be heard. Linda puttering in the kitchen cleaning up their dinner, the television set to ESPN, the worst watchdog in the world snoring at the foot of my dad's chair.

Anxious, I flip my long hair, laser-focused on the front door from my perch on the landing of the stairs, hidden from view. A devious smile spreads my lips when Dad finally grips the door handle, turning, pulling it slowly open.

He peers through the screen.

"Johnson." I hear the censure in his voice and grin wider. "What the hell are you doing here?"

Silence.

"Well?" Dad demands impatiently. "Did something happen?"

"I…" Another long stretch of silence before Eric finds his voice. "I didn't know you lived here."

Yikes.

That sure as hell wasn't the right answer.

"Who did you think lived here, Johnson? Huh? You lost?"

"I don't know, sir." He sounds panicked, ill-prepared for a battle of wits with Harry Donnelly.

"Then what do you want? Speak up," he continues, lecturing, "Johnson, it's Friday night, on your one weekend off. How did you find yourself on my doorstep?"

"I have the wrong address, sir."

"You boys pranking me? Is that what this shit is about?" I can see him moving toward Eric, leaning over the threshold so he's nice and close, intimidating. "You think I'm going to forget about the hazing bullshit you pulled last year with your pal Gunderson? Do you?"

"No, sir."

"Then I'm going to ask you again: what the hell are you doing on my porch in the middle of the godforsaken night?"

Middle of the night?

That's a stretch—it's barely seven o'clock.

Eric can't summon up a reply, so my dad fills the silence for him. "You better have the wrong goddamn address, son. If you're here for the reason I think you're here for, you better hop back in that piece-of-shit car you own and drive away. I don't wanna see your face *anywhere* besides the goddamn gym, do you hear me?"

"Yes, sir."

"And stop calling me sir. It's grating on my last damn nerve."

"Yes, sir." He gulps. "Sorry, sir. Shit. All right. Sorry."

My father huffs, aggravated. "You have three seconds to get off my goddamn porch."

Through the upstairs window above the doorway, I watch him stumble backward across the lawn as my father slams the door and locks it. Slides the deadbolt in place. Stands, hands on his hips, peering through the sidelight windows as the junior wrestler turns tail and power walks across the yard. Jumps into his red, beat-up pickup truck and guns the engine.

Screeches away from the curb, drives off without looking back.

It's almost comical.

"Dad, who was it?" I sound innocent and guileless.

My old man turns, glowering up the stairs, leaning on the newel post. "Don't be coy with me—you know damn well who that was."

I can't stop the laughter that bursts from my lips. "I'm sorry, Dad. I couldn't resist. He's been driving me crazy at school and wouldn't leave me alone."

"How?"

"I go to the gym to workout, not get hit on, and that guy cannot take a hint. I just wanted you to scare the shit out of him. He needed to learn a lesson."

Nothing is mentioned about the bet or how I've been battling about whether or not to tell my parents.

Dad's brows shoot up into the brim of his cap. "I'll do more than scare the shit out of him tomorrow in my office."

"Dad, please. Tonight was enough to cure whatever notions Eric Johnson has about pursuing me." My voice holds a warning. "He's wicked stupid if he continues harassing me after tonight."

Dad's meaty arms cross. "He's a good wrestler, but no one has ever accused him of being smart."

I make my way down the steps, yoga pants a little too long and dragging along the carpet, oversized sweatshirt engulfing my entire frame. I envelop my father in a hug, inhaling the familiar smell of him: the gym, sweat, and the same cologne he's worn since I was little.

He pats my back awkwardly, not comfortable with displays of affection. "You're not going out tonight?"

"Not until later, Dad—no one goes to a party this early. I have a few contract law flashcards to make. Torts and malfeasance don't learn themselves, you know."

His gaze sweeps my face, analyzing my expression. "You start apartment hunting yet?"

"Apartment or *house*?" I can't keep the optimistic inflection out of my tone.

Dad's head lolls from side to side, a low "Ehhh," rising from his throat. "We'll see about a house. I'd prefer you in something more secure, somewhere with locks and gates and guards."

"They don't have those here, Daddy." I don't call him that often, but for whatever reason, the word just seemed to fit, felt right. "My last apartment had a wooden fire escape and a couch with a giant hole in the middle. The springs would stab us in the ass if we sat down too fast."

He hefts a heavy sigh. "How did I not know this?"

"Because I never said anything when I sent you a copy of the lease. I wanted you to sign it, not tell me I couldn't live there."

"I would have forbidden you to live there."

"I know!" I rise to my tiptoes, giving him a loud peck on the cheek. "I'm going to hibernate before I go out, maybe take a shower." Plant another kiss on his weathered face. "Thanks for taking care of Eric Johnson."

"I've got my eye on him."

My eyes narrow. "Trust me, so do I."

"Drunk me loves creating
awkward situations
for sober me."

Anabelle

I am going to a party tonight, and I am going to drink those assholes out of my system. I'm going to forget their idiotic plan and what the douchebags were planning for me.

One.

Drink.

At.

A.

Time.

Why does it bother me so much that a bunch of half-grown men would make a stupid bet involving me? They don't even know me, couldn't identify me in a lineup. I could have been any girl on campus—or the planet, for that matter—and they still would have done it.

So why did it make me cry?

Why did it piss me off so bad I'm at this dumb party getting wasted so I can forget about it for one night?

Because it was humiliating. Hearing yourself talked about like that, in such a derogatory way, by complete strangers? Terrible. Not climbing down off that elliptical machine and defending myself is something I'll regret for a long time, even though the two guys talking about me were defending me.

Well, not defending me, but they didn't condone Eric and Rex's behavior, either, and to me, that's enough for now. In a way, that makes them semi-decent guys who probably didn't deserve me going psycho on their asses.

Another reason I'm out tonight is my new friend Madison. I met her today in one of my classes when she pulled up a seat during the one lab I have this semester to complete my science gen-ed credit, and we hit it off. Apparently, every Friday night she and her friends hit Jock Row—the off-campus party scene comprising student athlete housing—to chase jocks, hook up, and get drunk.

Which Madison has yet to do.

She's remained somewhat sober until this point while I've admittedly been tipping them back faster than a frat boy. I'm pretty sure whatever's in her red cup isn't running out as fast as mine.

"Are you sure you don't want to switch over to water or something?" she asks when I stare down into my empty cup. "I did."

"It was ten bucks for this thing and I'm getting my money's worth."

"I mean...beer downtown is cheaper," she points out. "And it doesn't have all that foam."

True.

"But look how cute I am with a foam mustache." I lick it, laughing. "Where do you even find water in a place like this?"

It's packed, the only visible liquid beverage in the form of the keg or a shot.

Madison takes a drink of her beer. "I went rooting through the fridge, they had it stocked. Also, it was unlocked, so that was convenient."

"They lock their fridge?"

"I guess?"

"That's weird."

"Ya think?"

"What's the deal with this place? Don't people usually party on Greek Row?"

"Yeah, but a few years ago the alumni donors started buying up houses for the student athletes, fixing them up really nice, and it just became another place to go. It's basically a meat market on the weekends because, guys."

"My dad says meat market!" I giggle.

"Didn't you say he works for the university?"

"He's the head wrestling coach."

"Wow. So you're like a big flashing target."

"What do you mean?"

"Are guys lining up to date you?"

"Not exactly."

"I mean, wrestling is a huge sport in Iowa. Those guys are treated like royalty around here. You would think once word got out that the coach's daughter goes here…"

I chug miserably at Madison's innocent reminder of why I'm here in the first place—drinking my woes away.

"Oh, word got out all right."

"Why do you say it like that?"

"Some blowhards"—I hiccup—"on the team decided to have a little fun with it and made a disgusting bet about who could sleep with me first."

"Shut up, no way!"

"Way. My dad told everyone on the team to stay away from me—like, first of all, thanks Dad. Secondly, it's some guys who have already been in trouble for this kind of thing."

My new friend is fascinated now. "No way."

"Yes! And it's been terrible the last couple of days, because it's humiliating and the guys are all talking about it. I was bawling in the library yesterday after I found out."

"How'd you find out?"

"I overheard it in the gym. I guess not everyone knows I workout in there. Keep your voice down at least!"

Madison reaches out and squeezes my arm. "Hey, you didn't do anything wrong. All you have to do is tell your dad and I'm sure he'll take care of it. Guys like that don't deserve to shit in our same zip code when they do crap like that."

My head dips, the last few healthy chugs of beer taking effect. "Ugh, I would, but I just moved here, and my dad and I are just getting to know each other again—no way could I tell him. I hate being dramatic. I'm his little girl."

"Right…" She drags the word out. "That's why you obviously need to tell him. Dads want to take care of that shit for their kids, Anabelle, and these guys—who, by your own admission are repeat offenders—need to be taught a lesson."

"You sound like such a lawyer."

"I'll take that as a compliment." She grins. "Even though I'm studying nursing."

"I'm still not telling my dad. I want to handle it myself. I just need to figure out how."

"Okay, but do you really think getting trashed at a house party is a good way to handle it?"

"You're the one who wanted to come out!"

"I know, but look at me!" Her hands flail up and down her torso. "I'm having a great time! I'm going to remember this entire night tomorrow!"

"But you still can't drive us home." I scowl.

She pouts. "True, but I'm not the designated driver."

That's right—we came with her friends, who have gone completely MIA.

"You know, we should probably go look for them."

I give her a wobbly, drunken nod. "You go. I'll wait here."

One.

More.

Drink.

That's it.

Then I'll leave with Madison and her friends.

That's all I need, to drink those assholes out of my system, to forget their idiot plan, the mortifying words, and what they were planning for me.

One.

Drink.

At.

A.

Time.

"Alcohole:
the person who turns into
an asshole after just a few drinks."

Elliot

The last person I expect to see drinking on Jock Row tonight is Coach Donnelly's daughter, but that's just who I spot over the rim of my plastic cup as I tip it back to take a gulp.

It's been a long week, and the cold beer sliding down my throat is a welcome distraction.

Donnelly's presence has me doing a double take. I'm barely able to reconcile her with the girl I found crying in the library. That girl was upset and disheveled but confident, sad but still friendly.

This one is piss-ass drunk.

I continue watching her from my corner of the room, leaning nonchalantly against the makeshift bar at the far end. It's crudely built but serves its purpose, lined with empty bottles that used to hold vodka and cheap liquor, painted black and gold, Iowa's school colors.

Coach Donnelly's daughter is chugging from a red cup like a seasoned partygoer, the beer in her hand almost a permanent attachment on her mouth, her throat working to swallow, her hand wiping away dripping liquid, dribbling.

Beer must have landed on her sweater, because she takes a second to glance down at her chest, narrowing her eyes.

Takes an uncoordinated swipe at what must be a wet spot, tongue out in concentration as if the movement requires all her concentration.

I wouldn't have pegged her for a sloppy drunk.

But I suppose her intoxication makes sense, given that she's out trying to make friends. Throw in the fact that she's had a fairly shitty week...

She doesn't look the same; she looks sad and tired, and of course, she looks fucking *drunk*.

It doesn't matter that everyone else here is too.

Somehow on her it just seems *wrong*.

Out of character.

I notice she's here with a small group of girls, girls I recognize as frequent visitors to the house—another thing surprising me tonight. They're partiers, out for a good time and to meet athletes. Having lived with two of the university's champion wrestlers, I've seen enough jock chasers to meet my lifetime quota, and the girls Donnelly is with are a stereotype.

Short skirts.

Tight, midriff-bearing tops.

High heels despite the casual nature of the party's atmosphere.

I glance over again to find Donnelly's daughter standing by herself again; they're not sticking together as a group. Drunk, lethargic, clumsy.

So I watch.

Like a fucking creeper. Not caring if it's weird, I watch, setting down my own beer. Gesture to the dude serving behind the bar and request a water.

Wonder what would happen if the guys here found out the drunk girl in the corner was the wrestling coach's daughter. Wonder what that information would do to her reputation if they saw her like this.

It really isn't smart for her to be so reckless; Jock Row isn't the place to come when you're trying to hide from your troubles.

This is where you come to be seen.

When Coach's daughter wavers on shaky legs, I'm at full attention, accidentally bumping the guy next to me, causing him to spill his beer. He plays baseball and lived in this house before they opened rooms to freshmen; too many bodies and he was out.

"Dude, what the hell is your problem?"

I ignore his salty glare.

"Rowdy, see that brunette over there? I think I might need to take her home."

He claps me on the back. "Atta boy, Elli-nor! It's about damn time you dipped your wick into someone from Iowa."

Rowdy's crude reference to sex doesn't faze me—my roommate Sebastian was a hundred times worse.

"I meant because she needs help out of here, not so I can sleep with her." I give him a shove.

"Everyone's too drunk to be here, or haven't you noticed?"

"That one, that girl right there." I turn his body toward Donnelly's daughter. "Her."

"Yeah, yeah, okay, I see what you mean," he concedes, nodding his head up and down, examining her from across the room. "She might be too shitfaced to stay. It can't possibly end well. Wanna take her upstairs and put her in Rookie's bed to sleep it off?"

Terse shake of my head. "I should get her out of here, away from the alcohol."

Besides, since when is it safe to leave an incoherent drunk chick in an unlocked house full of intoxicated assholes? Last time I checked, the answer was never.

"You want help getting her to the car, you let me know."

"Thanks, man."

"Should I let everyone know you're offering babysitting services to complete strangers now, Elliot?"

I laugh. "She's not a complete stranger, not really—I kind of know her. She's going through a rough time."

I don't tell him she's the wrestling coach's daughter; that little factoid will stay a secret, at least for now.

"You sure you weren't a boy scout in a past life? Always helping people, doing nice shit for the elderly and such. How many badges do you have on your vest at home?"

"I'm not always helping people, lay off." *Jeez, why do I sound so defensive?*

His brawny shoulders heft in a shrug. "Whatever, suit yourself. You'll find me in this exact spot, holding up the bar if you need me." He takes a swig of beer. "I have *one* more month until spring training starts and my life starts sucking major balls."

Balls. "Was that a baseball pun?"

"You're funny Elli-nor. Remind me to laugh at that later."

I walk away, squeezing through the crowd, shouldering people every now and again, sights focused on one thing.

The girl.

Who is totally sloshed and in need of rescuing. No doubt she'll be nursing a hangover in the morning, and based on how she's slamming down beer or whatever it is in that cup, she's nursing some pretty damn hard feelings.

I know she's miserable.

I know she's new here.

What I don't know is her first name or where she lives, but I'm going to help her anyway.

I make my way toward her through the thick crowd, the house getting more congested by the hour. I curse these weekly parties but still show up.

Thank fucking Christ I don't live here.

I get slapped on the back in greeting every five feet; it takes an entire ten minutes for me to cross a twenty-foot room. Everyone thinks they know me. Everyone wants to be my friend because of who my roommates were. Zeke Daniels and Sebastian "Oz" Osborne, two of the most celebrated student athletes on campus, both of whom have graduated and moved on.

They moved in with their girlfriends while *I*, on the other hand, am still working on my degree, working toward grad school. Having declared a major late in the game, I fell behind, putting me a year behind.

How those assholes managed to play a sport *and* graduate on time is beyond me.

I keep pushing forward, excusing myself the entire way, annoying some people, bumping into others.

"Donnelly."

Her smile is lopsided when she lifts her neck to look up at me, eyelids droopy. "Oh! It's you!"

"Yup. It's me."

"Library guy, why are you always coming to say hello when I look shitty?" Her mouth turns down in an exaggerated frown. "It's rude."

"You don't look shitty." *You look drunk.*

She lifts a hand to her dark brown hair self-consciously. It falls in messy waves over her shoulders. "I don't?"

"How are you feeling?"

"Ugh," she groans, pressing a forefinger to her lips. "Don't tell anyone, but I'm *drunk.*"

My smile is wry, my arms crossed. "You don't say."

"Yes, really really drunk." Back against the wall, she slumps, white off-the-shoulder top sagging to one side, threatening to lower indecently as the fabric catches then drags along the wall.

"Don't you think you should stop drinking if it's making you feel like crap?"

She ignores my question, instead lodging complaints. "My head feels *ugh* and I know I'm going to have the spins when I get home." The heel of her hand presses to her forehead and she moans. "Do you have any chocolate milk?"

"Chocolate milk?"

"Yeah, it's good for a hangover," she slurs. "It's hydrating and will help raise my blood sugar."

"I was not aware of that."

"My cousins drink a lot."

"And you don't?"

"No, can't you tell? I don't know where all the beer came from."

"The keg. It came from the keg, and now I think it's time for us to go."

"I don't want to go because if I do, I'll go to sleep, and if I sleep, I'll get the spins, and I'm so scared of the spins."

"What are *the spins*?" Is this girl code for something?

"Here, I'll show you." She demonstrates, twirling her hand in circles. "When the room goes round and round and round until you wanna puke." Her head gives a remorseful shake. "It's the worst."

"Sounds like it."

"Know what I think?" She's slurring again, peering into her red cup with one eye squeezed shut. Even intoxicated, the gesture is endearing.

"What do you think?"

"Beers is gone." Her cup gets thrust into the space between us. "Think I need another one."

"Pretty sure you've had enough."

Her lip juts out, pouting. "You're no fun."

"Yeah, I get that all the time."

"Guys are dumb."

Can't argue with that.

"I don't mean *you*," she says hastily. "You're nice and so cute."

I pause at that, hesitate.

Take a step closer into her personal space—not to be creepy, but to remove the beer cup suspended from her fingers, setting it on a nearby windowsill.

"Hey! Why'd you take my drink!" As loud as she manages to protest, her head dips, brown hair falling in a long sheet—can't even hold her neck up.

"I'm thinking you've had enough for one night, huh? Trust me, you won't remember any of this in the morning, and maybe you'll even thank me later."

Loud sigh.

I lean down, dipping low so she can hear me. "When we're in the car, you're going to have to give me your address so I can take you home, okay? Think you can do that?"

Her limp head shakes back and forth. "No way. My father will kill me."

My brows furrow. Great, a belligerent drunk—*just* what I need.

"I'm sure your dad will be glad you made it out of here without getting yourself assaulted."

I brace my knees, bending to scoop her up, tossing her over my shoulder like a sack of flour—not that I have any fucking clue what a sack of flour feels like, but I imagine it's lighter than she is.

She's pure dead weight.

"Come on party girl, you can argue with me in the car."

Getting her into my car is relatively easy—way too easy considering the fact that I'm a virtual stranger and it took little convincing to get her to come with me.

I make a mental note to lecture her on safety when she's sober.

But first, I have to get her home.

"What's your address?" I stall at the stop sign, waiting for directions. "Can you tell me?"

"Yes." A jerky nod. "I don't remember."

"How do you not remember your address?"

"I have it written down somewhere…I think."

"Okay." I wait patiently as she digs through her bag.

"But not in this purse." Her shoulders slump, dejected.

"Hey, it's okay. The address isn't really that important. Don't worry about it." I give her a sidelong glance, hand on the gearshift, waiting for directions. "Think really hard. Which side of campus do you live on? Near the stadium, or by the student union?"

"Oh, definitely farther than that."

"But which side?"

"Ugh, stop asking me questions! It's making my head hurt." Her head falls back against the headrest. "I'm starving. Will you stop at McDonald's? I'm hungry."

Now she's whining. Perfect.

"I *really* need you to focus—can you look out the window and show me which way to go?" Her head lifts but sways in my direction. "Do you recognize this corner? The admin building is right along this sidewalk."

"I don't think this is the right way."

"So maybe over by the cafeteria?"

That's completely on the other side of campus.

"Yeah, try that."

I hang a right, frustrated by all the stop signs and crosswalks, the streets filled with students walking to and from parties, the majority of them inebriated.

A loud sigh fills my car. "Mmm, it smells nice in here."

"Thanks."

"You have a really nice profile. I like the bridge of your nose."

Oh Jesus.

"Was that a weird thing to say? I'm sorry."

I clear my throat uncomfortably, pointing across her torso, out the window. "Does this street look familiar to you at *all*?"

We've made it halfway around campus, passing various landmarks along the way, none of which she recognizes as being near her street.

"I think the other way."

"Are you serious right now? Why didn't you say anything?"

"I'm so hungry!"

"Donnelly, I really need you to focus. I know it's hard right now but I have to get you home."

Her head hits the seatback with a thud and she moans. "Do you have any French fries? God, I want salt."

I frown, sweat breaking out on my brow. "You need to *focus* and help me out here. We've been driving around the block for fifteen fucking minutes."

She pats me on the shoulder, squeezing once. Twice. "Thank you, that's so sweet." Closes her eyes.

I pray for patience. "Do *not* fall asleep on me."

"Mmkay." Her head lulls, pert little mouth falling open.

Shit.

"Seriously. I am not equipped to deal with this, Donnelly."

Not right now.

Not tonight.

At the next set of lights, I glance over to study her under the streetlamps, dozing lightly, a small smile playing at her lips.

Dark hair. Red lips. Bare shoulders.

So pretty.

I can't take her back to the party, and there's no way I can take her to *her* house now that I have no goddamn clue where she lives.

Basically, I'm fucked.

Stuck with her.

My car hits a pothole and she chooses that moment to groan.

"Please don't barf in my car," I beg.

Her arm reaches out in an attempt to give mine another reassuring pat. Too heavy to execute the action, it flops down on the center console with a thud.

"Mmkay." Her pretty head rolls toward me, eyelids cracking open. She gives me a wobbly smile. "I won't barf in your truck."

It's a car—a black Mustang, to be exact—not a truck, and I'm entirely convinced she's going to vomit at any moment, big doe eyes sliding closed, dark lashes fluttering against her smooth cheeks.

Damn. Even passed-out drunk, she's *really* fucking attractive.

I hang a left, trying not to notice her appearance.

Drive two blocks. Turn right. Pull up in front of the one-room rental I moved into at the end of last semester once my roommate Zeke moved his girlfriend into my old place since he owns it.

Education.

Career.

Those are my priorities.

Gone are the days where I piss away my nights partying, though I certainly enjoy hanging out with my friends on the weekends, enjoy playing pick-up soccer when I have the time.

My rental house is small, painted a disgusting shade of yellow, in the center of the block. Grass overgrown, siding and trim in desperate need of repair, but that's not my problem, it's my landlord's, and he doesn't give two shits about the exterior of the house.

The upside? It's mine until I graduate.

The rent is so affordable it makes having a piece-of-shit landlord worth the hassle of having to fix things on my own. I can do whatever I want, whenever the fuck I want, without answering to anyone.

I cut the engine and unbuckle, turning my torso toward a girl whose name I do not know. She's slumped in my passenger seat, and I still know nothing about her, except that her father is the wrestling coach here—a man who's respected and revered across the nation and the entire NCAA.

A girl who was dumped on by a few of his idiotic wrestlers without a lick of any goddamn sense.

Bunch of fuckers.

A snore escapes her lips when I reach to unbuckle her seat belt, a snore that tells me she's in no condition to walk herself to my front door.

Wasting no time, I climb out of my car and jog to the passenger side. Pause. Hike up my short sidewalk in a few long strides, yanking open the screen and unlocking the door. Push through it, propping it with the nearest heavy object—a twenty-pound weight—satisfied it's open wide enough so I won't bang her head when I carry her limp body through.

Quickly, I jaunt back to her slumbering figure; the young woman doesn't stir at the sound of the door easing open.

Not even when I slide my hands behind her back, skimming one arm under her ass to hoist her. She's lighter than she looks, but still heavier than a sack of flour.

Ha.

Awesome. I'm so delirious I'm making stupid fucking jokes to myself.

Jesus, Elliot, get a grip.

I heave, raising her up, sliding her out of my car, which isn't an easy task. Maneuvering her without knocking her head on the metal doorframe of my car is damn near impossible. It's a miracle I don't give her a concussion.

Kicking the door shut with the bottom of my foot, I lift her, shifting so I have a steady grip.

I've never carried anyone in my arms before—drunk or sober—but here I am, carrying a veritable stranger across the threshold of my shoddy college rental.

Walking straight to my bedroom, I don't have the chance to straighten my covers, choosing to lay her as gently as possible in the center of my bed. I set about removing her shoes, little black boots with a gold zipper up the side.

Her feet are dainty, like her hands, and when I peel off her socks, I notice her toenails are a shocking shade of blue.

She wiggles them then, as if she knows I'm looking, rolling to her side. Her shirt hikes up, revealing a flat, pale stomach.

Innie belly button.

Easing my comforter from under her slim frame, I pull it up and over her body, blue sheets still trapped beneath her. She stirs, hands clasped beneath her chin like one of those angel figurines my mom used to collect, looking innocent and sweet, not drunk and incoherent.

Snuggles deeper into my mattress and pillows.

Sighs.

Groans.

Leaving her on my bed, I flip the light off, backing into the hallway with a quick glance over my shoulder. Grab the garbage can from the bathroom and place it next to the bed.

Pull the door closed behind me but leave it slightly ajar. I flick the bathroom light on in case she wakes in the middle of the night.

Shit.

What if she *does* wake up in the middle of the night and freaks the fuck out because she has no idea where she is? What if she wakes up then wakes me up?

What if she barfs in my bed?

That would be my worst nightmare, but I'm so tired I don't have the energy to think about it anymore. Being a good Samaritan is fucking exhausting.

I settle my ass on the couch, pulling off one shoe at a time, then my socks. Yank on a hoodie I tossed on the coffee table earlier because *where the hell is my snuggle blanket?*

Oh, there it is.

Disgruntled, I snatch up one of the couch cushions to use as a pillow, grabbing the *one* throw blanket I have and tossing it over my legs. It's gray, and approximately the size of a postage stamp— it barely covers anything. Cursing into the cold air, bad insulation, and sky-high monthly electric bills that keep my heating needs unmet, I hunker deeper into my Iowa hoodie.

I'm too tall for this shit.

For this couch.

I stare at the ceiling, eyes wide in the bleakness, grateful for my sweatshirt, scrap of blankie, and pitch-black living room. Still...knowing there's someone *else* in my bedroom that I made myself responsible for has me awake, mind reeling.

For whatever reason, this girl has ended up in my path three times in one week, and I lie there wondering about the odds of that before flopping over, rolling to stare in the general direction of the television.

I blow out a frustrated puff of air, too large and long to get comfortable on this fucking sofa; it's lumpy and dumb and I'm going to be awake all damn night, I just know it.

In fact, I'm already scheduling myself a Saturday afternoon nap. *That* thought mollifies me somewhat as I lie motionless for what feels like an eternity.

9

#DOUCHEBAG

"Any guy who takes away
the fries and nuggets
is not to be trusted."

Anabelle

*A*m I dying?

I must be.

I press a palm to my forehead, feeling for a temperature. Pat my cheeks, feeling the burn. *Oh God.* I feel like utter shit, stars dancing behind my closed eyelids.

The spins.

The headache.

The nausea.

My hand flies to my stomach, then to my mouth when I try to move, rolling to the side of the bed. I reach my arm over the side, feeling blindly until my fingers find a bucket.

Thank God.

Wait, who put this here?

I flop back on my back, dizzy.

Don't puke, don't puke—you are not going to puke. Get it together, Anabelle. You are a grown woman.

I peel my eyelids open, slowly blinking back the sun that's shining through a window that is most definitely not mine.

Where the hell am I?

This isn't the ceiling in my bedroom at Dad's house.

These ugly beige walls aren't pink.

These navy blue sheets that smell like cologne? *Definitely* not mine.

I pull them up my chest, to my nose, giving them another whiff and concluding: this bedding unquestionably belongs to a male. Aftershave or woodsy shower gel, it matters not—these sheets smell fan-freaking-tastic.

I'm inhaling the fabric, breathing in the wonderful scent of some nameless, faceless guy, when I notice a lingering figure leaning against the doorjamb, white ceramic mug in his massive paws.

He has a lazy grin on his face, a warm, friendly smile with zero hint of any sexual connotation.

I peer over the hem of the sheet, wanting to curl up into a ball and die, but for entirely different reasons.

I know him.

From the library.

Shit, shit, double shit.

"Morning." His voice has that low, bottomless, just-woken-up sound men have that I adore, so gravelly you want to climb inside it. He has a morning voice *so good* it's giving my drunk self actual shivers.

"Um, morning?" I, on the other hand, sound like a frog, croaking out my pitiful greeting.

"How ya feelin'?" He's wearing a cutoff navy T-shirt and gray sweats, and I'm hung-over but not freaking *blind*. My eyes, bless them, travel south to where his pants hang low on his hips, appreciating the view the entire way down.

Down his legs, to his bare feet.

"Hi," I croak. "Good morning."

Jesus Anabelle, you already said that! This couldn't be more awkward.

"Sorry, I already said that." I press two fingers to my throbbing temples. "I'm a little out of sorts."

That's putting it mildly, an exaggerated understatement.

"I'm never drinking again."

I don't know why the sight of him standing there is affecting me so much, but his hard, toned arms and slick skin do something to my already muddled, alcohol-soaked brain. Being in his house—*hung-over* in his house while he stands there drinking coffee, freshly showered and squeaky clean—makes me feel disgusting.

Embarrassed.

I can see from here that his green eyes are assessing me as I sit in the middle of his bed. They're alert and aware as if he's had plenty of sleep.

"You had a rough night." He states it as a fact, and I search his tone for judgment.

There doesn't seem to be any.

"I did, and I—did I sleep here? Duh, obviously I slept here." I laugh nervously then groan. *Oh God, my head.* "Is this your house?"

"It is." He shifts on his heels, and my eyes roam once again to his bare feet. "I hope you don't mind that I brought you here last night, but I couldn't get you to tell me your address."

My lips barely move as I whisper an appalled, "I am so sorry."

"And not to sound like a fucking stalker, but once I recognized you and saw how drunk you were getting, there was no way in hell I was leaving you at that party."

"Why?"

"You couldn't even stand up, and sorry to be so blunt, but you shouldn't have been drinking so much—it was a dumb thing to do."

No doubt I was wallowing in my sorrows. The humiliation from having those wrestlers talking about me and making bets behind my back is embarrassing enough; getting so drunk I don't remember this guy bringing me home is almost worse.

Anything could have happened last night. Terrible, bad things.

"So you brought me home?"

He sips from that white mug, and I wonder what's inside. "Yeah, sorry. I didn't really have any other choice. You weren't able to tell me where to go and then you passed out when I wouldn't take you to McDonald's for French fries."

"Oh my God."

I can't say I'm sorry he didn't take me home—me showing up on my father's doorstep completely intoxicated would have destroyed him. He's never seen me this way, has never seen me as anything other than his perfect little girl. I don't know what he would've done or how he would've reacted, but I know he would not have been happy to have some strange guy dropping me off in the middle of the night.

"How did you sleep?" said strange guy asks, fiddling with the handle of the mug, which says, *Day drinking from a mug to keep things professional.*

Oh the irony.

Despite my throbbing head, the quote makes me smile. I lift a hand, fingering my temple, massaging the tender flesh there, wincing.

"I slept great, thank you. Like the dead."

"Good. I didn't quite know where to put you."

"How did I get in here?"

"I carried you."

Well this just gets better and better with every passing moment, doesn't it?

My eyes fly to his arms—toned and taut, not overly bulky. Perfect. He's not a meathead, but he's in great shape, and I blush at the smooth tanned skin of his upper arms. His biceps.

Seriously, they are some of the most beautiful arms I've seen in my entire life, though maybe I'm still drunk from last night.

I have observed a lot of arms from visiting my dad, have admired a lot of bare torsos. I've appreciated the sight of guys traipsing around in nothing but thin, polyester wrestling singlets, and those leave nothing to the imagination.

The guy clears his throat when he catches me eyeing him, lifting the white mug to his lips and taking another sip, breaking the eye contact.

Man, he is so *cute.*

A blush that matches mine spreads across his cheeks.

He clears his throat again, straightening to his full height. He's tall, probably around six one, just reaching the top of the doorframe.

"Um, I hate to bother you, but do you happen to have any ibuprofen I can take? My head is *killing* me." I groan out loud this time, wanting to burrow back under his covers.

"Sure, in the bathroom." He offers me a pleasant smile just as my eyes land on the small gray garbage can next to the bed. Thank God I didn't have to barf in it or this morning would have gone from bad to worse.

"I didn't…I didn't, uh, throw up in your car last night, did I?"

I might have been completely blitzed out of my mind, but I do vaguely remember a conversation where he specifically asked me *not* to puke in his car. I have to wonder now if I did.

His head gives a lazy shake as he laughs. "No, but I think it was close. I seriously thought you were going to toss your cookies."

"I'm…really glad I didn't."

Talk about horrifying.

Not to mention, I had Mexican food last night—me throwing up in his vehicle would have been a nightmare for both of us.

Library Guy stays put, still in the doorway, watching me lie on his bed like a beached porpoise. I roll forward, intent on slowly dragging my feet over the side of his mattress, which is easier said than done when you're hung-over.

"Please don't watch," I murmur, only *half* joking.

He moves toward me a few inches, unsure. "Do you want a hand getting up?"

"No! No, I'm good. I got this." Deep cleansing breath in, deep cleansing breath out.

"Take your time, Donnelly, or you'll be yacking it on my carpet."

Dear Lord, did he just call me by my last name? I suppose it makes sense given that he knows who my dad is, but still, kind of weird.

"If you don't mind, I would love to at least use your bathroom, get that headache medicine—my head is pounding."

"I can get you some water, too. You need to hydrate."

"Do you happen to have any choco—"

"Chocolate milk? No, but you did ask for it last night." He chuckles again, this time into his coffee mug.

"Please, can we not talk about what I said last night? I don't want to know—I don't know if I'm emotionally equipped to handle it." I groan when my feet hit the carpet; they're bare, shoes and socks neatly placed by the door.

I gaze up into his expectant face…his tan, handsome face.

I stumble, grabbing for a nearby dresser, righting myself so I can stand. It's not easy; everything aches, and also *I'm dying.*

I've never wanted to crawl back under the covers and hide so much in my entire freaking life. My face, cheeks, and chest are a blazing inferno of shame.

Ugh. Shoot me now.

Seriously, put me out of my misery.

"Thank you." I hesitate, wondering how to broach the next subject, pointing to the rumpled sheets on the bed. "Did we, uh…"

"No, of course not." He sips from his mug. "I slept on the couch."

"Oh thank God."

His brows shoot into his forehead, and I realize that statement sounded worse out loud than it did in my head—my pounding, throbbing, spinning head.

I wave it off. "I didn't mean it like *that.* I just meant…I can't remember anything from last night and I woke up in your bed and I have no idea how I got here and I'm just really…" *Deep breath, Anabelle.* "Thank you for being a decent human."

"No, I get it. It's fine."

"I mean it, thank you—and I'm sorry you probably didn't get much sleep last night being on the couch. That's so awkward, I'm sorry. I can never sleep on mine."

His toned, tanned shoulder goes up in a shrug. "I've slept in worse spots than the couch, trust me."

I lean a few feet, capturing my shoes. Socks.

Slide one on, then the other, all the while managing not to fall on my ass.

Rising, I grab my boots. "Where exactly is your bathroom?"

He jams his thumb over his shoulder. "Straight across the hall, can't miss it."

"Thanks."

He moves, giving me a wide berth as I stick my head into the hallway, not sure what I'll find. I don't know where I am or how many people live here.

How many guys are likely to see me doing the walk of shame? One? Three? Five?

"I live alone," his deep voice calls, interrupting my thoughts from what I presume is the kitchen. "It's safe to come out." Pause. "You want that water now or something?"

Or something. Like, for example, a stun dart to my ass so I can pass out, wake up on a different day (or century), and remember none of this.

I make the short trek across the hall, using the wall as support, shutting the door behind me and exhaling a loud, relieved breath.

What I need right now is a warm shower, sleep, aspirin, water, and more sleep, in that order.

His bathroom is a decent size, mostly bare save for a few essentials laid out on the countertop. One sink, but a nice, long counter.

One navy blue hand towel folded into a neat square.

It's not the cleanest bathroom I've ever been in, but to be fair, I would have been surprised if it *was*. He is, after all, a guy living alone—what reason would he have to keep the place spotless?

I brace my arms on the counter, one hand on either side of the sink, raising my eyes to gaze at the reflection in the mirror. It takes a few seconds to focus, the face before me blurred…until it's not. I lean in closer, pressing my middle and forefinger into my cheeks, pulling at my bottom lids.

Verdict: I don't look as terrible as I thought I would.

Okay, that's a lie—I look like total shit.

Ugh.

Staring at the reflection, my expression is horrified. I gape at the sight of my hair, smudged mascara, and tired, red, bloodshot eyes. I'm so embarrassed by the way I look right now, embarrassed that my evening got so out of hand that a stranger—this guy I've only ever met once at the library—brought me home with him to keep me safe.

To his house.

To keep me *safe.*

The thought of all the things that could have happened to me because I was completely drunk? Shameful, upsetting. I could have ended up as one of those girls you see on the evening news or read about online.

Horrible decision to get drunk.

Horrible decision to go out while I was indulging in a pity party.

Horrible decision to allow this guy to bring me home, although I was passed out and couldn't make the decision for myself.

Stupid, stupid, stupid.

This is so unlike me.

I hunt down a clean washcloth, running it under the cold water and scrubbing my face clean. Try to locate a little moisturizer but only find aftershave lotion instead. No brush, but I do find a comb, one that barely pulls through my snarled locks without pulling my hair out.

Ouch.

I train my blue eyes on my clothes; they need to come off and hit the laundry. *Gross.* There's a huge, yellow stain on the front of my white top, the flared sleeves wrinkled and looking worse for wear.

Pulling the cap off a tube of toothpaste, I squeeze it onto my finger and rub it along my teeth, the least effective technique for getting them clean, but it's all I've got. Holding my hands under the water, I make a cup, drink, and swish water around my mouth, spitting the water and toothpaste into the sink. Repeat.

Crossing the bathroom, I hook my finger on the shower curtain, drawing it back to peer inside at the beige-colored tiles. Hmmm, a tiled shower? Not bad for a college rental. I wonder what he'd think if I hopped inside and took a quick shower with all his stuff. Would that be weird?

It definitely wouldn't be any more impolite than crashing his pad and taking up his entire bed.

Contemplating, I grasp a long chunk of my hair, giving it a long whiff: stinky and gross.

I smell like I was in a dirty dive bar, not a harmless house party on Jock Row, and there wasn't even anyone smoking. Even so, sweat, beer, and too many bodies can't lead to any good.

My fingers brush the metal faucet. On one hand, I desperately want to jump under the shower spray; on the other, I'd have to put my dirty clothes back on afterward.

Crap.

There is no winning this one.

I let the shower curtain go, backing away.

Heft out a sigh, giving myself another glance in the mirror before tugging open the door. I pass the bedroom I slept in, my curious gaze shooting into the only other room off the hallway. Large wooden desk. Bookshelf. Iowa pennants. Some kind of framed award.

An office? A spare bedroom?

There's certainly no one living in there.

Hmm.

I trudge down the hall, shoulders back and chin up. Though I didn't grow up living with my dad, he still taught me some life lessons: do everything with conviction, hold your head up.

My walk of shame begins here.

I can do this. I can walk into this guy's kitchen and look him in the eye, thank him for everything he did for me last night. I will suck up my pride and have an adult conversation whether there is black mascara smudged under my eyes or not.

I owe him that much.

He's leaning against a wooden countertop when I walk into the room, that white coffee mug still grasped in his large, mammoth hands.

"Hey." He nods in my direction. "Feel better?"

"Somewhat human, thanks."

"You should drink this." He holds another cup toward me and I take it, bashful now that he's still being so nice.

He should have kicked me out by now, and I wonder why he hasn't. I've been nothing but a pain in his ass. When will he have had enough?

I sip on the ice water in my hands, grateful for the liquid, which feels wonderful sliding down my throat. I watch him from above the rim of the cup. He's not creepy at all, despite his size. Tall and built, I can tell he works out. Maybe he plays intramural sports? Goes to the gym? He does *something* for sure—his arms are way too toned for him to be sitting around doing nothing.

His green eyes never stray from my face, laugh lines appearing at the corners, wrinkling when I plop down in his kitchen chair with a loud sigh.

"I know I've already said this several times, but I really am sorry about all this." I pause, fiddling with the plastic cup in my hands.

"Right place, right time."

"Yes." I bow my head, staring down at the cup, reading the screen-printed label on its side. Raise my eyes, shooting him a crooked, wane smile. "You don't even know my name. I don't know yours."

There's a long silent pause.

"Elliot."

"Elliot," I repeat. "What's your last name?"

He shifts against the counter, stuffing one hand in the pocket of his sweatpants. "St. Charles."

Elliot St. Charles, ooh la la.

It's an awesome name I let linger in my mind, turning it around and around, romanticizing it. St. Charles.

Saint Charles.

Charles.

Saint.

"Saint—that's a nice way to think of you, since you've rescued me twice in one week." I say it softly into the confines of his tiny kitchen; it's so tiny, there's barely room for both of us at this small table. "I'm not normally the kind of girl who needs rescuing, let alone this many times within the span of a few short days."

"Saint." His expression is impossible to read, his mouth…those *lips*…an impassive line. "I don't know if that's how I'd describe myself."

"But it seems to suits you."

Those gorgeous lips twitch. "How would you know?"

My butt wiggles in the chair. "First, you came over to console me in the library."

"That's because you stole my spot."

"I did? How?" *What on earth is he talking about?*

"That's the table I sit at when I study."

I laugh.

Wince because *ouch*, that hurts my head.

"I'd say I owe it back to you then."

His nod is slow, deliberate. "I'll allow it." Sips from his mug. "What else have I done to earn the nickname?"

"You brought me to *your* house to keep me safe," I explain. "A complete stranger. I could have been a complete psycho."

God, what if I'd puked?

"I could have been a complete psycho, too. Maybe I still am."

My face flushes red hot, a blush so deep I feel it move from the top of my head to the tips of my toes.

"You are not."

"How would you know?"

"I opened your cabinets—you don't have any medications."

We both laugh, and when he sits down across from me at the small wooden table, I can't stop the heat warming up my entire body.

His large wide shoulders and smooth exposed skin.

"I might have overstepped my boundaries, but I couldn't leave you at that party. You were way too drunk."

Yes, he could have.

He *totally* could have, and he also could have taken advantage of me, of the fact that I was *three sheets to the wind* drunk. Trashed. Wasted. Blacked out. Unconscious.

But Elliot didn't.

He could have done all sorts of terrible things to me and he chose to…keep me safe. What a nice freaking guy.

"Elliot, I'm sure you've seen your fair share of drunk chicks about to pass out at parties. What was it that made you leave with me?"

He stares toward the window. Purses his lips. "I knew why you were getting trashed." Turns to face me. "And trust me, I was trying to get you to your house, but you couldn't tell your left from your right."

Taking me home, back to Dad's would have been a blessing and a curse.

I briefly imagine Elliot taking me to my father's house, dumping me on the front stoop. Ringing the doorbell and having Dad answer, most likely in his robe, furious.

At me.

At Elliot, because he no doubt would have misinterpreted the entire situation.

Elliot studies me, an easy grin brightening his face, white teeth way too perfect. He's altogether too alert, way too cheerful considering he spent the entire night on an uncomfortable-looking couch. I give it a glance over my shoulder—no way did his tall frame fit on that thing.

"You've only met me once."

His chuckle is deep. "Let's just say I have a stronger moral compass than most of my friends. I'd rather see you safely home than take the chance and leave you to the wolves, to the jock-holes."

"Jockholes? That's a new one."

"You like? I made it up."

I like. "Friends with any?"

"Most of my friends are athletes, so yeah, I'm surrounded by douchebags and jockholes."

"Oh jeez."

"I lived with two guys on the wrestling team for the past two years. It was a test in patience most of the time."

"Where'd they go?"

"Graduated."

"What year are you?"

"Technically I should have gone through commencement last year, but I declared my major too late, and there are a few classes I needed to take before graduating. And one enrichment class."

An enrichment class—is this guy for real?

"Uh, so you're taking that class for…?"

"Enrichment." He casually sips his coffee while I stare at him, confused.

"Which is another word for…"

"Fun?"

Oh Lord. I'd never purposely take a class for fun—not even badminton. Okay fine, *one time* I took that as a gym class and had a blast, but for real, it costs a fortune just to screw around for an entire semester.

Lesson learned.

"Which class?"

"It's a science class. It's not required, but I think it will be beneficial."

"I'm sure it will be."

"You can never know enough, uh…" Uncomfortably, his sentence tapers off, missing an important piece. It's then that I realize, *I never introduced myself.*

"Oh my God, Elliot, I never told you my name! I'm the worst!" I stick my hand out self-consciously. "I'm Anabelle."

"Anabelle," he echoes quietly. Leans back in the chair to watch me before unfolding his arms and reaching to slowly slide his palm across mine, pumping my hand once before dropping it.

Nope. Not awkward in the least.

"Anabelle. I've been wondering what your name was." When his smile disappears into his mug, I dip my head and stare down at my lap, fiddling with the fabric of my jeans, biting back my own, stupid smile.

Elliot's silent, lazy scrutiny is doing bizarre things to my already quaking insides—plus, he's one of the good guys, which makes him even more attractive, if that's even possible.

Unlike those assholes Eric Johnson and Rex Gunderson, who I never want to see again.

"I used to hate my name growing up. It was always so hard for me to spell, and no one gets it right." One N, not two.

Elliot grins. "Really? I think it's cute. Anyone ever call you Annie? Or Ana?"

"My dad sometimes. Ana Banana. Jelly Belle."

"Huh."

"Yeah."

The room is awkwardly still while both of us rack our brains for something new to say.

Then, "Oh, before I forget, here." He produces a smartphone from his pocket that looks suspiciously like mine, sending it gliding across the kitchen table in my direction. "This was in my car last night—I remembered to grab it while you were in the bathroom. It's been beeping like crazy."

Tucking an errant hair behind my ear as he looks on, I remove the phone from the table, palming it. Slide my thumb over the screen to unlock it, cringing when I see that my father has texted me *eight* times in the past twenty minutes.

Great. He obviously thinks I'm dead.

Dad: *Where the hell are you?*

Dad: *Did you come home last night?*

Dad: *Anabelle, answer me goddammit.*

Dad: *You better be dead in a ditch somewhere.*

Dad: *Anabelle Juliet Donnelly*

Dad: *Young lady, answer your phone. You're starting to worry Linda.*

Dad: *Anabelle, if you don't text me back within ten minutes, so help me God, I'm calling the campus police and the state patrol.*

Dad: *Five minutes.*

Hastily, I tap out a reply: *Sorry Dad, just woke up. I stayed at a friend's house last night. Too much alcohol to make it home.*

He wastes no time asking questions.

Dad: *Which friend?*

Me: *Daddy, does it matter?*

Dad: *Daddy? Now I know you're up to something.*
Are you trying to manipulate me by sweet-talking me? I smell
bullshit. Who were you with last night? Was it a guy?

Dad: *Has your mother ever given you the sex talk? Do you*
know the number one disease on college campuses is
syphilis? That's not a rock band or a rash, it's an STD and
you get it by being foolish.

Oh my God.
My phone pings again.

Dad: *These college boys only want one thing, Anabelle Juliet.*

Okay, now he's laying it on a little too thick with the middle
name business. I'm approaching twenty-two years old for crying
out loud. Talk about heavy-handed parenting.

One more reason I need to move out, into my own place.

Me: *I'm sorry Dad, but I didn't want to wake you last night.*
It was late and I was in no condition to even call for a cab.

Dad: *You're telling me you were so drunk you couldn't even*
text your father? What the hell is wrong with you? Have you
gone and lost all your common sense?

I take a deep breath and pray for patience.

Me: *Dad. I stayed with a friend. It was the best decision last night.*

Dad: *You should have called me to come pick you up.*

I almost type *It's bad enough that I live with my parents* but delete it, instead sending him a terse: *I appreciate that Dad, but if I'm going to make friends and fit in here, I can't be calling you to bail me out. I'm not a kid.*

A few moments go by before he replies.

Dad: *Fair enough.*

Dad: *When can we expect you home? Linda is making potato salad for lunch and I have to be at the gym for a two-a-dayer.*

I sigh. He's never going to get it.

Me: *Tell Linda not to wait, I don't know when I'll be home. I'm probably going to stick around town for lunch, grab a coffee. I'll be back in a few hours, definitely for dinner.*

Elliot is watching me but pretending not to, his eyes roaming my face, interested in my expressions as I frantically reply to my dad's text messages.

I finally set the phone on the table, face down.

Sigh.

"I really should get going."

"You need a ride?"

"Nah, I'll catch an Uber."

"Anabelle, it's no big deal."

I reach out, covering his hand with mine. Pull back when his skin sizzles. "I know, but you've done enough, gone above and beyond already." I would die of mortification if he did me one more favor. "I appreciate you helping me, coming to my rescue. I probably won't ever forget it."

He demurs. "Don't worry about it."

I rise. "All right, well...thanks." Palm my phone, scrolling through the few apps I have downloaded for transportation, choose one, and click for a ride. "There's a car less than two minutes away. It's supposed to be nice today, so I'll wait outside if you don't mind."

He nods as I smooth a hand down my frizzy hair self-consciously.

"Bye Elliot." I give him a wave, despite the fact that I haven't left his kitchen. "See you around."

"See ya. Take care, Donnelly."

I grin, biting down on my bottom lip. "You, too, Saint Elliot."

#DOUCHEBAG

"I'm still so hungover that
when I walked into class late,
I tried to buckle my seat belt."

Anabelle

"**A**nabelle, hey."

I hear his voice before I see him, sitting at the table I've been occupying on the sixth floor, the one I apparently stole from him and have now happily surrendered as a thank you.

"Hey to you, too, stranger."

I haven't seen him since that morning in his kitchen, but I've thought of him every day. He's a sight for sore eyes, spread out at that corner table, the entire surface a mess of books, laptop, and pens.

"You just get here?" he asks politely.

"Yeah. Thought I'd check to see if this spot was taken."

"Have a seat."

"Gosh no, I'd hate to interrupt. You were in the middle of something."

"Big deal. There's plenty of room." The chair across from him shoots out, his foot propped on the seat. "More than that shitty desk over there."

"Okay. All right." I set my bag down on a different chair and he removes his feet, sitting up taller.

"How have you been?"

"Good. How 'bout you?"

Elliot slides down in his seat, slouching against the back, legs spread. "Same shit, different day. You know how it is."

"That good, eh?"

It doesn't take long for me to settle in, for us to quietly begin working on our own tasks, comfortable with the companionship. It's not necessary to fill the void with words or chatter; it's nice being in his presence.

Every so often we exchange glances—friendly smiles—but work in peaceful silence.

My phone vibrates.

Vibrates again.

When I finally flip it over, I see it's a text from my dad, asking if I plan on being around tonight to watch his favorite series on cable.

My groan is louder than I intend.

"I have *got* to get out of that house," I mutter, plopping my phone face down with an irritated huff so I can't see the screen light up *again*.

"Trouble in paradise?"

"Yes. My father is driving me nuts."

Elliot's brow rises.

"I don't know if I told you this, but since I transferred, I've been living with my dad and stepmom. They're both great, but…"

"But you're living with your dad and stepmom?"

I laugh. "Exactly." Sigh. "I love them to death, *obviously*, but they've completely forgotten that I'm twenty-one years old and not fifteen."

"When I go home to visit my folks, my mom still tells me to hit the sack at ten o'clock. Then she'll come in my room to turn off my light if I'm up reading too late. It's so obnoxious."

"That is my life. Every. Single. Day." I want to bang my head on the table repeatedly.

"Dude, that would suck so hard."

"It does suck, harder than you know."

"No comment." He laughs, tipping his head back. "What's your plan? I mean, are you going to stay with them all year or what?"

It hasn't been very long, and I won't last much longer without losing my mind.

My fingers shred the end of a sheet of paper as I mull over his question. "I don't know if I have a choice. I'm keen on living with a roommate, but it's second semester and everyone is settled, so finding one has been impossible."

Someone needs to take pity on me.

Soon.

"Yeah, the timing kind of blows."

Blows *hard.*

I blush, dipping my head so he won't see it.

As soon as he says the word *blow* with those gorgeous lips, my mind wanders south on his body. *All the way south.*

I clear my throat. "I think at this point, my best option might be to rent an apartment, which I was hoping would be a *last* resort. I don't want to pay the full rent on a place."

The last thing I want is my dad shelling out money for me to live on my own.

Elliot agrees, nodding his head. "That part of having a roommate is nice. I kind of miss having someone else around, you know? Coming home to an empty house sucks sometimes."

"How so? Because right now, it sounds like it would be paradise."

"Well..." He tips back in his chair, balancing on the back legs, hands braced on the table. "For example, my last two roommates were kind of assholes. The walls of the house were really thin, you know, and they'd barge in on me sometimes—"

I raise my brows, and now we're *both* blushing.

"That's...no. I didn't mean it like...Jesus, I just meant they constantly went where they weren't supposed to, and brought girls home when they were single, and had one too many parties."

That doesn't actually sound all that terrible, but I scrunch up my face anyway and make the appropriate sympathetic noises.

"But you kind of miss having someone around?"

"I totally do."

I'm suddenly very interested in the tabletop and worry my bottom lip, an idea taking root, one I'm afraid to voice out loud.

What if...

"Hey, Elliot?"

I still can't look at him.

"Yeah?"

"What, uh, what are you doing with that extra bedroom in your house?"

"What extra bedroom?"

"The one across the hall from yours, with the desk and bookshelves in it."

"Oh, it's not technically a bedroom because it doesn't have a closet. I've been using it as an office and a place to store my shit."

"Do you think a twin bed could fit in it?"

"Not with all that stuff in there."

I roll my eyes. "What if we took it all out?"

"We?"

"Yeah. What if you turned it into a bedroom?" I hold my breath.

"My storage room?"

It's taking every ounce of my self-control not to blurt out my thoughts. "What would half your rent be?"

"Three hundred something."

Just three hundred dollars a month for my own space?

Sign me up!

The wheels in my head start spinning, my heart rate getting faster. "Would you hate the idea of having someone move in with you?"

Elliot shrugs, non-committal. "Meh, it's been nice living alone, but I guess I wouldn't care if I had a new roommate. Covering the entire rent sucks up most of my savings during the year."

"Right." I brace myself, holding a breath. "Would you object to having a *female* roommate? Say, if someone female wanted to rent the room?"

"A girl? I can't see how that would matter." He seems to scoff at the notion. "How different could it be than living with a dude?"

"What about living with *me*, specifically?" I suck in another breath, waiting. "I know the last few times you saw me I was a hot mess, but I promise you Elliot, I am *not that girl*. I swear, that was one bad decision, one I regret and thank God you were there." I hate that he saw me drunk, hung-over.

I hate that he might have gotten a terrible first and second impression of me, ones I can't erase from his mind.

"But I'm other things, too. I'm really tidy, and I bake the most ah-mazing French butter cookies—and nothing unhealthy for dinner, promise. I'll be so good for your diet."

I beam at him, hopeful, trying not to look like the kind of girl who cries in the library and passes out drunk on a regular basis. Normal. Rational. Calm.

The perfect roommate.

"Hmm." Elliot taps his pen on the table, thoughtful. "You serious? Because I really don't care if you're a girl or not, I'd just like someone who's going to pick up their shit and pay half the utilities—on time."

"I'm really tidy, I swear, and I only brought clothes and school supplies from Massachusetts. You won't even know I'm there."

"You moved here with just clothes? How is that even possible?"

"I have almost no worldly possessions." *Annnd* now I sound like a hobo. "The last two places I lived were furnished, which was awesome, but it means I have nothing to my name. Blessing and a curse."

Judging by the look on his face, he is not hating this idea.

"Let's say, hypothetically, I did move into your storage closet—what would I need?"

"A bed?"

"I could arrange that. Anything else?"

Just then, Elliot's phone begins playing a mariachi tune, vibrating enthusiastically across the study table. "Shit. Can we finish this conversation later? I have to go."

"Oh. Okay, yeah. Sure." I pause. "Do you have a class?"

"No, a pick-up soccer game. There's a big group of us that plays a few nights a month whenever we can."

"Really?"

He's packing up his bag, shoving the laptop inside haphazardly, suddenly in a rush. "Yeah, down at Hadley Park." Glances up at me. "You should come sometime and watch."

"I would love that. I actually play soccer."

He stops. Stares at me. "You do?"

"Varsity, all through high school. I was a halfback." I flash him a grin, running a hand along my long, sleek ponytail. "Man, was I fast."

Elliot studies me a few more moments. Quirks a brow. "You interested in playing? That's what a pick-up game is—anyone can join."

"Seriously?"

"Yes, seriously. Are you interested?"

"I...yeah. I mean, sure! Maybe I'll come watch you play tonight then I can have my mom send my cleats? I'd have them by next week."

"Cool." Elliot stares down at my bag as he hefts his onto his broad, sexy shoulders, nodding toward the exit. "You coming or what, Donnelly?"

"Yes! Yes, I'm coming."

11

#DOUCHEBAG

"The only thing getting
head tonight is my pillow."

Elliot

"St. Charles, you bringing dates to the games now or what?"

"Huh?" I'm down on the ground, tying my cleats when my teammate Devin hovers over me, giving my shoulder a nudge with his knee.

He's wearing black shin guards and a shit-eating grin. "Bro, I asked you three times if you're bringing a date to our games now. You're not even paying attention."

"A date? Why would you ask me if she was my date?"

"Because you brought a girl here and she's been watching you the whole time?"

I look up from my laces, gaze colliding with Anabelle's. She shoots over a small wave.

"Oh yeah, her—I should probably introduce you."

"You got a girlfriend you forgot to tell us about?"

"Uh, no. I think that's my new roommate?"

"Roommate?" Devin Pierce takes his turn glancing over at Anabelle Donnelly, legs crossed on a lawn chair, watching us intently. "*Her?*"

"We haven't talked through all the details yet, but yeah, she's probably going to move into my house."

"Her? *You're* going to live with *her?*"

My eyes narrow and I stand, pulling at my shin guards and adjusting my shorts. "Why are you saying it like that?"

He stares at me like I've lost my damn mind. "Because, there is no fucking way you're going to live in a house with her without wanting to, you know…"

Dev takes his hand, makes the symbol for *okay*, and then takes the forefinger from his other hand and pokes it through, over and over. Immature asshole.

I shake my head. "You are out of your fucking mind. Anabelle and I are just friends."

Sort of.

"Men and women can't be friends, yo, and they sure as shit can't live together."

"Why not?"

"Feelings and sex and shit."

"That's not going to happen, but thanks for the warning."

"Hey man, I'm not saying it's a bad thing! I just think you're two reasonably attractive people with functioning downtown equipment. It's going to happen."

"Have you always been this annoying?"

"No. You're just being sensitive because you know I'm right." His eyes stray to the sidelines, hands propped on his waist. When he begins speaking, it's as if he's talking to Anabelle, but only I can hear him. "*You totally dig him already, don't you? Yup, yup, I see you watchin' him, girl. He's got real fine legs, don't he?*"

"Shut the fuck up, would you?"

He ignores me. "*Stare a little harder, honey, he ain't gonna notice. He's got you planted firmly in the friend zone.*"

"Stop talking like that. She's watching us, not staring—there's a huge difference."

"You're saying you haven't had any dirty thoughts about her?"

"No."

Dev laughs. "You will."

A whistle blows in the distance and our feet start moving, our forward facing our goalpost, kicking the ball back to me.

I tap it still. Pause.

Run, moving it up the field a few yards before a defender from the yellow team invades my space. Pass it left to our midfielder.

Try to block out the image of Anabelle on the sidelines. She's risen from her folding chair, clapping, hands around her mouth, shouting and calling my name.

Cheering me on.

The game is fast-paced and high energy and over before I know it, ninety minutes gone by in a flash.

Anabelle is waiting when we're done, long ponytail swaying back and forth as she walks toward me, holding out a water bottle.

"You thirsty?"

I brought my own bottle, but her gesture is sweet. I reach for it. "Thanks."

Chug.

I stop walking in my tracks. Blurt out, "I think we should do it."

"*Do it* as in…"

"Move in together."

She sucks in an excited breath, hands clasped under her chin. "You *do*?"

"Yeah. Why not?"

"Really?" she squeals, beginning a small hop that makes her boobs bounce. "Oh my gosh, Elliot, I could kiss you right now!" On her tippy toes, Anabelle folds me into an enthusiastic hug, squeezing the stuffing out of me, burying her face in my chest. "Thank you!"

Then she does kiss me, right on the underside of my chin, along my jaw. One quick kiss and another hug before she backs away, practically leaping in the air.

Talking a mile a minute.

"How soon can I bring my stuff over," she jokes, doing a little fast footwork around an imaginary ball. "I don't have much, so this is going to be so easy!"

"This weekend? Tonight?" I joke. "I don't know, what works for you?"

"This weekend? Tonight!" she kids back. "Seriously Elliot, I am so freaking pumped." Her arms go up and she jogs ahead of me. "Eek! I'm moving out of my dad's house! This is the best day ever!" she yells into the night air.

I bite back a smile, staring down at the ground.

When I glance up, Dev is shaking his head from side to side, a knowing grin on his asshole face.

Anabelle

"**D**addy, I have something to tell you."

It's late, half past eleven, but he had a long practice tonight with the team and has only just gotten settled in the living room, feet up on an ottoman, remote pointed at the television.

When he tips his head to the side, ear in my direction, I know he's listening.

I can barely contain my excitement.

"I think I found a place to live."

My father doesn't move a muscle, eyes trained on the TV screen.

"Dad, I said I—"

"I heard ya, pumpkin. As soon as you called me Daddy, I knew you were up to something. It's just taking me a few seconds to absorb the information."

I step farther into the room, sitting next to him on the couch, twisting my body to face his even though he's staring straight ahead.

"It's such a great place, Dad," I babble. "Small, but there isn't any maintenance, and I'll have plenty of room for my stuff and a roommate. Just one, so, kind of perfect."

He finally looks at me. "Where is this place?"

"Just on the opposite side of campus, near the university center. One block over—you'd be able to pop in sometimes to see me!"

"What about fire escapes? How many of them are there?"

"Uh, none? It's only one level."

"Smoke detectors?"

"I, uh, I didn't count."

My dad's jaw twitches. "I suppose you didn't look to see if there was a fire extinguisher, either."

"No, but I can text my roommate and ask."

"Who's the landlord?"

"Uh, I'm not sure. I'm, uh, subleasing."

"Do you have a signed contract?"

"Not yet, but I will—tomorrow," I lie, making a mental note to find out about all those things so my father doesn't have a coronary.

Dad's mouth remains pulled into a straight line, somewhere between pursed and expressionless.

He looks kind of sad, actually.

"Dad, what's wrong?"

"Nothing's wrong." He's being dishonest, something he's never been good at, and I frown, too. If he's already not happy about me moving into my own place, how is he going to feel when I tell him I'm living with a guy?

It can't happen.

At least not tonight.

He will find out soon enough and he. Will. Be. Pissed.

"I'm really excited, Dad. This place is perfection." I know it's rotten, but I lay the groundwork for a little guilt-tripping, unable to handle his silence. Wanting to move out but wanting to do it with a clear conscience. "You know how hard I've been looking...I thought you'd be happy for me."

"I am."

My arms go around him and I squeeze. "Aww, are you being a big grump because you're going to miss me? You are, aren't you?"

He mumbles under his breath, "What kind of a dumbass question is that? Of course I'm going to miss you."

Nope, not subtle at all—not my dad.

I let out a loud laugh before releasing him and fall back onto the couch cushions, giving his hair a tussle.

He grumbles. "Tell me about this roommate of yours. What's she like?"

Oh shit.

"Uh, well…" *Let's see, how can I put this without being specific?* "Plays soccer. Is good at, uh, science. Has everything we need so all I have to do is find a bed!"

Dad considers this information. "You can take the one in your room here, or we can get you a twin if a queen is too big."

He says it with authority, pleased to have solved my problem.

"A twin is probably best, thank you Dad."

"What's this girl's name?"

I step headfirst into the lie. "Ell…Ellie."

"Ellie?" He squints at the television. "What's her last name?"

"St. Charles."

"Ellie St. Charles." His eyes narrow farther, never missing a beat. "Why does that name sound familiar?"

Crap. What if my dad has met Elliot because his roommates used to be wrestlers? My housing solution would come crashing down around me before it began.

"Not sure. Do you know lots of Ellies?"

He doesn't answer. "When you planning on moving in? Next month? Beginning of next year?"

"Not exactly. We—Ellie and I—were talking, and we kind of think moving this weekend would be best, if that's possible."

He is *not* pleased by this news. "I won't be here this weekend—we have a meet in Indiana."

Excellent.

"Oh, well don't worry about it, Ellie and I have it covered. Shouldn't be a big deal."

"But I should be here to help, don't you think?"

I pat his arm. "Dad, stop worrying, it'll be fine—it's just a mattress. How hard can that be?"

"It's my job to worry."

"I know, but this is a piece of cake, and I'm just on the other side of campus. Seriously, draw a short line between the two houses and there you are."

Disgruntled, he lets out a puff of air. "Fine. If you think you can manage the move without me."

"It's a few boxes, and I can have the mattress delivered from the store." I lay a reassuring hand on his forearm. "I'm not a kid anymore, Dad. Everything is going to be fine."

"All right Ana Banana. I trust you."

"You are messaging me during
sexting hours. Tread lightly,
as innuendos are taken seriously."

Elliot

"I can't thank you enough for letting me move in with you, Ellie."

"Would you stop calling me that? It's weird."

"Sorry, I'm just so freaking excited! If my bed was put together, I'd totally be jumping on it like a little kid."

"I don't think the springs on mattresses are boing-y enough to make them bouncy."

Anabelle rolls her eyes, skirting past me into her new room. She wasn't lying when she said she didn't have much. Half a dozen boxes and an inexpensive bed that was delivered earlier in the day. I'm standing in the doorway, box hoisted on my shoulder, waiting for instructions.

"Stop being so literal, Elliot. It was a metaphor for my level of excitement."

"Oh. Sorry."

"Can you come in here and help me with this bed frame? It's awkward maneuvering in here. If you could hold that end up while I screw in these bolts, I'll be good to go."

She's arranged herself on the floor, grabbing a brown metal piece and resting it in her lap like a boss, ready to kick this project's ass.

"I sound like a broken record, I know, but my God, I am so pumped. Do you think it's because you're a guy and I'm used to only living with women?" Anabelle gushes again, holding the two metal parts together, fitting them into place.

"Maybe."

To be honest, now that Anabelle Donnelly is sitting cross-legged in the middle of her new room—my old storage space—I'm a little fucking nervous.

Fine, a lot nervous.

There are things I clearly didn't think through before inviting her to move her shit into my house, such as:

What if I walk in on her naked while she's showering and she thinks I'm a pervert?

What if I accidentally leave the door open while I'm taking a piss and she sees my junk?

What if she decides to walk around the house with no pants on and I have to see her ass cheeks? What if I like it?

Why do I keep worrying about all these naked, nonexistent body parts?

Fucking Devin and his nagging about living with a girl, that's why.

Christ.

"How long are you planning on standing in the doorway holding that box? I know you have those firm muscles and all, but you can set it down if you want. I don't expect you to stand there all day." She laughs, concentrating on tightening a screw, oblivious to my inner turmoil.

"Shit, sorry." I give my head a shake. "Where should I put this?"

"How about on the floor there, maybe in the corner so it's out of the way? It's course books from my first year, and I probably won't be needing them—I don't know why I even brought them here."

"You want to try to sell them?"

She shoots me a radiant, content smile. "I should, shouldn't I?"

"I would, yeah."

"All right, how about we put them back on the porch? I'll sort them later and list them online."

"Sure thing, roomie."

Anabelle shoots me a look, a smile breaking out on her face. "Oh my God, it feels so good hearing someone other than my father saying that! He really was starting to drive me crazy."

"If I still lived with my parents and was going to college, I'd want to drive my car off a fucking cliff."

Anabelle winks, watching as I lift another heavy box from the hallway, damn near toppling to the side.

"This is going to be fun. I can feel it." She giggles.

"What's so funny?"

"You. You're so big and strong, and here you are, tipping all over the place."

Big and strong?

Shit, that's like...music to every guy's ears—except when I look over to study her face, I see no hint of flirtation there.

She looks happy and comfortable sitting on the floor of this tiny room that's not really fit to be a bedroom, surrounded by her unpacked boxes.

Anabelle emits a few grunts, twisting the wrench in her hand, face turning pink. "Ugh, can you give me a hand? This is so *hard* to push in."

Hard to push in...did she seriously just say that? In that breathy tone?

Devin opened a floodgate to the gutter, and I can't keep my mind out of it.

"Sure."

"Great. Can you just hold that end?" She wiggles her fingers toward the end of the bed frame. "I'm almost done. Then if you could help me flip the mattress on, I can start putting on the sheets."

Together, we finish her bed frame, arranging it in the center of the room. Add the box springs and mattress to the top. Anabelle disappears and returns with a white, padded cover. Fitted sheet.

Shaking the top, it billows into the air like a cloud, white, crisp, and fresh. It flutters onto the mattress, resting there gently, and my roommate fusses around, tucking here, tucking there, until the bed is neat as a pin.

White sheets.

White quilt.

White pillows.

Immediately, I wonder what her dark hair would look like fanned out on the stark, snowy bedding, her pale skin…

Stop it, Elliot.

Get a grip.

Fantasizing about your new roommate will lead to no good, and she's already had shitty luck with men at this university; there's no need for her to trouble herself with one more.

"I'll be here! Oh! Wait."

I poke my head back into her room.

"Are you hungry for anything? Maybe we could start thinking about dinner?"

Am I hungry for anything?

I wasn't.

But maybe I am now.

I crash in my room a few hours later, flopping on the bed and grabbing my phone. Ten missed messages, all of them from my old roommate, Oz.

Swiping my thumb to open the messenger app, I shoot him a return text.

Oz: *Hey dude, what's up? We haven't talked in ages.*

Me: *Hey. Not much going on.*

Oz: *Really? Because I've been trying to get ahold of you all week.*

Me: *What are you, my girlfriend?*

Oz: *No, but if I was, I'd feel neglected enough to not give you a blow job.*

Me: *Sorry man, I really have been busy.*

Oz: *Busy doing what? Since when do you do stuff?*

Me: *Real funny asshole. I was helping someone move into the spare room of my house.*

Oz: *Shit, that's cool. You finally have a new roommate?*

Me: *Yeah, it's nice not having to fork over the entire rent and shit.*

Oz: *Who'd you end up with? One of the guys from the team? They still hanging around you like flies on shit?*

Me: *Nah, just someone who really needed a place to stay. I lucked out not having to look.*

Oz: *What's his name?*

Me: *Anabelle.*

Oz: *LOL that fucking sounds like a female's name.*

Me: *That's because she is a female.*

Oz: *I don't get it. I thought you said your roommate was a guy.*

Me: *I never said that.*

Oz: *Hold up, you're living with a GIRL? One with tits and everything?*

Me: *Yeah, she was kind of desperate to get out of her parents' house.*

Oz: *Her PARENTS? Please tell me she isn't a minor and is over the age of eighteen? DUDE. Elliot, what the fuck? Are you living with jailbait?*

Me: *You wouldn't even believe me if I told you.*

Oz: *Oh really? Try me.*

More than a few minutes tick by while I debate telling Oz Osborne my new roommate is his ex-wrestling coach's daughter, but I hesitate, not sure how he'll react to the news.

Oz: *Dude, I'm waiting. You're giving me blue balls.*

Me: *It's complicated.*

Oz: *What the fuck does that mean?*

Me: *Had you heard that Coach Donnelly has a daughter?*

Oz: *Yeah. Daniels might have mentioned he saw her in Coach's office a few weeks ago shooting the shit with him. Said she's cute.*

Me: *She's my new roommate.*

Oz: *Come again? I'm sorry, what?*

Me: *Anabelle Donnelly.*

Oz: *Yeah, I got that, but I thought you just said you're now living with COACH FUCKING DONNELLY'S DAUGHTER, but that can't be right, because only a fucking moron would do that.*

Me: *Why? It's not like I'm dating her—she just needs a place to stay. And I'm not on the team so what difference does it make?*

Oz: *Because Coach warned everyone away from her. He will blow his shit if he finds out she's living with a dude, trust me.*

Oz: *Was he there the day she moved in?*

Me: *No.*

Oz: *Yeah, you're fucked.*

Me: *Seriously, stop saying shit like that. I am not fucked.*

Oz: *Has she told him yet? That you're a guy?*

Me: *How the hell should I know? She's 21, she can do whatever the hell she wants.*

Oz: *You can't see me, but I'm laughing my ASS off so hard right now. You're so cute and naïve, Elliot. So fucking cute.*

Shit. What if he's right? When I agreed to letting Anabelle live with me, call me a fool, but I honestly didn't think her parents would give a shit about her having a male roommate.

Me: *I'm not telling her she can't live here, dude. She just moved her shit in.*

Oz: *Hope she doesn't have a lot cause she's gonna be moving it all back out, LOL.*

He can be such an asshole sometimes.

Me: *She's just renting the spare room—it's not even a bedroom, dude. That's how desperate she is to get out of his house. And I really need the money for rent, so...*

Oz: *Okay man, whatever you say. Keep the lies coming.*

Me: *What the fuck, Ozzy?*

Oz: *Look, all I'm saying is, keep your dick away from Anabelle Donnelly and you should survive the rest of the semester. That's just some advice from one friend to another.*

Me: *I've been on the receiving end of your advice before, but I'm not one of her dad's wrestlers so I'm not going to worry about it.*

Oz: *Seriously Elliot?*

Me: *Dude, trust me. I won't even know she's here.*

Won't even know she's here?

Who the hell was I trying to kid?

It's like an Anabelle Donnelly bomb was dropped on my house overnight and detonated—her presence is everywhere. Her makeup is in my bathroom, on the counter, and in the cabinets. Her adorable baby blue narwhal slippers are by the front door, and the perky little coffee mug she plunked down next to mine winks up at me as I slough into the kitchen.

Taunting me.

Grabbing an orange from a basket, I peel it as Anabelle enters the tiny room, hair piled on top of her head. Makeup-free.

Beautiful.

She's wearing a short gray robe made out of some satiny material, brushing past me when she reaches to pull open the fridge, bending to peer inside, ass in the air.

I turn to stare out the window so I'm not staring at her butt; this space is way too fucking small for both of us now that she's no longer just an overnight guest.

"Morning," she singsongs, clearly in high spirits. Leans against the counter, sizing me up. Twists open a bottle of water.

It's the weekend and there are a few errands I have to run, but first I want to stare at her, this girl in my kitchen, both out of place *and* belonging here.

I'm staring because I simply cannot help myself. Anabelle Donnelly in the morning is a sight to behold. Chipper, cheerful, and looking none too worse for the wear.

I just assumed she would look the way she did that morning she was hung-over, but I'll be the first to admit, she most certainly does not.

This could be a problem; she is way too good-looking and wearing far too few clothes.

"Morning," I mutter.

Anabelle takes a sip from her water, smiling around the bottle. "You feel weird right now, don't you."

"Kind of," I admit.

"Because you're not used to having a girl sleeping in the next room, or..."

Or because I'm starting to seriously doubt my decision to let her live here based on the fact that I find her attractive, that I'm attracted *to* her, and if it's not fucking cool getting a semi-boner while eating breakfast together for the first time, someone didn't send my dick the memo.

"Are you always this awake in the morning?" I deflect, avoiding her question.

"Most of the time." Her gaze rakes me up and down, dark brows rising. "But it's not that early. Aren't you a morning person?"

I grunt, peeling off an orange slice. "Not usually."

Not when I lie in bed all damn night, awareness that everything inside the house has changed hovering like a goddamn storm cloud.

"What are you doing today?" she asks, making casual conversation.

"Running to the mall to pick up something I ordered online. If you have nothing going on, you wanna come?" *Jesus, Elliot, what are you saying?*

"I would love that! We can bond." She winks. "Get to know each other better."

Super.

Nonetheless, I just hammer the nail deeper into my coffin. "Maybe we can stop somewhere before we come home and get dinner?"

"When do you want to leave?"

"I don't know, the mall doesn't open for a few hours, but if you want we can stop to get coffee and shoot the shit."

"Okay! I'll get changed. Just knock on my door when you're ready to go."

Which ends up being exactly one hour later.

By nine, Anabelle is walking out of her bedroom in a fitted pair of jeans, wedges, and a tucked-in gray T-shirt that says *Good Vibes Only* in white block letters.

"Ready?" She pushes a pair of sunglasses to the top of her head, tucking a purse under her armpit, and when she breezes past me toward the door, I catch a whiff of her perfume.

"Ready."

As I'll ever be.

Which is not ready at all.

13

#DOUCHEBAG

"I'm catching feelings
like a damn amateur."

Elliot

"I don't understand why you just let these guys treat you like shit."

We're walking along the food court, sipping on smoothies from Jamba Juice, and I don't know how the conversation turned to guys, but it stops Anabelle in her tracks.

"I'm not letting them treat me like shit. This thing isn't my fault—they're the morons who made the stupid bet, I'm just the collateral damage."

"Sorry, that's not what I meant. I meant, you should confront them about it instead of not doing anything."

"If only it were that easy. I don't want to cause a bunch of drama, especially with my dad being the coach here."

"You know what I think you need to do? Give those two assholes a taste of their own medicine. You do know that wrestlers are like the bottom feeders on the athletic food chain."

"Stop it, they are not." She gives me a little smack on the arm.

"Yes they are—have you seen their ears?"

"What does that have to do with anything?"

"I think you need to teach those dicks a lesson, and you know what else? I'm the person to help you do it. There's no bigger asshole than me if I want to be, and you're not going to teach them jack shit if you don't fight fire with fire."

"Okay now you're just starting to sound like my dad, and you are not an asshole—like, at all."

"I'm not? Shit. I try so hard, too."

Anabelle rolls her eyes, bumping me with her hip. "You wish. You'll never achieve douchebag status. You're doomed."

"Next you'll be slapping a nice guy label on me and telling me I'm sweet, asking me to stay in on the weekends and paint your toenails."

"Why do guys think being called nice is an insult? I'll never understand that."

"It's in our DNA to rebel against it."

She laughs. "You're doing a shitty job rebelling—pardon my French."

"Okay smartass." We pass by a jewelry shop, wandering past clothing store after clothing store until I stall us both in front of the sporting goods store where my new soccer gear awaits. "Before we go inside, I just want you to think about speaking up against these guys. These dicks don't get to treat you this way."

"A revenge plot Saint Elliot? Really?"

"No, no, not a revenge plot—I just think someone needs to call them on their bullshit. We can do it."

She cocks a brow. "We'll see."

Anabelle

I cannot believe I'm having this conversation.

A revenge plot? Seriously?

I don't think I have it in me, and I certainly don't have any desire to be the kind of girl who does.

We're at the front counter of an athletic store, Elliot waiting for the clerk to retrieve an order from the back room—a new pair of black and white indoor soccer shoes.

I lean toward him conspiratorially. "So when you say *get back at these guys*, like, what exactly do you mean?"

He shrugs. "You know, the usual. The punishment should fit the crime."

"Crime? Settle down, drama llama." I stare at him, not sure how to respond, speaking slowly. "I have no idea what you mean by 'punishment fitting the crime' because I have no idea what they've done to anyone else—you weren't specific the last time we talked about it and I'm new here, remember?"

"Good point."

"So?"

"Specifically? When the new guy joined the wrestling team last year—nice guy, right? He comes from Louisiana and likes to keep to himself. Quiet, studies a lot. Anyway, Rex and Eric were living with him. Get drunk one night and decide Rhett—that's his name—needs to get laid."

"Wait, *they* decided? Like it's their decision to make?"

"Yeah. Anyway, they're totally lit one night, and they make photocopies of a flyer with Rhett's face and phone number on it and hang them all over campus."

I gasp. "What! That's terrible!"

"It was bad. Girls were calling his number and messaging him for months."

"Oh nooooo!" My hand flies to my mouth, muffling my horror. "Then what?"

"The guys laid off for a while—except a few other people pulled pranks on the kid, copycat hazing. Let me think for a second...I know those two morons have done other dumb shit. They used to drive my old roommates up the fucking wall."

"Hypothetically, if I were going to do something to teach them a lesson, what's something that would *piss* you off if you were a guy?" He gives me a pointed look and I roll my eyes, poking him in the bicep. "Knock it off, you know what I mean."

"I don't know, maybe we can Google some ideas? I'm not a dick, and I've certainly never hazed anybody. It would make me feel like the biggest piece of shit."

"Don't you think it should be something public? Like...at a party or in class or something? I have a class with Rex, it would be so easy to embarrass him."

"Maybe it would be easy, but you would probably end up getting in trouble, or worse, come out looking like the asshole."

"You're probably right, I would. I have the worst luck when it comes to guys."

Elliot looks over at me then, pauses, hands hovering over the credit card reader as he studies my face, a peculiar expression passing through his eyes. His mouth is downturned at each end, not quite a frown, but not exactly a smile either.

"I highly doubt that."

"Trust me, I do. The last guy I dated dumped me because I wouldn't sleep with him on the second date."

"That's not you having bad luck, that's dating a guy who ended up being a fucker. You can't predict that shit—it's like... standing in line for a ride at the fair, getting on, and finding out too late it's a roller coaster."

"Uh, okay..."

"Like being on a Ferris wheel. It looks like a fun ride, but in reality, it's scary as hell."

I'm not sure how we went from talking about dating to carnival rides, but here we are.

"You mean a wheel of terror?"

"You don't like Ferris wheels either?"

"No!" My face contorts into a grimace.

The clerk hands Elliot his purchase after checking to make sure both shoes are the same size. Together, we walk out the door, stopping once more at the entrance.

"So now what?"

I grin up at him, gently remind him, "You promised me food."

Elliot shifts on his heels, his eyes doing a scan of my body before he clears his throat and looks toward the far end of the mall. "I did."

"Then let's go!"

"Dick is everywhere.
Chemistry isn't."

Elliot

S he's only lived here for a few weeks, but there's already a palpable air of comfort and familiarity in our house. We've grown to really like each other's company, probably a little too much—the relationship we've established is unlike any I've had with previous roommates, and I've had plenty in my four years at Iowa.

We're both private, preferring to be home where it's quiet.

We both laugh at dumb comedies.

Since she moved in, we've made dinner together more nights than not—spaghetti, soup, pasta, hamburgers on the charcoal grill I have on the back stoop.

We like each other.

A *lot*.

And we agree that maintaining our older friendships is more important than forcing ourselves to make new ones. I'm about to graduate, and I'm applying for master's programs. Anabelle is a second semester junior transfer with a bunch of friends from Massachusetts. My friends might have graduated, but they're still in the area and still in contact.

Partying isn't my scene, and it isn't Anabelle's either.

So, it's a surprise that one evening when we're both getting ready to park our asses on the couch and watch TV, there's a knock on the front door.

A loud, masculine knock.

"Hey!" Anabelle calls out, sticking her head out from behind the bathroom door. "I just got out of the shower—did you hear that knocking, or am I imagining things?"

"No, I heard it too," I call out from the desk I hauled back into my room when she moved in. Setting down my pencil, I rise, starting for the door. "Don't come out until you've got clothes on."

"Yes, Dad."

She couldn't have said anything more ironic.

Because standing on the front porch when I pull open the door is Coach Donnelly.

I recognize him immediately—I've seen him numerous times in the course of Oz and Zeke's wrestling careers, having attended many of their home meets and seen his face on the television during live broadcasts.

"Sir."

I push open the glass storm door so he can step inside.

And he does, wasting no time, stepping into the living room, onto the welcome mat Anabelle laid out the weekend she moved in.

It's round and blue and says *Hello, You Look Nice Today!*

Her father steps in the center of it, his presence filling the doorway, not looking nice at all.

"Who the hell are you?" He wastes no time with pleasantries.

"I'm Elliot, sir. You must be Anabelle's father. I'm a friend of Zeke Daniels and Sebastian Osborne—their old roommate, actually."

"What are you doing in my daughter's house? Are you dating her?"

"Uh, no. Not exactly."

"Where is Anabelle? I only have a little bit of time." He jingles a set of car keys in his hand. "The bus pulls out for Ohio in an hour."

"She's just getting out of the shower."

Shit. Wrong thing to say.

Coach's lips pucker, bushy brows dipping into an unpleased glower.

He squints at me. "What did you say your name was?"

I open my mouth to respond when my roommate breezes into the room—*thank fucking God*—to rescue me from her father, throwing her arms around him, looking fresh and clean and smelling even better.

Her hair is wrapped in a bright white towel, turban-style on her head, slender body swathed in her gray, silky bathrobe.

Coach's glower gets darker.

Jesus, is she trying to get me killed by wearing that damn thing? Coach looks murderous.

"Dad! Why didn't you tell me you were stopping by?"

"I didn't realize I had to." He shoots me an icy glare, glancing between Anabelle and me. "Where is your roommate? Are the two of you here alone?"

"Well, funny story about that…" She stares down at her narwhal slippers, giving them a wiggle.

I'd think it was a totally cute move if her father wasn't standing in our doorway hating on me.

"Funny story about what, young lady? Cut to the chase."

"Dad, you didn't stop by to yell at me, did you? I think we still have some leftovers from dinner if you're hungry?"

"Answer me, Anabelle. Who is this kid? That's the bullshit I'm trying to wade through here."

"Should we go into the kitchen to talk?"

"No. I'm not moving from this spot until you start talking."

There's an awkward stretch of silence before I excuse myself, taking a few cautious steps toward my bedroom. "Okay, well, I'll just go make myself scarce so you two can have some privacy. You won't even know I'm here."

"You stand right there, son. You're not going anywhere."

"Dad, how do you know this isn't my boyfriend?"

"Is it?"

"Well, no…"

"Then explain to me, if this isn't your boyfriend, why he's in this house and you're wearing a bathrobe." Coach crosses his meaty arms across a brawny chest. "Go on. I've got thirty minutes." He raises his forearm, staring down at his watch. "Go."

"See, the thing is—remember that night I didn't come home and stayed with a friend?"

Her dad gives a jerky nod.

"This is that friend."

When she moves to stand next to me, I back away slowly, afraid to get too close, not wanting to set Coach Donnelly off. She's wearing a sexy robe for fuck's sake. The last thing I want is him getting the wrong idea.

Her hands move, gesturing as she explains. "And he was living here all on his own, with a spare room he'd turned into an office. When I saw it, I thought it would be perfect converted into a bedroom."

Her old man glares at me as if it was my evil intention to lure his daughter into my den of sin from the beginning. "How convenient."

"I know, right?" Anabelle, bless her heart, doesn't hear the sarcasm in her father's voice, too relieved that she's finally able to tell him the truth. "So I asked him if I could move in. I'm sorry I didn't tell you, Daddy, but I thought you'd freak out."

"Freak out," he deadpans, looking me up and down as only a father can. "So you lied, because I specifically remember you saying your roommate's name was Ellie."

"I might have?" She chews on her thumbnail.

"I guess with a name like Ellie, I didn't realize you came with a penis. I assumed you'd have a vagina."

"Oh my god, Dad!"

"Well, I've heard very little about him, what did you expect?" Coach shrugs his solid shoulders, studying the living room.

"Now would be a good time to say something, son."

"I honestly had no idea you didn't know she was living with a guy, sir. We never talked about it."

"Is that so."

Anabelle lays a hand on her dad's arm. "I swear, he didn't know. I never told him about our discussion. I was just so excited, and Elliot—that's his name—has been so great. It's like living with a girl."

Awesome.

"He's been the best."

Once again, Coach Donnelly trails his eyes up and down my body, scoping me out, shoulders relaxing with a sigh of relief. "So you're saying he's gay."

Anabelle's laugh is light and twinkling. "No, I didn't say that."

"This is lying by omission. You led me to believe you were living with another young lady. How many times did you call him Ellie during our conversations?"

My brows go up.

She did?

"Dad, he's the best roommate I've ever had. Please just give it a chance, okay? I'm not moving out. Elliot is my friend, and I haven't been this happy in a long time."

"Not even when you were in Mass?"

"No, not even then. I don't want you to be mad, okay? I want you to trust me."

"Even though you lied, you want me to trust you."

"Dad, it was one little white lie—I never *actually* said I was living with a girl."

"Young lady," he warns, tone low.

"All right, all right, I was wrong. I'm sorry." She sidles up to her dad, putting an arm around his waist, squeezing. "Dad, this is my roommate Elliot. Elliot, this is my dad."

Jesus, could this be any more fucking awkward?

There's a knock on my door and before I can respond, a set of delicate hands are easing it open, Anabelle sticking her head through the crack, pert nose playing peekaboo.

"Are you decent? Is it safe to come in?"

I laugh. "Yeah, it's safe."

She pushes it all the way open. "Thank God—I'd die if I ever walked in on you. That's like, breaking roommate code, right?"

"Uh, that must be a girl thing, cause I wouldn't really give a shit. I've showered with a room full of guys."

"Oh, good point."

I swivel toward her in my chair, tossing my pencil on the flat surface of my desk. "What's up?"

"I just wanted to come in and apologize again for what happened earlier with my dad. I know it was a real shitty situation to put you in."

"Not gonna lie, Anabelle, it was fucking awkward. I felt like a ten-year-old being scolded, and I didn't even do anything wrong."

"I know."

I look at her now, standing near the door, her long hair dry, hanging in loose waves. Eyes bright and alert and lined in black. Concerned—for me. She inches closer, dressed in jeans and an Iowa sweatshirt, feet bare. I can't help fixating on her toes, the long length of her legs, the pretty sight of her pink glossy lips.

Guilty, I glance away, staring up at the trophies lining my wall on a shelf my dad helped me build at the beginning of the year when I moved all my shit into this dump.

Anabelle closes the space between us, inviting herself farther into my room, perching on the edge of my bed, making herself comfortable like we're familiar, like we've chatted like this a million times before.

"Are you going somewhere tonight?" I ask curiously, changing the subject.

"Yes, just for a little bit." She leans back, resting with her elbows on my quilt, swinging her legs off the end of my bed. "I met this girl in one of my classes and we really hit it off. She just texted me and thought we could meet up and have a coffee or something."

Coffee at night? Anabelle is going to be flying off the walls later.

She reads my mind. "Don't worry, I'll drink hot chocolate or something. She just wants to talk—I don't think she has many friends, either."

"Which class?"

"It's one of the science classes I needed to fulfill a gen-ed requirement—biology. She's actually one of the TAs."

"This isn't going to be a repeat of the night I brought you home that first time, is it?"

Anabelle groans. "I can't believe you're bringing that up, and no, it's not going to be a repeat because we are just going to sit and talk at a coffee shop."

"Whatever, it's none of my business."

My roommate leans over, patting my leg. "Yeah, sure it isn't."

"For real. It's none of my business."

"Oh come on—you don't take an active interest in what I do? Don't lie, we spend all our time together."

That's true. We have been spending a lot of time together. "Fine. Maybe I do give a shit about what you do, but only because I care and want you to be safe."

"Right, only because you want me to be safe."

Anabelle stares me down, blue eyes boring into me at the end of the bed, biting back a smile, wanting to say something else. I can see it in the way she's worrying her bottom lip, in her eyes—the twinkle in them.

But she doesn't just blurt out whatever she's thinking.

I admire that about her, the fact that she doesn't just say what's on her mind, that she knows when and how much to say. She's not nosy and she's not overly tenacious; that in itself makes me want to tell her things I wouldn't share with anyone else.

"Anyway, I should go. I just wanted to pop in and tell you again how sorry I am for what happened when my dad was here, but you understand why I didn't tell him, don't you?"

"Yeah, I get it."

"I really wanted to live here and I didn't want him to try to stop me. He would have had no problem with a female, which is dumb because living with girls has been nothing but drama. This has been like a vacation." She pauses. "Well, except for tonight. That was embarrassing."

"It's fine. It's over." And hopefully he won't be back to give us a hard time, because I really don't want her moving out, either.

I like having her here.

The house wouldn't be the same without her.

It certainly wouldn't smell as good.

"No more drama, I promise."

"Maybe the love of my life
got stuck in a condom."

Anabelle

I beat Rex Gunderson to class.

Unfortunately, there are far too many open seats available, including two on each side of me, presenting him with the perfect opportunity for him to plop down next to me when he finally gets here.

I'm seated halfway up, in a middle row, a bird's eye view when he strolls through the door at the front of the room.

He's wearing a different version of the same outfit I've seen him in every class: khakis, an embroidered Iowa wrestling polo, brown belt, tennis shoes. If he's trying to look the part of a team manager, he's certainly doing a bang-up job.

Rex reaches my row, shimmying his way down the aisle until he's pulling a desk next to me, inching it closer, close enough that I can smell a heavy-handed dose of aftershave and notice the hairs on his chin he missed while shaving.

He's still wet from his shower, shaggy dark hair falling in damp, sloppy strings.

"Hey. Thanks for saving me a seat." He yawns.

"I wasn't saving you a seat."

He sighs. "You know what I mean."

"I was just stating the obvious, Reginald."

He narrows his eyes. "I hate that nickname."

"It's actually not a nickname, so…"

I'm being a brat and don't even care.

"If we're going to be friends, you'll have to call me Rex." His grin is patronizing, and I'm embarrassed that I ever found it charming.

It's not.

It's strange and annoying and it makes me want to pop him right in the kisser.

"Did you get the notes I emailed you from class?"

Before I discovered what a sleaze he is, I borrowed lecture notes from him. Our professor talks really fast, and I never took pictures of the projection screen, so I had Rex email me his.

"Yes, I did. Thank you." My lips purse.

Fiddling with the laptop, I decide to take notes longhand instead since I'm quicker at it than typing on a keyboard.

"Busy weekend?" he asks, making small talk.

"No."

Short, sweet, and to the point.

Maybe he'll get the hint and stop talking.

"What do you have going on tonight?" He leans in closer, shooting me a flirtatious smile. "Feel like doing something?"

Wait—is he going to ask me out? "What are you suggesting?"

"You're new to town. I could show you around."

"Yeah? Where would you take me? Because I've already been to the park, a house party, and the mall."

He scratches his neck. "That doesn't leave us with many options."

I stare straight ahead at the whiteboard, eyes scanning the previous class's notes, acting bored. "Not many options? That's too bad."

"What about a date or something?"

"A date? With you?"

"Yeah, I could take you out. We could go dancing or something."

"Dancing? Where?"

"Mad Dog Jacks has a dance floor."

"Mad Dog Jacks?" I let the sound of indecision enter my voice, pursing my lips. "Isn't that a biker bar?"

"It used to be."

"But it's still a bar, right?"

"Sure, but they have a dance floor."

I tap on my chin, pretending to ponder his offer. "Hmm, let me think about it."

"Take your time. We have the entire class."

"How magnanimous of you."

Gunderson winks. "No problem, babe."

Babe.

Gag me.

Elliot

"**K**nock, knock."

"Door's open."

Literally, it's wide open—I have no idea why Anabelle is actually knocking.

She appears in the doorway, fully dressed to go downtown, looking fucking fantastic, not at all casual like she did for her night out with the girl from her class.

My stomach drops and I sit up straighter in the middle of my bed, where I've been studying, transcribing notes for a class I've been struggling to ace, thinking that maybe when I was finished, Anabelle and I would spend the rest of the night watching movies or playing a game, or maybe go for a drink.

Together.

"You're going out? I thought we could do something later."

"We *were*, but then Rex asked me out—dinner and dancing—and I thought it would be the perfect opportunity to feel him out a little. You know, do a little reconnaissance work? Kind of like an undercover FBI mission where I infiltrate enemy territory. See if it's worth my time to get back at the smarmy bastard."

"Oh." I flop back against my headboard. "That's cool."

Passive aggressive much, Elliot?

Anabelle's brows shoot up. "Why are you saying it like that? Do you want me to stay home? Because I will. We can hang out."

That's even worse—Anabelle would sit on the couch with me out of some twisted obligation? Because I sound pathetic? *No thank you. Hard pass.*

"No. Whatever, it's fine—I've got to catch up on this." I hold up the exercise science textbook I'm reading. "This class is kicking my ass."

She raises her arms, hands smacking her thighs on their way back down, exasperated. "Seriously Elliot? Science on a Friday night?"

"I'm trying to graduate with my GPA intact, Donnelly, so I can get into a stellar grad school. This shit is hard."

"You can take one night off to have some fun."

She has a point. "I suppose. Maybe I'll see what the guys are up to."

"That's the spirit. Anyway, I just wanted to know what you think of this outfit for tonight. Is it too casual?"

Too casual? Ugh. Yeah, *no*.

Tight jeans, high black boots. Black fitted shirt. Dark, long hair down, messy. Glossy lips.

Anabelle looks both conservative *and* smoking hot at the same time.

"I thought you said this date was *fake*." This sure as shit looks like a real date outfit to me, the way she's fussing about her clothes and touching her hair.

"It is."

"Then why…" my voice trails off.

She props her hands on her waist, jutting out her hip. "Why what?"

"What's with the outfit?"

She looks down the front of her shirt. "What's wrong with it? It's just jeans and a shirt."

Maybe, but her tits look fantastic.

"Nothing is *wrong* with it. You look nice."

Anabelle laughs, poking a big hoop earring through the hole in her ear and tightening the back. "I thought the whole point of going on a date was to look nice for the other person."

"That's the point when the date is *real*."

She pulls a face. "Why are you being weird? Rex is a complete douche, but I have a feeling he's harmless, and I want to find out."

Harmless?

Is she for real? "You're fucking with me, right? I thought we established the guy is only trying to get into your pants to win a bet, and now you're getting all dressed up for him. That's all I'm saying."

"He *is* a douchebag, but I mean, it might be worth it to go out with him, just to see? I feel like his whole problem is Eric Johnson, and that's the guy I have to watch out for. He was super pushy that day in the gym."

"What do you mean, super pushy?" The hair on the back of my neck prickles.

She fiddles with the silver hoop in her right ear. "Elliot, if we get into the whole story right now, I'm going to be late."

Late for her fake date.

I let out a puff of pent-up, frustrated air.

"You think Johnson will be there tonight?"

"I don't know…I hope not. Rex thinks this is a date, so I'm assuming he won't want his friends around. I'll cut him some slack, there's no harm in that."

Is she fucking serious? The more she talks about it, the more pissed off I get thinking about the whole damn situation.

"Are you so lonely and desperate you're willing to give this guy a chance? He's an asshole, Ana. Everyone on campus fucking knows it."

"Desperate? *Wow*, Elliot, that was low." She stands in the doorway of my room, hands on her hips. "I'm not giving him a chance, so screw. You."

Shit. That was a really dick thing to say. "I'm sorry. I didn't mean it like that."

"How about you worry about your own crappy relationship problems and let me worry about mine, okay?"

"I have a crappy relationship? I don't have a girlfriend—what are you talking about?"

"Precisely." Anabelle scoffs, nose tipping into the air with a sniff. "These walls are thin, you know. I might be across the hall, but I hear *every*thing."

They are? She can?

I sit up straighter, adjusting the reading glasses on my face. Set down the book I've been holding. "Like what?"

Her shoulders shrug.

"Why are you shrugging?" *What does that mean?*

She inspects her nails. "I just know you have a lot of time to yourself, if you know what I mean. Maybe if you put yourself out there, Elliot—if you were in a relationship, you wouldn't have to...*you know*."

When she lifts her head, her brows are raised, both of our gazes sliding down my torso to the flaccid dick lying against my thigh—the dick she obviously hears me jerking in the middle of the night from across the hall.

Jesus.

Christ.

My face flushes but I manage not to flinch. "I do put myself out there. You're not making any sense."

"*Do* you though?" She crosses her arms, plumping her breasts above the collar of her shirt. Anabelle has obviously taken great pains with her appearance, spray-tanning herself to a golden perfection.

I return my gaze back to her eyes.

"You're so passive aggressive, Elliot. I don't think even *you* know what you want."

"I am not. Just because I'm not out there hitting on every goddamn girl stepping in my path does not make me passive aggressive."

The thing is, I know she's right. I have been chicken-shit lately. If I wasn't, I'd have already told her I'm starting to have feelings for her.

That it kills me not being able to wrap my hands around her waist when she's standing at the sink, wearing that gray robe, hair pulled up atop her head. That I find her long, delicate fingers fascinating. That the sound of her voice instantly lifts my mood.

"Okay, you're not." Another shrug. "Cool."

"Cool? What does that mean?"

"Oh my God, I'm not going to stand here all night and list the things you could be doing if you wanted a relationship! I don't have the time. I just meant you could put yourself out there more. That's it. Or maybe you don't want a relationship and I'm wasting my breath, I don't know. It's none of my business."

"You're the one who brought it up."

"Only because you're giving me shit about my outfit."

"Otherwise you never would have said anything?"

Her shoulders rise and fall, breathing hard because she's gotten herself all worked up. "Maybe I would have mentioned it eventually." She rakes both hands down her stomach, smoothing out the hem of her top. "Do you like this top on me or not?"

"Yeah, it's fine."

"Just fine? *Ugh.*"

It's better than fine, actually. She looks gorgeous, and if circumstances were different, I'd tell her so. But, she's my roommate, she hasn't indicated she wants to change things anytime soon, and the last thing I want is Anabelle getting the wrong idea by me hitting on her.

Not when she's living across the hall.

Not when I have to see her in that damn silk robe every morning.

"You look good."

Really fucking good.

Hot.

"You're sure I shouldn't go change?"

"Nah. You look hot."

"Why the hell didn't you say that to begin with?"

"Because, you're not sticking to the plan!"

Now I have her laughing, thank God. "I am the only one following the plan! I'm letting him take me out for *free* food! And to start, I'm going to order a bunch of appetizers and drinks, not eat or drink a single one of them, and make him pay."

"Are you going out after your dinner?"

"Yes." She picks at her navy blue nail polish. "For dancing, remember?"

"Seriously Anabelle? You're going to let him wine and dine you?"

"I repeat: *free. Food. Fake.*"

She's exhausting. "Is he coming here to pick you up?"

"No, I'm meeting him downtown. I thought it would be best—you know, no awkward goodnight walks to the front door, no fending off a goodnight kiss."

I don't even want to try imagining that scenario playing out on *my* fucking front porch.

"Can you do me a favor? Don't lose sight of the fact that Rex bet one of his teammates he could fuck you for the chance at a bigger bedroom, okay?"

All the way from my bed, I can see her chest getting red. "Who would forget a detail like that? Do you think I'm an idiot?"

"No. I just think you're being too nice."

"Disagree." She sticks her forefinger in the air. "I sent Eric Johnson to my dad's house already, remember? He won't be bothering me again."

"*Bet* he does."

"Haha, very funny. Don't you start with that *betting* crap."

"I was joking. Lighten up."

"Fine." She relents. "It was a decent play on words, though I'm not too proud to admit it."

"Should I get dressed and come with you?" I set the book down on my comforter, starting to rise from the bed.

Anabelle throws her hands up to stop me, waving them in the air. "Oh my God, don't you dare! I do not need you hovering, *Dad*. He'll know something is up."

I beg to differ. "No he won't—Rex Gunderson is a fucking moron. I've seen his brand of genius at work many, many times."

"Still, don't you dare show up." She sends me an accusatory glare.

Not intimidated, I ignore her, thinking I might actually show up on her fake date—you know, scope it out, check out the situation. Make sure he keeps his fucking hands off her.

If I can't touch her, he sure as hell can't.

The last time Anabelle went out to party, I carried her semiunconscious body through my door and tucked her into my bed to sleep it off. I've earned the right to be overprotective of her.

She's my friend.

The thought makes me throw up in my mouth a little.

"Oh!" I say a little too loudly. "I have an idea before you leave. Should we have some kind of Bat Signal? In case you need me?"

"*Sure*." My roommate rolls her eyes. "Or I could just text you like a normal person."

"This whole revenge plot thing is becoming anti-climactic, seeing as you've forgotten what a tool this dude is."

"Oh my God, *twist my arm*, we'll have a panic word! What do you want the signal to be?"

I sit up on my bed, resting against the headboard. "How about 'take me out to the ball game' and I'll be there within five minutes."

"How unoriginal."

"I was going to suggest 'balls deep' as a soccer reference but didn't want to offend you."

"As if I've never heard that zinger while hanging around my dad's practice gym. Still, it was very considerate of you not to suggest it." She laughs. Stops laughing. "Wait, what do you mean 'be there in five minutes?' That would mean you were close by."

"Don't worry about it. Just know I'll be within five minutes away."

"Elliot! Did I not just say I didn't want you spying on me!"

"I won't! I've decided to go downtown. Not in the same bar, I swear."

She squints one eye closed. "Why don't I believe you?"

"Because I'm full of shit and we both know it, that's why."

I grin, determined to find out where she is and make sure I'm in the area. I don't trust Rex Gunderson, and neither does anyone else. I don't want to just burn the bridge he has with Anabelle, I want to drain the lake beneath it and fill it with concrete.

Anabelle is spending the night out with a fucking loser.

"Can we just get this night over with please?"

"You are *so* bossy when you're crabby."

I throw my legs over the edge of the bed, stretching. "Having a roommate was supposed to be fun and not cramp my lifestyle."

"It is fun—don't be a baby. Get dressed and we can ride together since you insist on stalking me. I'll even let you drive."

I get to drive, drop her off downtown for her fake date from hell with a complete tool, and then lurk for the rest of the evening?

Awesome.

Exactly what I wanted to be doing on a Friday night.

16

#DOUCHEBAG

"It could be raining men
and I'd still be single."

Anabelle

I will admit, coming out with Rex Gunderson hasn't been one of the worst ideas I've ever had.

In fact, other than the fact that he's ignoring me by replying to incoming text messages, I've had way worst dates.

We're at a small restaurant in town, and even though I'm just wearing jeans and a black shirt, I'm still overdressed. This is more of a diner—a greasy spoon, as we call it back east—serving beer, burgers, and fried appetizers.

I push aside the napkins in the center of the table, clasping my hands, waiting for my fake date to put his phone down and notice me.

If Rex Gunderson is trying to win a bet so he can have sex with me, his effort is seriously lacking. How do girls find this behavior appealing?

He isn't paying any attention to me.

He's doused with cologne.

And he keeps referring to himself in the third person.

Annoyed, I tap on the table, nails clicking against the wooden top. "Are you almost done? I'm getting bored."

"Yeah, give me *one* more second, babe." He shoots me a toothy grin that's meant to be charming. "Team bizness."

I wish I hadn't come out with him.

I'd give anything to be snuggled up on the couch with Elliot right now, watching a show or reading a book—something I haven't done in forever.

Rex sets his phone on the table, seeming ready to finally give me his full attention. "So, this is fun."

"Really? You think this is fun?" I lean forward. "Is this what you normally do with your dates?"

"Bring them here? Yeah. It's the perfect setup. I can sit and watch the game"—there are flat-screen TVs everywhere—"and the ladies can sit and watch me. It's a win-win."

"You're kidding me. You did not just say that." I fall back in the booth, back hitting the seat, laughing. "Do you have a sheet of paper and a pen? I want to write that down."

Classic.

I wipe the tears now spilling from the corners of my eyes, determined to remember every bit of this night.

I seriously *can't* with this guy.

He is too much.

And he is for real.

"Can I ask you a question?"

"Totes."

Totes? I do a mental eye roll. No one uses that word anymore.

"I've heard a few things and wanted some clarification."

"Things?" Rex studies me somewhat warily, throwing his arm on the seatback behind him. "Like what?"

I thank the waitress when she sets down our appetizers then focus my energy on the twerp sitting across from me. "I heard that last year you pulled a few pranks on a guy who's on the wrestling team. What were they?"

"Oh man, my reputation precedes me!" He laughs. "You heard about that? It was crazy, man—legendary."

"Legendary, huh? How so?"

"Anabelle, you're sitting across from a legend. Obviously, if you've heard about it, they're going to be talking about it for years."

"Talking about what?"

"Okay, so there was this new guy, right? And he ended up living with me and my roommate cause he didn't know anyone in Iowa." Rex takes a chicken wing, dips it in sauce, and bites down. Chews. "Anyway, the dude never went out, right? Like, ever. So, my roommate and I thought we'd help him out, ya know?"

I nod along. "K, then what?"

He cleans his face, swiping at the ranch dressing at the corner of his mouth with a napkin. "We make these signs—totally shit-faced from drinking all night—and sneak into the dorms without ID cards. The chick at the front desk had a major lady boner for my roommate."

"Uh huh."

"We make all these copies of a flyer—"

"What did it say?"

"Uh, let me think." He regards the ceiling, squinting, thinking hard. "*Are you the lucky lady who wants to pop our roommate's cherry? Must have a pulse. He will reciprocate with oral.*"

"Was he seriously a virgin?" Not that it matters, but since he brought it up…

"Nah, I don't think so. It was our marketing hook, just had more mass appeal, know what I mean? Ladies dig virgins."

"They do?" This is news to me.

"Oh yeah, totally. The whole thing blew up, right? Chicks texting and calling nonstop, wanting to bang him. All in all, a total success."

"Isn't that an invasion of privacy, putting his actual phone number on posters?"

"Totally legal."

"Is it though?" I make a mental note to look it up as Rex continues his story.

"So anyway, it ends with a happy ending because he has a girlfriend now and they're shacking up."

"Are you sure he didn't move out because of the prank?"

"No way man, he should be thanking us—we're matchmak-ers. Without those flyers, he never would have hooked up with his girlfriend. She was one of the chicks who texted him."

Oh.

Well.

How interesting.

"Are you friends with her?"

"Nah, she hates us." Gunderson laughs, and it's loud and so full of humor, I laugh along with him. I mean, come on—how could you not? You'd have to be stone cold not to find this guy the teeny *tiniest* bit amusing.

He *is* a complete numskull.

I can say with full confidence that Rex Gunderson, honest to God, thinks he is ruler of pranks, and he sees nothing wrong with pulling them. In his opinion, they are harmless fun, and the truth is? I am highly entertained, one hundred percent.

I couldn't make this shit up if I tried.

I want to climb inside his brain and find out what makes it tick.

"Is there more? Did you pull any other pranks last year?"

"Let me think—after I eat this chicken wing."

He stuffs one in his mouth, whole.

Chews. Swallows.

Grabs another one, wash, rinse, repeat.

Cleans himself off with a napkin, moaning with pleasure. "Damn those are good. I could eat here every night of the week."

Yeah, he *could*, because it's a cheap bar that serves cheap fried food, not an actual restaurant.

I hand him a wet wipe for his chin. "You were saying?"

"Right, pranks. Oh! Duh. I brought my roommate's girlfriend up to a cabin once and left her there with him alone, without a car."

I blink. "What?"

"Yeah. I told his girlfriend—well, she wasn't his girlfriend at the time. I don't even think they'd banged yet..." Rex pauses, thinking a little too hard. "No, they definitely weren't dating. So I give her this sob story about this bonding weekend up at Coach Donnelly's cottage and said all the girlfriends and shit were going to be there—they weren't—and if she didn't want him to be the only loser there without anyone, she should go up and surprise him."

"Did she?"

"Totally."

"And?" *Jeez, get to the point!* This story is taking forever.

"And I drove her up. Then when they went upstairs to dump her luggage and stuff, we disappeared. Left them there." Another pause so he can scarf down a few more wings. "Man, he was so pissed, no way was I going back. Besides, I wasn't the only one involved so it wasn't my fault."

"Whose idea was it?"

"Well, *mine*, but someone could have stopped me."

I genuinely think Rex Gunderson is just a careless human being. He's selfish and callous, thinking only about himself.

It's not that he doesn't consider consequences, it's that he lives for the moment.

Lives for fun.

Thinks he's damn near invincible.

I wonder what it would take to break this guy. What would have to happen to make him take a hard look at himself? To *change* him?

After sitting with him, hearing him talk, I'm not sure if the answer is *time*.

Maybe maturity?

"He moved out after that?"

"Shortly after, once the semester ended, yeah."

"And now you and your roommate have an extra room?"

"Yup."

"The big room."

He stops dipping a piece of celery in the ranch dressing to watch me. "Yup, the big room."

"You know, not too long ago, I needed a place to live." I smile, twirling my straw innocently. "I could have taken that big room."

"No shit? That would have been cool—having a girl room-mate."

I cringe, wondering what life would be like living with a goon like Rex and a jackass like Eric Johnson. It would be a nightmare, that's what. I bet they're complete slobs, careless, and inconsiderate.

"Cool…hmm, I wouldn't be so sure about that. How long has it been since you vacuumed?"

"Vacuumed?"

My head tips back as the bubble of laughter climbs up my throat. "You know, a vacuum, the machine that sucks dirt and crumbs off the floor, keeps the house clean."

"I don't think we have one of those."

He doesn't *know*? "How do you clean?"

"Clean what?"

"Uh, your house?"

"Oh. Sometimes when we have girls spend the night, we have them clean the bathroom and shit before they leave in the morning."

"For real?"

"It's a pretty sweet deal actually, and so much cheaper than hiring someone to do it."

"I can't believe you just said that."

"Why? You've never heard of hiring someone to clean your place?"

"No, not *that*. I can't believe you said you have the girls you have sex with clean your shit up in the morning. We are on a date."

Rex Gunderson scrunches up his goofy features. "I'd never ask *you* to scrub my toilet, that I can guarantee you."

He winks.

I cannot stop laughing.

"You're…I don't even know what to say about you right now."

"Trust me, many have come before you, tried, and failed."

I don't know why, but this makes me laugh even harder.

Gunderson has brought me to a biker bar.

Perfect.

Way to woo the ladies, Gunderson.

He's disappeared into the crowd, presumably to schmooze and get us adult beverages, although now that I think about it, he never asked what I wanted.

What a gentleman.

I scan the crowd, bodies packed into the building far beyond capacity. Bright blue lights strobing, loud music vibrating the speakers.

"What's the verdict?" a deep voice asks near my ear, warm breath brushing the outer shell and tickling my neck. It makes me shiver.

Has me swinging, nailing my roommate in the stomach with the back of my hand.

"Shit! Jeez, don't sneak up on people, Elliot! And never do that at home—you'll give me a heart attack."

His presence gives my heart a kick, sending it into mild palpitations I've recently become familiar with.

"How can I sneak up on you in this place? It's packed!" He has to dip his head so I can hear him, and I'm not exactly put off by his nearness.

Not in the least.

Because by leaps and bounds, Elliot St. Charles is growing on me. Gives me butterflies. Has me lying awake, staring at the ceiling, listening hard for the sounds of his—

"Where's your *date*?" he asks, emphasizing the last word with air quotes, a sardonic smirk spreading his lips. "I saw him scurry off like a little rat."

"I had to run to the bathroom and he maybe ran to get us drinks, not a hundred percent sure."

"You are not going to take a drink from him. No fucking way."

I lean in to hear his reply. "What do you mean?"

"Hello—date rape drugs? I don't know anything about that dude other than the fact that he's a complete fuckwit, but I definitely wouldn't take a drink from him."

I slap a hand over my mouth, eyes wide. "Oh my God, you're right! I never thought of that."

"I'm not saying he's going to, or that he's the kind of guy who would. Just be careful."

I rise on my tiptoes, planting a kiss on his warm cheek. My lips linger near his ear. "Thank you for caring enough to look out for me."

When he laughs, I laugh, our eyes meeting under the dim blue lights of this sketchy bar.

"Are you having fun?"

"Rex Gunderson isn't horrible, he's just…" I purse my lips. "A smidge clueless."

"Just a smidge?"

I raise my arm, extending my fingers. "Little bit crazy, lot bit naïve—*not* a stellar combo."

"Ya think?" he deadpans.

I glance around the perimeter. "Are you here with anyone?"

"Honestly? No. I tried enlisting my old roommates to join me on this recon mission, but they're both presently occupied."

"With what?"

Elliot is tall, so he has to lean down, upper torso dipping, leaning into me until I feel his heat in my personal space. "My old roommate Sebastian and his girlfriend went to visit his folks, and Zeke is, well…I think he's planning some shit for his girlfriend. I don't know, it sounds like he's getting ready to propose."

My brows go up. "Propose? *Marriage*?"

Elliot chuckles. I can't hear it, but I can see the humor reflected in his eyes. "Yes, marriage. I mean, you have no idea how far this guy has come—he used to be a real piece of work."

"I've seen him around—he still helps my dad out. Dad said he spends crazy amounts of time with his girlfriend. Violet is her name, right?"

"Violet, yeah."

"How old are they?"

"Twenty-two, about to turn twenty-three."

"Wow. They must really be in love."

"Head over heels and all that." Elliot's gaze shifts, homing in on someone in the distance. "Shit, there's your dipshit of a date. I'm going to catch up to him real quick before heading out."

My eyes narrow suspiciously. "Be nice."

"You want me to be nice? *Why?*"

"I don't think he can help himself, Elliot. I've deduced he lacks the common sense gene."

"No promises to be nice, but I'll do my best."

I pat him on the forearm. Squeeze. "I know you will."

"But I'll probably be a dick."

"Elliot!"

"What?! I won't be able to help it. I'm bored, let me have some fun."

"You're the worst."

He boops me on the nose. "Stop. Flattery will get you everywhere."

Elliot

“The two of you seem pretty chummy—what’s the deal?”

I sidle up to Rex Gunderson, the most popular unpopular guy on campus. He just walked out of the bathroom, still fussing with the hem of his shirt. Still zipping his fly.

Sees me.

“Hey Elliot, what’s up.”

“Oh nothing, just popping in to check on my roomie cause I had nothing else going on and I’m a good friend like that.”

“What do you mean?”

“Oh didn’t Anabelle tell you? I’m her roommate.”

“Roommate?” He looks confused.

“Roommate. You know, we *live* together.”

“*You* live with Anabelle.” He pauses, scratches his balls. “She might have mentioned at dinner she’d been *desperate* for a place to live, but she didn’t say it was with you. Guess she wasn’t lying about being desperate.”

He smirks.

Dickhead.

“Everyone on campus has heard you and Johnson have an ex-tra room available—or are you still on that mission to have the big room all to yourself?”

He’s onto my wordplay, narrowing his beady eyes. “Does her dad know she’s living with a dude?”

“Not that it’s any of your fucking business, but yes he knows. Why, what would you do if he didn’t know? Tattle on her?”

Gunderson scoffs, disbelieving. “There is no way Coach Donnelly is okay with Anabelle living with a guy—no fucking way.”

“How ‘bout you mind your own business, Gunderson?”

He ignores me. "What's it like?"

"I just said mind your own business."

"Has she crawled into bed with you yet? Dude, that would be so fucking awesome."

Before he can say another word, I'm in his personal space, bumping my chest against his. "Say one more word about it and I'm going to—"

Gunderson's hands go up. "Whoa, whoa. Dude, what the hell is up with you tonight? Between you, Osborne, and Daniels, I always thought *you* were the gentleman—guess I was wrong."

"Guess so, or maybe I just don't like you. Never have."

He rolls his eyes, glancing over my shoulder. "And I'm real broken up about it."

Why is this guy so fucking annoying? "Enjoy your night. It'll be your one and only date with her."

"As if that's up to you." He snorts. "Wait a second..." He rears back to look me in the eye. "Are you—you are! You're jealous aren't you?"

"Don't be stupid, Gunderson. *No one* is jealous of you."

"You are. You're jealous I'm here on a date with Anabelle Donnelly."

He's struck a nerve and knows it, the little fucker. "No—I have a problem with the fact that you're a lying scumbag who's only going out with her to win a bigger bedroom."

"I don't know what the hell you're talking about."

"Everyone fucking knows, Gunderson. It's just a matter of time before Coach finds out."

But he's no longer looking me in the eye; he's scanning the room looking for an escape from this conversation.

I get right up in his face so he hears every word I say. "If you think for one second I'm not watching you like a *hawk*, you're out of your fucking mind."

"What is your damn problem, man?" Rex throws his hands up. "I haven't done anything to you, and no one has slept with her.

Trust me, she sent Johnson to her fucking dad's house, so he won't go near her with a ten-foot cock."

He laughs at his own joke, clever idiot.

"You're too dumb to stay away from her. You just can't stop yourself from doing stupid shit, can you? First that bullshit with your old roommate Rabideaux, now this crap with Johnson, and that's only the shit anyone has found out about. This isn't the first time the two of you have pulled a stunt like this, and if you know what's good for you, you'll apologize to her, because once her dad finds out, you and that pissant Johnson are going to be *fucked*."

Even under the dim lights of the bar, Gunderson is blanching, swallowing hard. Nervous.

"I haven't done anything," he repeats with conviction. A firm nod. "Maybe you should climb down out of my *ass* before I complain to the bouncer that you're harassing me."

"You're so fucked." I raise my arm, clamping my giant palm on his bony shoulder. "Consider this a friendly warning, eh?"

I straighten the collar of his polo shirt, wanting to smack my palm across his face. "Now act normal and smile, because I promised Anabelle I'd behave myself tonight." Pull back and get a nice, long look at him. "Keep your dick and hands to yourself, pony boy."

"I wasn't—"

"Hands to your *fucking* self."

"Jesus Christ, St. Charles, were you always as big a douchebag as Osborne and Daniels?"

"Yes. Obviously I learned from the best."

"My phone doesn't even autocorrect the word 'fuck' anymore. It knows me better than I know myself."

Elliot

laying the white knight is exhausting.

I'm sprawled out on my bed, the house pitch black except for the glowing television in the corner of my room, when out of the corner of my eye, I see Anabelle tiptoe past.

Quiet as a church mouse, but not quiet enough.

"Psst. What are you still doing up?" I call out to her in a voice barely above a whisper. We're both awake, but the lights are all off. The mood calls for it, bedtime having come and gone hours ago.

"I was thirsty," she whispers. "Going to the kitchen for a drink. I was trying not to disturb you in case you were asleep. I didn't realize you were awake."

"Yeah, can't sleep."

"It would help if the TV wasn't on." Her eyes land on the flat screen then flicker back to me, narrowing. "Wait a second—are you watching our show without me? You said you were going to wait!"

Oh shit.

I cringe, busted.

"I'm sorry! It's been driving me crazy and you've been at your dad's the past few nights so I thought I'd get caught up."

"Elliot, I'm not caught up either!" Her arms cross over her breasts, the thin, sexy tank top does nothing to conceal her breasts. "I feel betrayed. What kind of a friend does that?"

"I just started it!"

"That doesn't make it right! How am I going to forgive you?"

"Want me to rewind it?"

From the doorway, Anabelle rolls her eyes. "Duh, *yes* rewind it! You want anything from the kitchen?"

"Nah, I'm good."

My roommate isn't gone for long, the pitter-patter of her bare feet in the hallway returning within a few minutes.

Setting a glass of water on the bedside table, my roommate climbs into my bed—and it's not that I feel it's an invasion of my privacy, it's just different.

And let's face it, I was never in danger of being ridiculously sexually attracted to my last roommates like I am with this one.

"Do you mind if I crawl under the covers?"

"No, of course not."

Please do, I silently add, *so I don't have to sit and stare at your long, smooth legs.*

On all fours, ass in the air, Anabelle pulls back the bedspread to join me. The tank she's wearing dips, giving me a clear shot of her cleavage. I *try* to glance away when her boobs sway beneath the fabric.

"Oh my gosh, it's so warm in here." She makes a show of plumping the pillows behind her head, propping them against my headboard so she gets a better view of the TV, arms crossed over her chest. "This bed is so much more comfortable than mine. There's so much of it, I could get lost in here."

"Right." 'Cause really, what else is there to say? I can barely concentrate on the remote control in my hand, fumbling around for the pause button. Hit play, doing my best to settle on my side of the bed.

My side of the bed.

It sounds so…permanent.

My side. Her side.

Knock that shit off, Elliot.

Christ, if the guys saw me right now, they would be laughing their asses off at how awkward I'm acting. Amateur.

I shoot Anabelle a sidelong glance then focus on the show we've started binge-watching together at night, usually two episodes in a row—sometimes three—until one of us is too tired to keep watching.

We're on season four of a show showcasing a hyper-dysfunctional family living in the city, enduring one fucked-up scenario after the next.

It's riveting. We can't stop watching.

"Was that your foot?" Anabelle laughs. "Stop that, it's cold!"

"Sorry."

"Want me to warm you up?" she jokes, her toes wiggling under the covers, dangerously close to mine. She hunkers down deeper into my blankets, not unlike the night I carried her into my house, passed out in my arms.

Flopping on her side, she rests her cheek on her hand, watching me. "Did I tell you I got my cleats in the mail today? And my mom managed to find my shin guards and some socks. They're hot pink with black polka dots." Her laugh is low.

Cute.

I look down at her, startled by how relaxed she is compared to the inner turmoil I'm feeling. Seriously, she doesn't seem at all fazed by lying here so close to me.

"Don't you dare fall asleep on me. We've only been watching this show for ten minutes and you'll make me watch it all over again from the beginning."

Her lips curl into a catlike smile. "That's probably true."

She's not fussy or high maintenance, but she does like to know what's happening on her favorite shows. Hates when I watch without her. Makes me rewind if I'm talking during important parts. Makes me rewind if *she's* talking during important parts.

"Why is she going out with him? Tell me why," my roommate says to the TV. "I swear, if she screws things up with Steve, I will be so pissed."

I glance over. "I thought you hated Steve."

"I do, but of all the guys she keeps banging, I like him the best."

"But he's a criminal, and last week you said he was too skinny."

"He is."

"That makes no sense."

Anabelle sighs. "I just can't do skinny jeans on a guy, okay? It's weird."

"I wear skinny jeans."

"No you don't. Yours are tapered—there's a huge difference." I'm not going to argue with her when I have no fucking clue what she's talking about.

"Do you want me to rewind what we just missed?"

"Yes please," she simpers, nose buried in my sheets, and I actually hear her inhale. "These smell so good."

"Uh, thanks." I pause. "Thanks for washing them this weekend."

"Thanks for hauling the garbage cans down to the curb yesterday when it was my turn."

"No problem." It was her turn—I know this because she made a chart when she moved in so we could share responsibilities. There are only like, five chores, but if a chart makes her feel like she's contributing, I'd be an idiot to complain.

I rewind, go a little too far, and hit play. We watch again in silence until I wonder out loud, "Are women really attracted to guys who look like that?"

"Pfft, I'm not."

"Every guy she goes out with looks like a creep. I don't get it."

"It's fake, Elliot."

"I know that, Anabelle. I'm merely making an observation." I roll my eyes. "Out of all her boyfriends, who would you date?"

"Gross. You're going to make me choose from those guys? I can't. I'd rather throw up in my mouth."

"Just pick one."

"Fine. I'd pick Gus—not because I want to, but because you're forcing my hand." She rolls to her back, staring up at the ceiling. "We're going to be up all night if we keep talking."

I click rewind. "Should we just turn it off?"

"Yeah, maybe. I'm tired. My heart's not in it."

We laugh, and she sits up to take a drink of water. Falls back onto my pillows, hair piled on top of her head in a messy bun, lobbing from side to side when she moves.

"I guess I'll go back to my room."

I hesitate, not wanting her to go, already missing her but not knowing if it's appropriate for me to ask her to spend the night.

Casually, "Nah, you're already comfortable. If you promise to keep your hands to yourself, you can stay put."

"Yes, please. I'm too lazy to walk all the way across the hall."

"The whole ten feet?"

"It's *so* far." She chuckles in the dark when I hit the power button and my television goes off, making the room pitch black.

"Wow. This is dark." Her voice cuts through the night.

"Isn't your room dark?"

"Not *this* dark. I have a streetlight outside my window that keeps me up sometimes. One of these days I'll order some curtains, or maybe I'll buy myself a sleep mask."

"I can help you hang curtains."

Her hand finds me in the dark, patting its way up my forearm. Bicep. Giving me a squeeze.

"Good night Elliot."

I yawn, lying flat, rolling to my side, facing the door. "Night roomie."

Another soft chuckle and she yawns, too. "I love it when you call me that."

"You do?"

"Yeah. I don't know why—it's not much fun as far as nicknames go, but...I'm glad I'm here."

The room is silent as I think of what to say next.

"Same."

Anabelle

I don't know what time it was when we both fell asleep, but at some point in the middle of the night, we gravitated together, something I've never done before when in bed with another human. I'm wrapped up like a pretzel.

I don't know when I rolled up beside him, or when my cheek found the space above his armpit, resting there...or when I threw my leg over his thigh, tucking it between his legs.

Palm flattened out over his ribcage.

His arm around me, pulling me in.

When did we curl into each other?

Does it even matter?

His body is so warm, and I'm in no rush to unfurl myself, content to listen to the rhythmic sound of his heart. It's beating relatively slowly, so without having to look, I know he's still sleeping.

Bu-bump, bu-bump, bu-bump.

Steady.

Constant.

Just like Elliot.

Over the course of a few short weeks, he's become more than just my roommate; he's become my friend. Big. Strong.

Solid.

Every muscle on him is firm and toned. Tan from playing soccer with no shirt on, his upper body is carved to perfection, not too hard, not too soft.

Perfect.

Eyes still closed against the morning sun, the tips of my fingers do the exploring for me. Softly drift from their spot on his sternum, trailing across his ribcage, pressing into his hot flesh in slow, lazy circles.

Bu-bump-bu-bump-bu-bump.

His heartbeat quickens.

My hand runs over his skin, up along his collarbone. The space between his neck and shoulder, languid and carnal, back to his chest.

He smells good.

I always notice, but more so when we're piled on his bed watching television, every time he shifts on the bed. Fresh like a shower, like soap—no heavy cologne or body spray. Just water and soap and *him.*

I crack an eyelid when my fingers skim along the underside of his pecs, chancing a glance at his face.

He's awake. Watchful. Massive palm beginning a leisurely stroke up and down my back, his touch leaving a hot trail in its wake.

As my thumb caresses his nipple, my eyes travel down the length of his long, lean torso, settling on the front of his athletic pants, on the stiffening dick there.

Bu-bump-bu-bump-bu-bump.

Biting down on my lower lip, I continue to caress his skin. Chest, sternum, stomach. It's so smooth—he has almost no hair, nothing but the sexiest of happy trails. It's light brown and looks soft, starting at his belly button and disappearing into that mysterious place I can't help fixating on.

Happy trail. Pleasure track. Garden path.

Guh!

We don't even flirt. I should not be eyeing the goods.

Well, we do flirt occasionally, but not in the traditional sense. The routine we've fallen into goes way beyond comfortable. It's sweet the way he takes care of me when we're only roommates, buying my favorite foods and leaving the lights on so I don't have to come home to a dark house. Leaving me notes instead of just texting me.

Cute little notes with smiley faces on the bathroom mirror.

Twice, he's walked me to class.

Twice, I've walked him to his.

Last week, when I knew he had a late study group, I made him a sandwich to take along so he wouldn't starve. Yesterday, when I was running behind, he stood by the door holding my backpack, watching as I rushed around the living room, desperately trying to slide my shoes on. Ended up driving me so I wouldn't get locked out of class for being late.

Bu-bump-bu-bump-bu-bump.

His heart thumps and I'm not sure if I want to stop touching him, even though we've officially crossed an invisible line we can't walk back over.

Elliot's hand continues rubbing my back, sliding up and down my ribcage, his palm that big. Massive hands meant to touch my skin, fingers that play with the hemline of my tank top. Glide beneath the material, hiking it up, etching hot, burning lines on my spine.

His hand stops on my ribcage. Thumb strokes back and forth, grazing the underside of my breast.

It's then that our eyes finally meet.

I wish I could read his mind or see into his soul, because I can't for the life of me read his expression. Tired, half-hooded eyes, his mouth—those lips I've been secretly wanting to kiss—is impassive.

We don't speak. We don't have to.

I have nothing to say that wouldn't be awkward anyway, so I keep my lips sealed shut and concentrate on the way Elliot feels pulled up beside me. How it feels being wrapped in his strong arms.

How it feels having his hand almost touching my boob.

Glancing down again at his boner, I feel somewhat guilty that he has a hard-on and we're not yet at the point where I can do anything about it. So, I just watch it spasm every now and again, every time I touch him somewhere new above the waist.

Bu-bump-bu-bump-bu-bump.
A heart is racing but I'm not sure if it's his or mine.
I'm not sure whose heart is beating fastest.

18

#DOUCHEBAG

"*Well that didn't work:*
An autobiography."

Elliot

shift happened this morning.

I can feel it in the air as we get ready for our pick-up soccer game, shyly smiling at each other and joking all the way to my car.

I sneak a few covert glances at her over the hood of my car when she climbs in, her long hair pulled into a ponytail, her goofy grin confusing the shit out of me.

We listen to music on our way to the park, windows down all the way, cool breeze blowing Anabelle's ponytail into long wisps around her face. Every now and again she looks over and smiles, biting down on her bottom lip before turning back toward the window.

What was that look? Is she flirting? Just being nice?

Jesus, I can't tell.

I need a fucking manual.

On the field, we choose teams. There are twenty-five of us today, so it's a near even split to make two teams. I end up on one, Anabelle on the other, and we take our warm-up laps together once she ties her cleats.

She's so fucking cute.

So pretty.

Her black soccer shorts are thin, the socks she has pulled up her calves a bright neon pink and peppered with black dots. Her gray t-shirt says *Sweating like a Sinner in Church* and she has a yellow apron over it, her sports bra straps playing peekaboo with the collar.

Sue me for noticing.

Side by side, we jog around the field, Anabelle's ponytail swaying the entire way. It's jaunty and cute, and I'm excited to play against her today.

It's her first game with our group, and I can tell she's nervous because she hasn't stopped chattering the entire three laps we've made.

"What if I accidentally take you out while I'm using my sweet, sweet moves on you?"

"What kind of moves? This is regulation, you know, not gorilla-style."

She turns, jogging backward. "I don't know. First I'd come at you like this"—she swerves—"then I'd fake you out like this."

Anabelle does a few toe taps, mimicking some of the fast footwork we use during games, breasts bouncing beneath her shirt.

I avert my eyes. "You shouldn't be giving me all your best plays."

"You ain't seen nothing yet."

"Put your money where your mouth is Donnelly. The game hasn't even started yet—isn't it too early for trash talk?"

Her laugh rings out. "It's never too early for a little trash talk, St. Charles."

We run the lines of the field once more before the ref—who's just another player volunteering to sit one out—blows a whistle. Anabelle is at midfield where she feels most comfortable, while I play sweeper near the opposite goal.

Whistle blows.

Feet move.

Forty-five minutes later, the first half is over, a new one beginning. We don't take long breaks or stop for time-outs because no one wants the game to take all night.

It's fast-paced and fun, with lots of bantering.

I can hear Anabelle laughing at Devin, two sets of eyes angling my way during a penalty kick. My roommate hits my friend on the shoulder while they stand together, forming a wall to block their goal.

It doesn't work and my team scores.

Everyone scrambles to get back in position.

The ground is uneven in the park, the soccer field a hazard to run on, so when Anabelle trips in a divot and falls backward, I'm not surprised. I'm close enough to offer my hand and help her to her feet.

Our palms slide together, fusing.

I tug.

She stands. Swipes the grass off her rear, long legs marred with grass stains. Blushes.

"Thanks."

"No problem."

"Wait." Her fingers reach out, plucking at my hair. "You have a piece of grass stuck right…here."

"Thanks."

She smiles. "No problem."

I watch as she jogs away, eyes fastened on that ass. The long, colt-like legs striding back to her side of the field.

"What the hell do you think you're doing?"

Fucking Devin.

I turn and shoot him an irritated scowl. "Aren't you supposed to be on the other side of the field?"

"I took Brandon's spot, he had to cut out early for a study group." My teammate laughs. "Getting chummy with your roommate already, I see? Peel your eyes off her for one damn second, would ya?"

"Shut up."

His laugh is loud and annoying as hell. "I knew you fucking liked her! You can lie to yourself, but you can't lie to me."

"I said, shut. Up."

"It is too damn cute, that's all I'm saying." He falls into line beside me, way too far back to be in his correct position. "Like little puppy dogs!"

Curious, I can't help asking, "What were the two of you laughing about during the penalty shot?"

My knees are bent, eyes still trained on the ball being kicked around.

"You, obviously."

"Jesus, Devin, would you cut the crap? What did you say?"

He lets out a loud laugh. "I asked if you were being a kind and courteous roommate."

"You fucking liar."

"Yeah, I'm lying." He sniffles, wiping his nose on the sleeve of his shirt. "I asked her if she found you attractive, if she liked you as more than a friend."

"What the actual fuck! Why would you do that?"

"Because I was curious and I knew you wouldn't have the balls. Don't fucking lie and say your dick doesn't tingle thinking about her. She's hot."

She *is* hot, especially in those short soccer shorts, with those flirty pink socks pulled up to her knees.

"Well, what did she say, asshole?" He's driving me insane.

"What do you *think* she said?"

I want to strangle him so hard right now. "God I hate you."

"Do you? Do you though? Or do you wish your balls were as big as mine?" He grabs his dick through his shorts, laughing.

"Just fucking tell me what she said."

"Nah." He ignores me, watching the players move around the field. "I don't think I will."

Fantastic.

I don't know what's happening to me; I have Anabelle on the brain 24-7.

We're playing with fire, and we both know it.

19

#DOUCHEBAG

"I talk an awful lot of smack
for someone who trips
putting on their pants
in the morning."

Elliot

When I enter the house tonight, Anabelle is snuggled up in the corner of the couch, blanket over her legs, highlighter in hand, hovering it over a book I've never seen.

I can't decipher the title from here, but its hot pink cover catches my eye. Setting my bag down by the door and kicking off my shoes before entering the living room, I join her on the couch, plopping down on the opposite end.

"Hey."

She looks down at my feet, propped on the coffee table, happy to see me. "Hey. Welcome home."

"What the hell are you reading?"

"A book? I bought it on the 'Zon." She turns the cover toward herself, reading it with a snicker. *"How to Get Revenge on Someone and Stay Classy in the Process."*

"Oh Jesus."

Anabelle sighs. "Yeah. I've been thinking about this whole Eric and Rex debacle thing, and I'm just not ready to let it go. Like, I don't want to be a *psycho*, but I don't think they should get away with acting like complete douchebags. Know what I mean?"

"I hate even asking, but what does the book say you should do?"

"Well, it's not good news." Anabelle clears her throat, opening to the middle of the book, trailing her thumb along one of the pages. *"When you act in desperation to get revenge on an ex, this not only makes you look crazy, it can also make you look like a complete psycho. Seriously, you're better than that."*

"It says that? For real?"

"Yeah, for real. It's such a bummer."

"Why?"

"Because everything I've researched is telling me to let the whole thing go. It's depressing."

I shrug. "I mean…you could. Those idiots are never going to learn their lesson."

"Oh, and then there's this!" She clears her throat dramatically. "*Let karma handle the situation.*" Anabelle snorts, reading. "*You are not starring in a movie—this is real life. You might think you have the tools to pull off revenge flawlessly, but you do not.*"

The book flops down in her lap, and my roommate tosses the yellow marker onto the coffee table. It hits the hard surface and bounces to the floor.

"How do the authors know I don't have the tools to pull off revenge flawlessly? They don't know me—they don't know my life."

"*Do* you have the tools?"

"No, but they don't know that." Anabelle tosses the book to the side next to her on the couch. "Ugh, I want my money back! This book is garbage!"

"Anabelle, don't you think it's time to tell your dad?"

"Probably, but I want to explore all of my options first—and correct me if I'm wrong, but getting back at those guys was your idea."

"No, I want them to be held accountable for the shit they've been doing, not get *revenge* on them. They keep getting away with their crap. Telling your dad would finally put a stop to it."

"Elliot, I went out with the guy, remember? He's harmless enough. Honestly, I just think he's rather impulsive." Anabelle's arms go above her head, stretching. She changes the subject. "I am so sore, my shoulders are killing me. I thought I was in better shape than this, but these soccer games are kicking my butt."

"Should we chill out and watch TV? I can massage your back if you want."

"Yes, oh my God, would you? I would love that!" She sits up, animated, scrambling to her feet. "I'm getting my pajamas on. I know it's early, but I'm beat, and then you can give me a back massage."

She does a happy dance on her tiptoes in the center of the living room.

"Seriously? That's all it takes to get you excited? The promise of a shoulder rub?"

Her finger points in my direction, one eye narrowing. "You said *back* massage."

"Semantics."

My roommate rolls her eyes toward the ceiling. "Whichever way you want to rub me, I'll meet you on the bed in ten minutes. I'm not missing this opportunity—I haven't had anyone work on my back in ages."

Whichever way you want to rub me… Meet you on the bed…

Head out of the gutter, St. Charles. That's not what she meant.

I know, but I can't help it.

I trudge along behind Anabelle down the short hallway to my room, shutting the door behind me and peeling off the clothes I wore to my classes and while studying in the library, where I just came from.

I'm pulling on a pair of navy mesh shorts when she knocks, giving the elastic waistband a snap and opening the door.

"Oh, I didn't realize you were still, you know…getting dressed." She's gaping at me, intense blue eyes swiftly raking my bare chest and abs, standing in sleep shorts and a tank top. "Do you want to throw a shirt on or something?"

"It's fine, I'm good. Come in and make yourself comfortable—you always do."

She doesn't take offense at my good-natured teasing.

"Haha, but also, don't mind if I do." She almost literally throws herself on my bed, landing on her stomach, head at the foot, facing the television. Props her chin in her hands, waiting for me. "I brought this."

Magically, a bottle of lotion is produced, tossed on the comforter next to her. She stretches like a cat waking from a long nap. "For real, this is so exciting."

"You're the easiest person to please, I swear."

"Basically." Anabelle raises her head. "If I don't fall asleep, I'll return the favor, promise."

"You better not fucking fall asleep—I don't think I've ever had anyone massage my back."

This interests her immensely and she perks up. "Wait, you've never had a back massage?"

"No?"

"*Ever?*"

"Nope."

"Well, what the hell, Elliot? How can I, in good conscience, lie here letting you rub my back when you've never had anyone rub yours?" She scoots over, pointing to the mattress. "Lie on your stomach, I'll do you first."

I wave my hands in front of me in protest. The last thing I need is her warm hands roaming my body. "No, no, you don't have to. It's not a big deal."

"Are you crazy? Back massages are the best—like, better than an orgasm. You're first, so lie down."

"And you call me the bossy one?"

"Quit stalling and get on the bed, St. Charles."

Obediently, I climb to the middle of my bed in nothing but a pair of gym shorts, legs hanging off the side. Next to me, the mattress dips, Anabelle on her knees, approaching my side.

A finger glides down my spine. "It will be easier for me to do this if I'm sitting on you. Hope that's okay."

"Is that the approved method?"

"No, but my arms will get tired if I have to lean over you the whole time."

"Do whatever then, I don't care."

I stiffen when Anabelle swings one leg over my body, straddling my ass. Warm palms at my lower back.

"You're so tense, Elliot. Try to relax," she coos, making it worse. "Tilt your head to the side, that's it."

I hear the lotion bottle snap open. Click closed. My roommate's palms rubbing together, warming it up. "Sorry, I don't have any actual massage oil. This will have to do."

When her hands make contact with my back, I almost groan it feels so fucking good. Warm. Smooth. Pressure in all the right places, pushing gently into my muscles.

Slowly.

Slower still, caressing along my shoulders, thumbs and fingers working together to soothe the burning on my right side.

"Doesn't this feel great?" Her soft voice cuts into the silence. "You're loosening up. That's good."

I feel her leaning as her hands move up and down my spine until they stop, hovering at the base of my neck. Thumbs stroking the skin below my hairline, back and forth.

Kneading.

Her torso dips, hands maneuvering my arms, placing them at my sides. Palms slide up and down my biceps.

For several minutes, she rubs my arms and shoulders. Then she skims down my ribcage unhurriedly, in no rush, making little humming sounds inside her throat.

I know I'm not imagining the feather-light way her hands drift down my spine. I remain still, letting her touch me, basking in it.

Remain still when her lips kiss the tender spot of my shoulder where it meets my neck, nose nuzzling behind my ear, her breasts rubbing against my back and *what the fuck was that all about?* What does she think she's doing, trying to drive me insane?

"Okay! Done!" Just like that, her hands are gone and Anabelle is sliding off my body like she didn't just kiss me, innocent doe eyes widening when I glance up at her. "I'm sorry that was cut short but I'm *dying* for my turn." I watch as she lies down next to me, facing me, grinning. "Ready when you are."

I rise to my haunches, unsure. "You don't expect me to sit on you, do you?"

I'm afraid I'll crush her if I do.

She shoots another smile across at me. "You can if it's easier. You won't smother me. I trust you."

Right. She trusts me, and what better way to affirm that than my erection digging into her ass crack?

Yeah, don't think so.

Reaching for her bottle of lotion—it's shea butter—I squeeze a decent amount onto my palm, imitating the way she rubbed her hands together before starting her massage on me.

Get ready to place my hands on her back, pause. "Hold up, I just realized I have all this lotion on my hands."

"Yeah?"

"Where do I put it?" She's wearing a top, and now I can't lift the hem or it'll get it dirty. "Do I just rub my hands along your arms or what?"

Anabelle laughs, burying her face in my quilt. "No you goof, you put them under my shirt."

Under her shirt. Sure. "Got it."

Her tank top is threadbare, the hem sitting at the base of her spine, skin already playing peekaboo. Poising my fingers along the edge of the fabric, the pads press gently on her exposed flesh, tentatively.

Sheepishly.

"Don't be shy—a little lotion on my tank won't hurt anything," my roommate whispers, eyes already closed, smile playing on her lips. "Just rub my back, don't worry about the technique."

Jeez, I suck at this.

"Okay."

I have no choice but to hook the fabric with my forefinger, making room for my hands, giving them berth to glide their way up, under her top. They catch the cotton once, smearing. Twice, fighting their way up, awkwardly.

Anabelle chuckles. "Should I just take my shirt off?"

"What?" I can't have heard that correctly.

"Maybe I should take my shirt off. It might be easier—your hands are so big."

My hands *are* big.

Her skin so soft.

Smooth.

Warm flesh.

Perfect spine.

I marvel at it, under the incandescent lighting of my bedroom. Marvel at how intimate this moment is, how much faith and trust Anabelle is placing in me.

I haven't had a girlfriend in a really long fucking time, but I don't recall a single instance as intimate as this, not even the sex.

Transfixed, I watch when she turns away for privacy and peels away her shirt, tossing it aside. Settles, once again on her stomach, chin resting on her hands.

Sighs, content.

"Let me know if my hair is in the way."

"It's not." It's piled atop her head, a few loose wisps of the baby-fine hair escaping; I imagine it's tickling her neck.

Her waist is narrow, ribcage peach perfection.

Her breasts are flattened, side-boob creating a glorious distraction as I finally lay my hands on her skin, firmly rubbing her back.

"That feels amazing." She's quiet a few seconds. "Can you do me lower, right here?" Her left hand reaches back to grip my wrist, dragging it down, right at the waistband of her sleep shorts.

I place both hands on her obliques. Her iliac crest, just above her ass.

"Here?"

"Yes. Oh *God,* that feels good."

I can't tell if she's doing it on purpose—the moaning—but regardless, it's turning me on. This whole massage is, from Anabelle's bare flesh, to mine, to the little sounds she's making as she lies motionless beneath me.

I have no idea how *low* to go or where I'm allowed to put my hands. So, I play it safe, staying above her waist. Gently caressing her teres major, her deltoids and trapezius, all the places I'm learning about in kinesiology, but this is different than practicing on another student or a prop.

This is a woman I'm growing desperately attracted to.

This is my bed.

My room.

Our house.

Her skin.

"Elliot?"

"Hmm?"

"Is everything okay?"

"What do you mean?"

"You stopped."

"Oh." I move my hands to the base of her neck, kneading. "Sorry."

"It's okay." I can hear her smiling into the pillow. "Should we stop and watch a movie?"

"I can keep going if you want me to, it's no big deal."

She wiggles her ass. "You're sweet, but I can tell you're getting tired."

I'm not tired; I'm turned on. *Huge* fucking difference.

"Sure, let's watch a movie. I'm done with all my studying and you're done with that ridiculous book you're reading."

Anabelle rolls to her side, taking my comforter along with her, covering her breasts. "It wouldn't be ridiculous if it actually contained useful information."

I'm on my side now, too. "Face facts, Donnelly, you don't have the heart for revenge. You're too kindhearted for that life."

"That's true enough." Her hand reaches out, brushing a stray lock of hair off my forehead, and I almost rear back in surprise.

I've noticed her doing that a lot lately—touching me. Taps, poking, teasing. Not wanting to read anything into it, I chalk it up to comfort in our growing friendship, evidence of her trust in me.

Christ, it sucks being the good guy all the fucking time.

"My dad texted me today."

"Oh yeah?"

"He wants me to come to a wrestling meet soon. They have a big one at home coming up."

"Who are they wrestling?"

"I'm not sure, he didn't say. I think either Penn State or UConn? Someone blue." She laughs. "And I'd really rather not go alone."

I swear she's batting her fucking eyelashes at me. "What are you getting at, Donnelly?"

I haven't been to a wrestling meet since Oz and Zeke graduated. Neither of them had their parents in the stands on Senior Night, so I went to represent, with bouquets of flowers for both miserable bastards, even though their girlfriends were in the audience.

"Want to come with me?"

"Yeah. I could probably do that."

Anabelle's blue eyes bore holes into my bare chest, pink lips parting. "Thank you."

"No problem."

I'm still not wearing a shirt.

She's still not wearing a shirt.

We're on my bed, in the middle of the evening, flirting like we have an interest in each other. A sexual attraction. Crazy chemistry.

"Would you be so kind as to turn your back so I can put my shirt back on?"

I swallow, too chicken-shit to make a move and kiss her.

"Sure. While you do that, want me to grab us ice waters?"

"Thanks, Elliot." Her eyes sparkle. "You're the *best*."

Anabelle

Thanks, Elliot, you're the best?

Ugh.

As I mentally face-palm myself for sounding like his little buddy, I grapple for my shirt, yanking it back down over my head, flushing. Remember his big, rough hands running over my skin. Over my naked flesh, not once touching me inappropriately. Not once skimming down to accidentally caress my side-boob or lower back. Not once trailing his fingers anywhere indecent.

Damn him.

I sigh, giving the rubber band in my hair a tug, loosening my top knot and letting the hair fall around my shoulders. Free, uninhibited, like I've resolved to be around him.

But he's not getting the hints.

So, either I suck at flirting or he's clueless, *or* we're both just really scared to make the first move.

I've been touching him all week—little touches on the arm, bicep, chest. Teasing pokes, nudges. Laughing at all his dumb jokes. Following him around the soccer field, secretly admiring his masculine force. His speed, his skill. His calves and the back of his neck, wanting to lay my lips on the baby fine hairs there.

Last week at our soccer game when his friend Dev jogged up next to me and began peppering me with a million Elliot-related questions, I was taken aback by his direct approach. Was I attracted to Elliot? Did I want to be more than friends? Was it hard living in the same house with him and not having sex?

Yes, yes, and yes.

At an alarmingly increased pace.

I am attracted to Elliot.

I do want to be more than friends.

It's hard living in the same house with him and not thinking about sex all day, every day. It's impossible not to; Elliot is big and sexy and strong and sweet.

Polite.

Funny.

As a male specimen, Elliot is highly underrated by the female population of Iowa, and for that, I am eternally grateful.

God, moving in with him was the worst thing I could have done—the guy is too polite to put the moves on his roommate. Too polite to put his hands on me, even when I whip my shirt off during a massage.

I know it.

He knows it.

Devin freaking knows it, and he doesn't know me at all!

Guh!

I climb under the covers of Elliot's incredible queen-sized bed, the flannel sheets fresh from the laundry, a familiar warmth. Welcoming and cozy, we're well acquainted, his bed and I.

His bed. The ultimate tease.

If having me tucked under his covers doesn't make his mind wander, there really is no hope for him.

On the side closest to the wall, I give my shirt a tug, straightening it on my body, wishing I had the courage to remove it and bury myself in Elliot's sheet with nothing on but my underwear.

God, I'm a hormonal teenage boy.

Worse, actually.

And now that my hormones are screaming at the rest of my body and brain, there is no stopping them now. They're doing the thinking for me.

Skin against skin is what I *crave*.

Soft, gentle stroking is what I *want*.

Sucking is what makes me *squirm*.

Oblivious to my woolgathering, Elliot returns, still not wearing a shirt. His broad chest fills the doorway, wide shoulders and tan flesh making my girly parts tingle—his pecs are perfect. Nipples dark. Collarbone smooth enough to lick.

Maybe instead of staring, I should read a book. Climb out of this bed and back into mine and move on with my life. Find a guy who likes me back enough to pursue me, to put the moves on me.

"I was texting with Daniels yesterday and he was telling me about this show he and his girlfriend started watching, about four couples that get married at first sight, kind of like a blind date. The new season just started."

I sit up, intrigued. "People get married without even seeing each other first?"

He shrugs, setting the water glasses down on his desk. I *totally* check out his ass before he turns around to face me. Climbs on top of the bed, back against the headboard, legs atop the covers.

They're long, toned, soccer player's legs. Fit from running every morning and playing games regularly. We both played in high school but weren't good enough to play at the university level. Both like to run, but not long distances.

He crosses those legs at the ankles, resting his arms behind his head, and my eyes travel the length of him. Tall. Solid. Hard in all the *best* places.

I want to purr, but I also don't want to creep him the hell out.

"Would you get married to someone you've never laid eyes on before?" Elliot gives me a quick cursory glance, flipping through the channels.

"Yes, one hundred percent." I'm nodding vigorously because I totally would.

He looks surprised. "Really?"

"Yes. If I reached a certain age and wasn't in a relationship, you bet I would. What do these people have to lose? It seems like a fun experiment."

"You think you'd reach an age where you'd resort to marrying a complete stranger?"

"I don't think any of these people are settling. The way I see it, there is someone for everyone if you're open to it."

"But marrying a stranger, on TV? You think you'd be so single you'd have to?"

"Uh, *yeah*, it's a definite possibility. I mean, think about it this way. I'm in my twenties, in my prime, and there still isn't anyone on the horizon who wants to date me, douche canoes notwithstanding."

I leave the bait for him to disagree, and he takes it.

"That's not true." He says it slow and quiet, deliberate.

"Well, in any case, I think the idea is kind of romantic."

Elliot makes a low scoffing sound in his throat. "It must be if Zeke Daniels—the biggest cynic on campus—sits and watches it with his girlfriend."

I consider this information. "So basically we should prepare to become addicted to yet another TV show?"

"Basically."

"This constant bingeing on ridiculous shows is not going to end well, you know that right? At some point, you and I will have to leave the house for food, water, and sunlight. I can't remember the last time I even showered."

He makes a show of sniffing the air between us. "Very funny, Donnelly."

Donnelly.

I love it when he calls me that.

He does it when he's teasing me, when he's not sure what else to say, and I like to pretend it's his shy way of showing affection without being obvious about it, like he's secretly harboring feelings for me but can't let me know.

"It *is* very funny, St. Charles." I give it right back, sneaking a peek at his abs from under my lashes.

I don't think Elliot realizes his appeal to women. If he did, I doubt he'd be sitting around shirtless, looking like a romance novel cover hero.

Freshly showered. Bare chest.

Mesh gym shorts.

Those damn shorts do *nothing* to conceal the very obvious outline of the dick nestled inside, the navy fabric thinner than my tank top and making me squirm every time my eyes take a gander downward.

Which is every few seconds.

Arms behind his head, the undersides of his biceps are paler than the rest of his arms, the flesh tender. I fixate on his light brown armpit hair for a few heartbeats; I find it masculine and sexy. Very different than the parts on *my* body, deliciously so.

When the new show comes on, the impulse to commentate is impossible to resist. We're shocked, outraged, and awed by what's happening on screen. Annoyed, obviously, voicing our opinions during the first episode—until our lids get heavy with fatigue.

For a while, the lights stay on, illuminating the room; when my eyes start drooping, Elliot climbs off the bed to flip them off. Pulls back the cover when he returns, sliding in beside me, heating the small space between us.

I sigh, letting my lids close.

Content.

Body humming.

Sigh *again* when at some point in the middle of the night, the large hand on my hip skims down my thigh. Sleepily, across my waist it drifts, up the front side of my shirt. Floats up and down in relaxed, lazy motions over my stomach, pulling me in.

Elliot tucks me into his body, palm splayed on my abdomen.

If this is a dream, don't wake me...

His huge paw travels north, heated, thumb hooking the hem of my shirt and sliding beneath it brazenly. Unhurriedly caresses my ribcage, dangerously close to my breasts, back and forth...back and forth....

It feels like heaven.

It makes me ache with desire.

In a dreamlike daze, I drag Elliot's arm higher so his palm is cupping my boob. The pads of his fingers brush across my stiff nipples, first one, then the other, in slow circles. Rubbing gently. Plucking. Rolling them between his forefinger and thumb so slowly, the dull ache between my legs begins to throb.

Spooning, my ass is snug against his growing erection, so snug I feel it twitch inside his gym shorts. Straining.

Gradually, I rotate my pelvis, grinding into it.

His gluts flex.

Body stirs.

Fingers grip me tighter, flexing.

When his warm lips meet the back of my neck, hot breath fanning my skin, it's an ecstasy I could get *high* from. The simple act of his face being buried in my hair is so arousing, making me hot. I squirm, our bodies entwining.

Elliot's mouth kissing my shoulder, hand on my breast...

Arching my back, I reach behind me to pull him closer. Pull his head down, fingers plowing through his thick hair as his fingers pluck at my nipple from under my shirt.

Oh God, it feels so good.

I moan quietly.

He groans gruffly, hand snaking down my abs and stomach, inching its way below my belly button. Pads of his fingers reach into my shorts, find the valley between my thighs where it's warm and damp and ready.

Elliot plays, middle finger rubbing tiny little circles, round and round, in the center of my slit. Mouth sucks my neck while my back arches and I twist his hair.

When I can't stand it anymore, I ease away, flipping to face him; we're breathing heavy and only inches apart. In the background, an infomercial illuminates the room with enough light that we can see each other.

Just enough.

His lids are open now, too, blinking back at me. Nostrils flared. Chest heaving.

Dick swelling—I can feel it against my thigh.

Wanton.

Drowsy.

So good and *so* hard.

I don't know how long we lie there, staring each other down, slowly coming awake, hearts racing, but I know his heart is racing, too, because I can *see it* in his eyes.

They're wide and shining and full of veiled anticipation.

Using the dark as an alibi, I raise my palm to his shoulder, running it along his collarbone, memorizing every velvety line. Trace his jawline. Indulgently run the pads of my fingertips behind his neck, lazily toying with his hair.

When my thumb brushes over his beautiful mouth, his lips part, landing a kiss on the tip of my finger. Seizes my forearm, grazing the center of my palm with his mouth.

It tickles. Tingles.

Makes me shiver.

Then…

Elliot kisses my wrist, nose running along the sensitive skin on the inside. Up to the crook of my elbow, small intakes of breath escaping us both while he inhales the smell of my perfume, the soap from my shower earlier in the evening.

My eyes flutter closed and somehow, we find ourselves moving closer, our bodies finally pressed together. Elliot's tenacious erection demands attention.

His neck bends.

Mouth drags along my shoulder at the same time his hand moves over the top of my tank, cupping my breast.

Lips find the pulse in my neck, quietly sucking.

I moan, eyes fluttering open, staring at the ceiling, collecting fistfuls of his hair in my hands while Elliot tastes my flesh.

Then…our lips meet for our first kiss.

Press together once, exploring.

Twice.

Tongues connect, probing.

Hot, wet, needy.

So needy.

This is a side of Elliot I haven't discovered yet, this physical, unrestrained, sensual side. I'm on fire for him, my body a flaming calamity of want and greed and longing.

Everything about him is sexy. His warm hands on my skin. His wet, ravenous tongue inside my mouth. His full, pouty lips. The flat abs and happy trail leading down into his shorts.

That happy trail leads to a place I want to visit.

I reach between us, grasping for the hem of my top, pulling it up and over my head. I want to feel him, every hot inch of him. Tossing my shirt aside, I lean back against the plump pillow, inviting him to look his fill.

He does, eyes burning in the dark, gaze fastened on my breasts, hands hovering.

Head dips.

Elliot's hot mouth latches on and sucks at my nipple, the whole thing—not just the tip—curling my toes. Tongue swirling, he sucks while I dip my chin to watch, the desire between my legs igniting into tiny sparks of pleasure.

I get off on having my boobs played with, love when they're being sucked on—and suddenly it's not enough. I want the dull throb between my legs to burst into an agonizing blaze.

Suddenly, my shorts are an annoying, cumbersome burden, a barrier I can't wait to dispense of, now desperate to feel his skin against mine.

Mouths fastening together, we shove down the waistband of my shorts until I'm entirely, delightfully naked.

My hips begin a slow roll. I part my thighs so he can fit himself between my legs, his dick snug, mesh shorts dampening with every push and pull, in and out.

Dry-fucking.

His massive, gorgeous hands grasp my waist, tugging. Grapple at my ass, harder. Sucking. Grinding. Licking.

Kissing.

Dreamy. Awake.

He scoots to the center of the bed, hauling me on top, huge paws skimming up and down my bare torso. Sliding to my backside, teasing my spine. Squeezing my ass cheeks.

I lean down to kiss him, hair falling in long waves, and he grabs a handful, holding it back, out of his way so he can see my face.

I grind on him through his shorts, the thick head of his penis rubbing the swollen clit between my legs. He might be wearing shorts, but they're thin, and the head of his dick creates a glorious, unbearable friction I haven't felt from a man in who *knows* how long.

Months. Years.

Never—not at a conservative Catholic college.

We dry-hump like horny teenagers until we're both panting quietly, quick breaths masked by the sound of the television. Elliot's hands massage my breasts, squeezing gently, head tipped back in ecstasy as I ride him.

We want more.

But more isn't enough.

Lazy and slow and still in a daze, he raises his hips. Shucks his shorts down, not all the way, *just enough* for me to slide onto his hot, thick erection.

Bare.

Easing onto his dick, I impale myself on its round-tipped perfection.

G-Gasp.

Because…

Oh.

My.

God.

Our mouths fuse as he thrusts up, going deeper, over and over and over until I'm a useless, weightless ragdoll, rocking back and forth. Hair falling down my back, hands on his knees for support, I'm lost in myself.

And him.

Lost in the sensation of my own sexuality, finally getting what I want. Giving him what he wants.

And what he wants now is me on my back.

Flipping me onto my back in one instant motion, Elliot drives into me methodically, sedately, spreading me wider, hands holding my thighs apart.

Silent fucking perfection.

Slow, unhurried thrusting.

I've never heard myself whimper before, but I do, in time with Elliot's grunts. Our sounds primal.

When I raise my arms to push against the headboard for support—to prevent my head banging into it—he rises to his haunches, dragging me farther onto his pelvis, driving into me on his knees, brows creased. Concentrating on every deep, deliberate thrust.

His body tenses at the same time I throw my head back, mouth falling open, the waves of my orgasm pulsating around his cock. We come together, his face buried in my neck, teeth biting gently into his shoulder. Cock throbbing, spilling himself inside me.

I can feel it, warm and wet and breathtaking.

Intoxicating.

"Surprise sex is the
best thing to wake up to.
Unless you're in prison."

Elliot

*H*oly shit.

I'm naked.

It's morning. I'm in bed with Anabelle, and I'm naked.

Worse yet, I glance across the mattress at my slumbering, sleeping roommate *whom I fucked in the middle of the night.* Sweep an embarrassed hand down my face, groan.

Pass a hungry gaze over her body, because Anabelle is still naked, too.

Bare-assed naked.

Beautiful.

I allow myself the luxury of checking her out; her tits are incredible, rosy-tipped nipples playing peekaboo with the edge of my navy sheets. Dark brown hair fanned out on the pillow in messy tangles. She stirs, arching those beautiful breasts in my direction.

I glance down the length of my body at the exposed, half-hard woody begging for permission to stiffen against my inner thigh. I must have gotten overheated and kicked the covers off at some point while we were sleeping—after we finally dozed off—and I feel an embarrassed blush spreading throughout my body at the memories assailing me from last night.

Leaning, I reach for the quilt, concealing my junk, unsure of how Anabelle will react when she wakes up and sees me lying here buck-naked.

For now, I'm content to watch her, shoulders and clavicle and plumped cleavage. Pale, creamy perfection. I don't know how long I lie here, quietly fighting the temptation to reach over and touch her, but eventually she stirs, lashes fluttering against her pink cheekbones.

Blue eyes focus in my direction, drowsy, gleaming.

Peach mouth bows into a secretive smile.

Anabelle strokes a hand in circles against the mattress, drawing back the covers to beckon me into the center.

It's an alluring sight.

In the light of morning, I can see everything I didn't in the dark, in the glow of the television. The exact color of Anabelle's nipples. The groomed patch of hair between her legs. The skin tone of her breasts, stomach, and legs.

Quietly, we lie still, regarding each other before I scoot over, grasping her slim waist. Immediately, my fingers itch to wander, and she's satisfied to let them, lounging on the pillow, languidly watching me explore her body.

Reclining on the pillow while I hover, she props her hands behind her head. Eyes slide shut when I cup her breasts in my palms, stroking her nipples with my thumbs, getting them hard, getting us both turned on in the process, my semi-hard morning wood now a rock-solid boner.

When her hips begin a steady roll, I know last night wasn't a fluke.

I get excited, even her unsteady breathing is turning me on.

My mouth waters, wanting to go down on her.

"*What?*" she whispers, meeting my eyes, the word barely audible, licking her lips.

Instead of greeting her with words, I kiss her collarbone. Then the valley between her beautiful breasts. Pull a nipple into my mouth before dragging my nose down her stomach, tongue wetting her skin on the way down.

Instinctively, Anabelle spreads her thighs.

Eager.

My broad shoulders nestle between her legs, settling in. I spread her with my fingers, torso and tongue disappearing beneath the sheets.

She clutches the quilt, arching her back. Moans when I lap at her clit, splitting her apart.

"Don't stop, don't stop, don't stop," she says as she pants, begging.

I don't stop—*of course* I fucking don't.

I suck and suck until she's coming *hard* and I'm satisfied, drawing out her climax.

Climbing back up her limp, sated body.

"Anabelle?"

"Mmm?"

"Are you on birth control?"

Considering we had unprotected sex last night, it's a little late to be asking, but it's necessary. I don't have a single condom in this house—stupid, I know, but it's not like I was sleeping with anyone before last night.

"Of course I'm on birth control." She exhales lazily. "You think I would have let you come inside me last night if I wasn't?"

Come inside me last night.

Fucking A, that's one sexy sentence—almost as sexy as the sounds she made last night when I was inside her. Silent, breathy moans. Tiny gasps.

My eyes drop down to her naked tits. "I don't know. Would you?"

"No. The last thing I want is..." she pauses then wiggles her hips, causing the rushing blood in my brain to skyrocket to my dick.

It surges, giving me the green light to slide home.

Bracing my arms on either side of her head, I glide inside her slick pussy, still wet from my tongue, bearing down, all the way in.

Deep.

So deep, our pelvises connect.

When Anabelle's mouth falls open, head listing to the side, I suck on her neck, the mattress below us dipping. Headboard hitting the wall, bedframe squeaking.

Low moans.

The slowest tortured thrusting.

The world's most *perfect* morning fuck.

Her long, lean fingers fasten on my ass, urgently pulling me deeper. Emboldening me, urging me on.

It's so goddamn intense, I swear my fucking eyes roll to the back of my head.

"Oh *fuck*," I groan when my balls tighten. Body stiffening, one last grunt into her hair and I'm dumping my load inside her.

Heaven.

It's fucking heaven.

Me: *Dude. I have a major problem.*

Oz: *NOW what?*

Me: What do you mean, NOW what?

Oz: ***shrugs** Nothing, it's just that you've been texting me a lot lately.*

I have been texting him lately, but no more than usual.

Oz: *I'm in the middle of something, so can you get to the point? No offense, but I don't have tons of time.*

Me: *I had sex with my roommate.*

Oz: *How was it?*

Fantastic, but obviously that's not why I'm messaging him.

Me: *No, you're not listening dude. I had SEX with my room- mate.*

Oz: *No, no man, I understood you perfectly the first time, and mad props, bro. It's been forever since you've gotten laid— am I right, or am I right? HIGH FIVE.*

Me: *You are no help at all.*

Oz: *Moving along—was it a fuckfest, or just so you could get the lead out?*

Me: *Fuckfest.*

Oz: *See? Aren't you glad you're not living with a dude? How awkward would that have been this morning? Am I right or am I right?!*

Me: *Why do I bother talking to you?*

Oz: *Because I give good advice.*

Me: *No you don't—but your girlfriend does.*

Oz: *Yeah, that too.*

Oz: *I have to give you mad props—you put your hot dog in Coach's daughter's bun.*

I roll my eyes at his analogy.

Me: *He's not MY coach.*

Oz: *Hey, does that mean you won the bet Eric and Gunderson had going?*

Me: *Jesus Christ, you're such an asshole.*

Oz: *I believe the correct term is douchebag.*

Me: *Can we stick to the point?*

Oz: *If I knew what your point was, yeah.*

Me: *I'm freaking out—that's what my point is.*

Oz: *So you screwed your roommate. How many times was it?*

Me: *What difference does that make?*

Oz: *Trust me, it matters. How many times did you fuck her?*

Me: *Twice.*

Oz: *So what's the problem?*

Me: *I had sex with her TWICE.*

Oz: *When?*

Me: *Jesus, dude. Why do you want me to get specific?*

Oz: *Why can't you just answer the fucking questions? If you had sex with her once it can be brushed off as a "mistake", but twice? You're either really fucking horny or you like her, and the fact that she let you dick her multiple times in a 24-hour period is either really good news or really bad news.*

Me: *Explain.*

Oz: *It depends on whether you like her or not.*

Me: *I do.*

Oz: *Then why are we even having this conversation?*

Me: *I don't know if SHE likes me.*

Oz: *DUDE. SHE LET YOU FUCK HER TWICE.*

Me: *Good point.*

Oz: *Morning sex?*

Me: *Uh...*

Oz: *So I'll take that as a yes. Nice work. Morning sex is the fucking best! I always come so hard when I'm half out of it. It's like some serious out-of-body experience bullshit. If you're lucky, you'll wake up one night while she's giving you* *a blow job—you'll think you've died and gone to heaven. For real.*

Me: *How is it that every time I text you for advice, you never have any?*

Oz: *This was sex-related. What kind of advice could you possibly need?*

Me: *I had sex with my roommate. WHAT THE HELL DO I DO NOW?*

Oz: *You do it again. Duh.*

Anabelle

Elliot and I had sex.

Twice.

Three times if you count him going down on me, which I don't because there was no penile penetration.

But still.

Elliot and I had sex!

I've been sleepwalking through my day, light as air, my thoughts on one thing: last night. Orgasm, orgasm, orgasm. Then again this morning.

His face between my legs.

His dick inside me.

My face flushes, and if I had a notebook handy, I'd be burying my face behind it, cheeks flaming hot. Obviously no one knows what's going on inside my mind right now, but I feel like it's stamped on my forehead, tattooed in neon ink: *I HAD SEX WITH MY ROOMMATE LAST NIGHT!*

Hang a big red sign around my neck while you're at it.

I tug at the collar of my shirt, giving myself room to breathe. Is it hot in here? No? Just me?

"What's wrong with you today? You high or something?"

Rex Gunderson pokes me with a pencil I doubt he'll actually use this entire semester.

"No I'm not *high*. I just have some stuff on my mind."

"Ahh." He leans forward, balancing the desk chair on two legs. "Someone's been running through your mind all day. Was it me?" He flashes a devilish grin. "Let me take you out again, put you out of your misery."

If he knows about Eric Johnson showing up at my father's house, he's displaying no indication of it, but Rex knows I'm Coach Donnelly's daughter, I'm sure of it.

This guy is playing the long game, and he's playing it well. I'll give him credit for that.

"Thanks for the offer, Gunderson, but I don't think so."

"Shit. My friends call me Gunderson—are you friend-zoning me, Anabelle?"

"I wouldn't call it that, no." More like keeping him at a distance. Despite his odd charm and weirdly charismatic personality, I still don't trust this guy.

A few weeks ago I might have, even knowing what I know about him—that he's a douchey little asshole who makes harmful bets. I've concluded that Rex Gunderson is bored: bored with being the manager of the wrestling team, bored with Iowa, and bored with school.

He's creating drama. Generating fun.

The problem is people are getting hurt along the way. Not physically, obviously—no one has gotten sick or died—but what would have happened if Eric Johnson had shown up at my house and my parents weren't there?

What if he was so determined to win that bet he had forced himself inside? Or forced himself on me? I don't know anything about him, but he's aggressive, and the big bedroom in their house seems to be worth a world of trouble to obtain.

My mind wanders, drifting to Elliot as Gunderson babbles on and on about himself. Did he have sex with me because we were both half-asleep? Because he wanted to get laid? Does he care about me, or was it purely physical?

Feelings or physical.

Feelings... Physical...

Shit, I'm so confused.

We haven't spoken to each other in the past twenty-four hours, despite all the screwing, shyly going about our business this morning, both of us late for class after one last orgasmic quickie before the hustle.

I'm a mess today. Yoga pants, baggy sweatshirt, hair tossed up in a ponytail—I had zero time to get ready before sprinting out the door.

"So no second date?"

"Sorry, what?"

"I was asking if you wanted a second date."

"No second date. Sorry."

"Why?"

Because you bet your friend he couldn't sleep with me!

Because you have a history of hazing!

Because you are sketchy as fuck!

"How about I check with my dad first? If he gives his approval, I'll go on a date with you."

I swear I wish I had my phone handy so I could take a picture of the expression on his face. Brows shooting up into his hairline, eyes wide, head rearing back.

"Pfft. Your *dad*?" He furrows his brows, acting perplexed, nose scrunched up like a baffled rabbit. It would be kind of cute—if he weren't such a putz.

I laugh, right in his face. "Oh come off it, Gunderson. *Any* day now you can quit acting like you don't know I'm Coach Donnelly's daughter."

He tips his head to the side, staring like *I'm* the confused one here. "Anabelle, I have no idea what you're talking about."

"I'm saying, if you're serious about dating me, I should check with my dad, Coach Donnelly, AKA your boss."

He clutches his chest. "You went out with me knowing I was a wrestler? We have rules about this!"

This elicits a big, fat eye roll. "Rex, you can't run around calling yourself a wrestler. You're the team manager, which is basically like being assistant *to* the regional manager."

"*That* was the height of rudeness."

I tsk. "How about I mention this to my dad? You wouldn't have a problem with that, would you?"

Rex Gunderson glances at me condescendingly, pursing his lips. "Anabelle, how old are you?"

What does my age have to do with this conversation?

"Twenty-one. Why?"

Gunderson shrugs, displaying forced nonchalance. "Aren't you a little old to be asking your dad's permission?"

I shoot him a fake, megawatt smile. "Not when it comes to matters of the heart, Rex. Not when it comes to matters of the heart."

I'm the first one to arrive home tonight, the light above our little kitchen sink offering a dim, welcoming glow. I set my bag by the door, kicking off my shoes and unknotting my rubber band until my hair falls around my shoulders.

It was a long, stressful day.

One in which I did more thinking about Elliot than I did concentrating during my classes.

But I hide from him.

Slink off to my bedroom, closing the door, afraid to bump into him in our kitchen...or our bathroom, or the hallway, and *oh my God I had sex with my roommate.*

Sex with my roommate.

My Lord, are there any worse offenses? Yes, because I've already committed several of them this semester: Cried in a public place (the library). Blacked out drunk after a party. Passed out in a stranger's bed. Went out with the campus idiot.

Had sex with my roommate, the same guy who saved me from myself, like a true friend would.

I cringe.

My body goes still when I hear the stirring of life at the front of the house. The door being opened and closed. Footfalls in the entryway. I imagine Elliot taking off his jacket and tossing it on the couch. Maybe sauntering into the kitchen to rifle through the fridge, leaning against the counter, shoes off, in his socks.

Alerted to his company, I cock my head to listen, waiting. Praying he doesn't try to come find—

A soft knock sounds at my bedroom door.

"Ana?" He knocks again. "You in here?"

"Yeah—yes." Fuss with my hair before answering, straightening my sweatshirt. "The door is unlocked, come in. I'm decent."

I groan at that last comment; what difference does it make if I'm decent? He's already seen me naked. He's seen my—

The metal doorknob turns, time lapsing in slow motion as Elliot eases the door open, his sweet, sexy face appearing in tiny fragments, small bits at a time.

When the door is open all the way, it hits me how happy I am to lay eyes on him after a long day—so happy I want to pounce on him, kiss his beautiful face all over just to watch the changes in him as he reacts to me.

Instead, I stay firmly planted in the center of my twin bed, textbook spread on the coverlet, highlighter poised in my hand, ready for business—or at least pretending to be.

Breathlessly, I wait.

Petrified of rejection.

What if he wants to pretend last night and this morning never happened? Or that it was a huge mistake? I'll be humiliated. Living across the hall from the guy you just slept with is the most awkward form of the walk of shame. It would be like a *marathon* of shame.

"How's it going in here?"

Instinctively, I sense him weighing his words, treading lightly. Unsure.

So, doing my best to appear nonchalant, I shrug casually. "Good. Just catching up on a paper I should have written but spaced out on. What about you?"

"I was at the gym." He leans against the doorjamb, broad shoulders slouching, hands in his pockets. Those big, capable man hands were on my body.

Every inch of it, just hours ago.

I peel my eyes away, sinking them down to my notebook, embarrassed, chest and cheeks turning red.

"How was it? Was it crowded?"

"Nah, not too bad. I think I beat the rush."

"That's good."

"I was surprised to find the house almost dark when I walked in."

"I was, uh…trying to save on electricity."

"Trying to save on electricity," he repeats, crossing his arms, clearly entertained. "Is that so?"

"You're lucky I didn't hide and try to scare the crap out of you."

Elliot smiles then, biting down on his bottom lip the way I do when I'm being coy. On him, it's even more endearing.

"I thought we'd eat together when I got home. Aren't you starving? It's almost six o'clock."

My stomach turns, but not from hunger. It's from nerves, thousands of them crackling to life in my lower abs. I place a hand there to quell them.

"I wouldn't get mad if you fed me."

"I threw that lasagna Linda dropped off Tuesday in the oven while you were at class." Elliot enters my bedroom, sitting on my bed, legs spread. Hands clasped in his lap. "Sorry I haven't texted you all day—I left my phone in my gym bag and it fell to the bottom. Was too lazy to dig it out."

"You don't have to tell me where you're at—I'm not your gatekeeper."

I'm also not his girlfriend.

"Maybe not, but still."

We sit in silence for a few moments, the only sound coming from the earbuds I removed earlier, the tiny speakers blasting a song so old and outdated I should be ashamed of myself.

I have terrible taste in music; all my friends tell me so.

My bed is a twin, so Elliot reclining back takes half the space, his hands patting down the area around him, patting down my white comforter, feeling it up.

He shoots me a look. "We'll never be able to sleep in here, this bed is way too small—you realize that, right?"

I lean forward so our noses touch. "Are you scoping out my bedroom, St. Charles?"

"I'm just stating facts in case you're entertaining the notion of me crashing in here with you."

Entertaining the notion. I love it when he uses big words.

"Last night wasn't about just sex—do you understand that?"

"Last night *and this morning.*" I laugh nervously. "But who's keeping track?"

"Answer the question, Anabelle."

My shoulders rise and fall. "Maybe. Just a little?"

"You've been sleeping in my bed for at least a week—not that anyone is keeping track," he jokes back. "Do you think I'd make you stop because we had sex last night?"

"I have not been sleeping with you for a week!" *Have I?* "I like my little bed—why would I want to leave?"

"Bullshit, you do not! We've done nothing but eat pizza and binge on Netflix for the past seven nights."

"Well that's because you have the only bedroom with a TV—duh."

His arms go around my waist, dragging me onto his lap, knocking half my crap off the bed in the process. I'm kissed soundly on the lips as highlighters, pens, and notebooks go crashing to the ground.

"You like my big TV," he murmurs into my mouth. "Don't lie, Donnelly."

"I do." I shiver. "It gets me all excited just thinking about it."

"I'll be honest. I thought about TV all goddamn day." His hand is making slow circles along my spine and he pats my rear.

"Really...*did* you now? TV with anyone in particular?"

"Wait, we are still talking about *actually* watching television, aren't we?" Elliot laughs, giving me a chaste kiss on the cheek, scooting me off his lap so he can stand. Stretch. "I'm going to take a shower—I stink."

"Wow, sexy. If you're lucky, I'll even be here when you get back."

"You're cute."

"So are you."

"Check the oven for me?"

"Are you cooking for me now, St. Charles?" I can already smell the pasta and Italian aromas wafting from the kitchen, my mouth watering, stomach growling.

"Sure am."

We eat standing at the counter when he's out of the shower, forgoing the table, lasagna on paper plates. We already dug into the pan the night Linda kindly dropped it off, so it's half gone.

I poke at one of the noodles, folding it with my fork and shove it in my mouth, feeling self-conscious when some of it slips out and I have to grab it with my fingers to prevent it from falling on the floor. Sauce drips from my chin, fingers, and the collar of my shirt.

Shit.

Elliot catches me, a secretive smile playing at his lips; he's a gentleman and hides it, turning his head and burying it in his shoulder.

Ugh.

Cleanup is easy; we just toss our plates, quickly draw some suds in the sink to wash the utensils, both of us dipping our hands beneath the water at the same time, grasping for the silverware to scrub them clean.

I bump his hip playfully, flirting, and he removes his hands from the sudsy water, drying them on a nearby towel, moves to stand behind me. Skims those glorious hands down to my waist, nose buried in the crook of my neck.

"I wasn't just thinking about TV all day, I was thinking about this." His lips find the pulse in my neck, kissing it. "About you."

In reply, my lids slide closed, hands still submerged in the water. "You were thinking about *me*?"

"Of course. Going to the gym killed me—I knew you were home and I wanted to be home, too."

I swallow. "That's nice to hear."

When he chuckles in my ear, it sends a delightful shot of electricity down my spine, warming my entire body with pleasure.

He has the best laugh.

The best hands.

Elliot St. Charles is one of the sexiest, smartest, and most irresistible men I've ever met—and he's got me by the hips, in our kitchen, mouth exploring the long column of my throat.

"You smell good," he croons, spooning me from behind. "I could eat you up."

"Okay," I say as I exhale, completely out of breath.

His hands slide up the back of my shirt, unclasping my bra, palms gliding over my ribcage, cupping my bare breasts.

Kneading them gently, thumbs stroking the undersides while his teeth nip at my neck.

It's bliss.

Pure nirvana.

I raise my hands out of the water, wrapping them behind Elliot's bowed neck. Bubbly fingers plowing through his thick hair while his hands rub down my boobs.

I turn my head and our lips meet. Tongues connect.

Then, I'm facing him and Elliot is hefting me up by the ass, setting me on the Formica countertop, fingers tugging at the waistband of my pants. I work the button on his jeans, frantically unsuccessful until he relieves me and finishes the task.

Anxious, I eagerly watch as he tugs down his zipper. Shoves those dark denim jeans down his lean hips, boxers shed along with them.

I lift my hips, pulling my leggings as far down as they'll go, bare ass on the cold counter. Elliot hauls me toward the end of it. Lines up his stiff cock. Together we watch as he slips his dick into my pussy, both our heads tipping back when he's buried to the hilt.

"Oh God."

For a few seconds he doesn't move, just stands there inside me, staring down at our joined bodies.

"I swear to God, Elliot, if you don't fuck me right now, I'm going to lose my mind."

He pulls out.

Pushes in.

We groan in tandem.

"Say that again."

"I swear to God, Elliot, if you don't fuck me right now…" My breath hitches when he pumps faster, over and over, my lower half quivering. He's the perfect height to screw me on the counter. We're effortlessly lined up, pelvises grinding.

He grabs my hips, tugging me forward into him, thrusting in and out, my legs wrapped around his waist.

"Not so fast—slow down," I moan. "Make it last."

"Take your top off," he says between pants. "I wanna see your tits."

"*You* take my top off."

We're getting rough, and I like it.

Hard and gentle.

Fast and slow.

I've been on the verge of coming twice now, a third time when he lifts my shirt off, letting it fall to the floor, my nipples sensitive to the cold. Even more sensitive to his tongue sucking on them.

I plunge my fingers into his hair when our mouths finally connect, tongues twirling. We're louder than we were in bed, the moans long and drawn out, panting, grunts guttural.

"Anabelle," Elliot chants, kissing me. "Anabelle."

Anabelle.

I'll never forget the way he says my name in that moment. Never.

"It's probably a terrible idea for us to continue living together—we need a chaperone."

"Should we get another roommate?"

"Fuck no."

We're in bed now—his bed—having cleaned up the kitchen, put away my homework, and shut off all the lights. His hand reaches for mine beneath the covers, lacing his fingers through mine.

"Elliot?"

"Hmm?"

"Don't you think at some point we should talk about this?"

"Talk about what?"

"You know, the fact that we've...that we're physical."

He shifts to face me. "What do you want to talk about?"

"I'm not trying to make this weird, but it's been on my mind the past few days. I'm not one of those girls who can do things casually. I just can't. So, before we get carried away, I want to talk about where this is headed."

"What do you mean?" He pushes a stray lock of hair out of my eyes, tucking it behind my ear.

"What are we *doing*? Does this change our relationship?"

"I hope not. I like you and I don't want to lose you as a friend."

"That's not really what I meant. I need to know if your feelings for me have changed now that we're having sex, because I like you."

A lot.

And I don't want to be fuck buddies.

I don't want us to be just roommates.

I don't want to be just friends, either.

"I like you, too, Anabelle. I just…"

Oh God, he's hesitating.

He hesitates so long it becomes awkward, and I'm afraid to pull back to get a better look at his face.

"What, Elliot. Just say it."

"This isn't a good time for me to be starting an actual relationship."

My bare shoulders tense against his cozy cotton bedding. "So are you saying you don't want one?"

"I do, Anabelle, but it's complicated." He says it kindly, almost consoling. "I'm applying to grad schools all across the country, but none here. Chances are, I won't be back after the end of the semester."

I did *not* know that.

I mean, I knew he was applying to graduate programs, but we've never discussed *where*. Not once did he tell me he was leaving at the end of this semester.

Which is in a matter of *weeks*.

"Right. I get that, I was just asking." I fake a laugh. "Relax."

I release his hand, rolling away from him, toward the wall, distancing myself so we're no longer touching. Stare at the beige paint and blank space, fighting back tears.

Elliot runs his hand up my bare spine; I want to shrug it off and tell him not to touch me, but I don't want him to see me pout. Or worse…cry.

"Anabelle…" The rawness in his voice is so thick, I ache for him, too, even though he's the one hurting me. "Anabelle, I'm trying to make something of my life. I didn't have it easy growing up—my parents weren't financially successful until I was older and wanted to make sure I had a strong work ethic. I'm not here on a scholarship, and they're only paying for a portion of my schooling."

I didn't know that either. "Where have you applied?"

"Michigan. Texas," he continues in a low, soothing voice. "LSU, and a few other smaller places."

Wow.

Just…*wow*.

My eyes sting, blinking hard, and I'm grateful he can't see my face. The last thing I want is for him to feel guilty. He's not my boyfriend.

He's my roommate and he's moving and I'd be wise to remember it. Just because Elliot is the sweetest, most thoughtful guy I know doesn't mean we were meant to be.

"When will you know where you're accepted?" I try not to sniffle.

"Soon."

"Oh." I dip my head into his soft pillow, letting the cotton soak up the tears that have begun to fall, doing my best to keep them out of my voice. "Where do you want to end up?"

"I don't know. I'm from Iowa, but I'd rather not stay in the area. There's nothing for me here."

A hard lump forms in my throat. "I see."

"Do you?"

The room is silent, and I stopped breathing minutes ago.

"Anabelle," he whispers gently. I wish he'd stop saying my name. "We've only had one semester together and we've never been on a single date—you know it makes no sense for me to stay."

We never went on any dates because he never asked.

"Do you care for me at all?" It's desperate and needy but I don't care. I only care how I feel in this moment, and the words I crave to hear, memories and words I can latch on to, to replay in my mind when he's gone.

He scoots closer, wrapping his arms around my middle, chin resting on my shoulder, burying his nose.

"If I were to stay behind for anyone, it would be you, but I can't give up my education or career for what-ifs."

I go quiet for a moment, thinking. "I'm going to miss you."

"I'm not gone yet." He's quiet, too, and I hear him swallow a lump in his throat. "Do you still want me to come with you to your dad's wrestling match tomorrow?"

"Of course I do," I barely manage. "If you're not busy."

"Are you still bringing that sign for Gunderson?"

"Yes."

"Then of course I'm coming—I wouldn't miss something like that. I want a front row seat."

"Good, because I don't want to go alone."

"You won't be alone. I'll be right there with you."

For now.

He doesn't say it, but we both know that's what he means.

Because he didn't apply to any grad schools in Iowa.

21

#DOUCHEBAG

"I give a little bit of a fuck.
Just enough to
keep me out of jail."

Elliot

"You're sure that's what you want the sign to say?"

"I'm sure. Best to leave things vague, don't you think?"

"Not really, but this is your thing, not mine."

"You put the idea into my head in the first place, remember? *'Get revenge,'* he said. *'It'll make you feel better,'* he said. Well, I'm not catty, and the book on revenge said acting on it will make me look psycho. Therefore, this sign is as good as it gets."

Anabelle is carrying a piece of neon pink poster board, on which she painstakingly stenciled the words: *HEY REX! WILL YOU STILL WANT TO "DATE" ME AFTER MY DAD FINDS OUT ABOUT YOUR BET?*

"I have no objection to walking in with a sign, but you don't think it's a little…wordy? And sparkly?"

"The words all fit, so I don't see what the big deal is."

"It's wordy and it's sparkly."

"That's the point."

"I don't get it."

She huffs a sigh. "My dad is going to see it, get mad, storm over, and then confront Rex about it. It's genius."

"Because you want to tell your dad and teach Rex a lesson about publically embarrassing someone?"

"Exactly. This is payback for last year—what he did to that guy was mean."

It was. However, "And you honestly feel doing the same sort of thing is going to make him change?"

"It's worth a try, don't you think?"

"If you say so." I glance down at her trotting along beside me down the block. "You want me to carry it?"

"No, I got it. I'm going to fold it up and hold onto it until the moment is right."

"When will the moment be right?"

"I don't know, probably when my dad knows I'm there and makes eye contact with me in the seats." She holds two fingers out on her right hand and points them back at her eyes. "He's always watchin'. Trust me, he'll see this—everyone will."

"What do you think he's going to do?"

"Get pissed. Fly off the handle. Kick Gunderson off the team." I've never seen her so resolute about anything.

"I mean, technically he's not *on* the team..."

"You're just saying that because you don't like him. A team manager is a big deal, Elliot. Make no mistake, Rex Gunderson's position is important." We walk along, both wearing Iowa wrestling T-shirts, jeans, and sneakers, making our way to the stadium. "Sucks that they're not going to have a manager after this weekend. Training someone new will be such a bitch."

"What about Eric Johnson?"

Anabelle waves off my question. "Rex Gunderson will make sure he goes down with his sinking ship, don't you think? Like a rat. Guys like him always take down their friends—he'll be clinging to him like a life preserver. Besides, they're roommates. It's inevitable."

I agree. "For sure."

We enter the building through the athlete entrance, flashing the badges Coach Donnelly gave Anabelle to give us special privileges while we're here. No lines, no crowd, no noise.

Not until we get to the arena.

It's a packed house, but our seats are down by the floor, and there is no way her father is going to miss this neon sign. In fact, there is no way *anyone* will miss it—not Donnelly, not Gunderson, not Johnson.

And the gang is all here.

Anabelle waits.

231

Waits through the entire meet, until the last man has been pinned and the wrestlers are on their knees, tipping back water, listening to their last lecture before heading into the locker rooms.

The sign is neon pink with glitter-covered letters, a blazing beacon in a room full of black and yellow that catches Coach Donnelly's eye almost immediately when she holds it above her head. Rocks back and forth on her heels, the glitter catching the light in just the right way to make the letters shine.

Coach glances up, searching the crowd for his daughter.

I watch the poor man do a double take.

Squint.

Read.

Read it again, lean forward, toss down his clipboard, and stalk toward Rex Gunderson. He grabs him by the shirt collar and points toward where Anabelle and I are standing, forcing Rex to read the sign. Pointing, jamming his fingers in our direction.

"Yeesh," Anabelle mutters. "It looks like he's about to have a heart attack."

"That does look like a very likely scenario."

She smacks me in the abs. "Oh shit. He's coming over."

Anabelle

"What the hell is the meaning of this?" My father stomps over, glaring at me, at the ridiculous sign. Rips it out of my hands and tosses it to the stadium floor, along with all the other garbage the students in our section have discarded.

"Hey! I worked really hard on that!"

"You think this shit is funny, Anabelle Juliet?" My dad is so pissed—but then again, what else is new? "You have two seconds to tell me exactly what the hell is going on. Then I'm going to drag Mr. Gunderson's bony ass over here and you're going to repeat it to him."

I take a deep breath, Elliot standing beside me, one hand on the small of my back. "There's something Gunderson and Eric Johnson needs to tell you."

"That they're gay?" he shouts over the noise, glancing back at Rex.

"What? No!" I laugh at my dad's confusion. "I mean, *maybe* they are, who knows, but that is *not* the point I'm trying to make right now."

"What is your point? If you're going to come into my house —my arena—with that tasteless sign and cause a ruckus, you better have a damn good reason for it, young lady."

My father's bushy brows rise expectantly, eyes shifting between Elliot and me. Noticing the narrow space between our bodies, and our hands—they're hanging at our sides but are almost touching. A palpable air of intimacy hangs between us.

"Get to the point, Anabelle—I have some skull-crushing to do in the locker room and not much time to do it."

I open my mouth to tell him…

…and the whole story comes out.

The bet. Overhearing it at the gym. Crying in the library then going out and getting wasted. Elliot bringing me home, back to his place. Going on a fake date with Rex but not hating it.

He's mad, but he listens, nostrils flaring out with his displeasure. Arms crossing, steam rising from his ears.

When I finish, he nods tersely, narrowed gaze sliding to a nervous Rex Gunderson, who didn't have the balls to join us.

Two days later, we heard through one of my dad's wrestlers that Rex had been fired as team manager, suspended for the remainder of the semester, and is no longer able to hold a job on campus. Eric Johnson lost his partial scholarship and eligibility to wrestle at any Division 1 school.

My feelings range from glad to guilty and every emotion in between, but that's not what has been haunting me.

Elliot is finally graduating, the end of the semester looming above us like a storm cloud, shadowing us wherever we go. With every box he packs up, every call from his mom to find out when he'll be home, it becomes more real.

Everything about us has been too easy. Everything about him is too constant and good. He's handsome and funny and makes me feel…

He makes me feel…

I glance up at him from my spot at the library table with an unsteady smile, pen poised above a notebook. When he notices my eyes welling up, he's quick to reach across the table and brush away the tears with his thumb.

And tonight, after we make love, he'll hold me with his strong, steady arms. It'll make me feel better, for a few moments.

Until it's time for me to let him go.

"I give a lot of fucks, actually.
I'm a prostitute of feelings."

Anabelle

"What are your plans this summer?"

I can't meet his eyes as he hefts a large box, carrying and setting it next to the door. Elliot's pile of boxes is growing, stacked in the living room.

The semester is over and he's packed up, ready to leave, a summer internship already waiting for him a few states over.

"Work." I shuffle my bare feet. "I'll probably try to see my mom for at least a week or two in Massachusetts. She'll expect a visit since it's been an entire semester, making me basically the world's crappiest daughter."

"You're hardly the *crappiest*." He laughs. "I'm sure there are worse daughters in the world."

I don't know what to say next, so I go with, "Thank you for leaving the couch—it would suck having to sit on the floor."

"No problem. It's not like I could have taken it with me anyway."

Everything he's taking along on his journey has to fit in his car, and it's not much. Just a few boxes, his bedding, computer, and toiletries from the bathroom.

"As it is, I only have room for a few more boxes, so…" Those mammoth hands of his get stuffed deep into the pockets of his cargo shorts.

I look around, surveying the landscape. The bare walls, the nearly empty rooms. "What about your TV?"

He hasn't taken that out of his room yet.

"I'm leaving it for you."

"Jeez, Elliot, I'm not keeping your TV."

"Anabelle, can you not make a big production out of it? You can have my bed and the TV and you won't have to sleep in that shitty twin anymore."

"It's not a shitty twin! It's just tiny."

Since I have one more year of school before graduation, I'm staying, in this town and in this house. Who knows, I might even find myself a roommate to rent out my old room.

"So this is it, huh? You're doing it."

Packing up and moving to Michigan.

"It's really not that far."

Six hours and forty-three minutes, or an hour-and-forty-five-minute flight...not that I Googled it or anything.

"No. It's not that far I guess. I'm excited for you."

But not for myself. I'm going to miss him, going to lose a bit of myself when he finally turns and walks out that door for the last time.

"We can text and follow each other on social media."

"Great."

"You don't seem excited."

That's because I'm not! I want to shout. *I'm devastated you're leaving!* My best friend is leaving to create a new life for himself, one that doesn't include me.

"I'm excited, of course I am, don't be silly. I'm just...I don't know, Elliot. I'm pouting. Don't even listen to me, okay? Don't let me ruin your day."

"Ruin my day? Do you think I'm happy about this?"

Then stay!

Stay and finish your education here.

I hang my head, unable to look him in the eyes, afraid of what I'll see there. "I'm just being selfish."

"It's not selfish, Anabelle. It just means you care."

A lump forms in my throat, and I swallow it painfully when he adds, "You've been a really good friend to me."

"Friends."

"I thought that's what you wanted—to be *friends*."

"Of course I do! But I already have enough friends, even if most of them aren't in Iowa, and now you'll be long-distance, too." Outside, cars drive slowly down the street. The sounds of the students a few houses down can be heard as they haul furniture to their curb. "You have to give me time to adjust, okay? I already miss you and you're standing right in front of me."

"Give you time? Time for *what*?"

"I'm losing someone I was just starting to, you know…love."

"You don't think I feel the same way?"

"As a friend? Of course."

"No, Anabelle, I love you—I do."

Why is he telling me this now, after all these months? Is he trying to destroy every piece of my already breaking heart?

"You love me?" I struggle to get the words out.

"Of course I do."

"But you're leaving, so tell me this… what difference does it make? Go chase your dream, Elliot."

There's an entire lifetime ahead of us.

"Anabelle, you know I have to move. Michigan has one of the best post-grad programs for kinesiology in the country, and I'm lucky to have been accepted. You just transferred, so I can't ask you to come with me. We practically just met."

"I know," I answer miserably.

He steps forward, cupping my chin in his hands. "You're so close to graduation yourself."

"I wish you'd stop telling me things I already know." I try to look away, but he won't let me.

"It sucks, but it's for the best. You're going to graduate, and I'm going to get my master's, and I'll come visit every once in a while when I can. I just don't see how long-distance can work right now."

"It's fine, Elliot. You already said you weren't ready for a relationship and I respect that. I won't pressure you. I'm mature enough to be okay with this. So, you can leave, and go with a clear conscience." I falter, swallowing. "We'll both miss each other, but we'll get over it."

Life goes on.

"Eventually, right?" His voice wavers. Shakes.

And I swear, I've never seen a guy's eyes well with tears before, but Elliot's are welling up now. I can barely stand looking at him. It's killing me inside. It's killing me knowing he's leaving, moving halfway across the country.

Knowing he's not going to be returning when classes resume in the fall.

"Jesus, don't you dare cry, too," I scold, bottom lip trembling when he wraps his strong arms around me, resting his forehead on mine. "Please, don't cry."

"I'm sorry, Ana." His face is buried in my shoulder, in my hair, arms wrapped around me tightly. "I love you, I do, but I have to go."

"You're going to do amazing things, Elliot St. Charles. You're the best roommate I've ever had."

"I'll be back for the holidays. It's not like you're getting rid of me forever."

"But you'll be old by then, maybe even have gray hair, and I'll probably start dating Rex Gunderson and won't remember your name."

"I swear to fucking God, if you start dating Rex Gunderson, I will literally—"

"Literally what?"

"I don't know, but it would crush me."

An alarm goes off in his pocket, his cell phone chiming a gentle reminder that it's time to leave.

He's needed somewhere else.

"I have to go or I'll be late meeting my parents."

"All right."

"Anabelle." Elliot's big, masculine hands take hold of my face. "I…I…"

I bow my head, wordlessly saying what my lips can't.

I know.

Me too.

He presses his lips to mine, and I can taste the salt from our tears, his and mine.

"Just go." I can barely get the whisper out of my throat, it's so raw from emotion. "Get out of here."

I give him a gentle shove toward the door and he takes a step over the threshold. Then another.

He nods, fighting back tears, but one escapes anyway and slides down his face, glistening in the sunlight.

I hate this. Hate it.

"Goodbye," he mouths.

"Bye," I mouth back.

Then I watch him walk away. Climb into his car, start the engine, idling.

He sits, staring at the little house we lived in together for one *amazing* semester—the best semester of my life—and I see him inhale a deep breath, clutching the steering wheel.

He sends me a quick wave.

I don't know how long I stand on that porch, watching him go, but it's long enough that his car disappears around the corner, out of sight.

Finally, I have the energy to raise my hand and wave back.

Except he's not there anymore.

He's gone.

"I love you."

Elliot: *Hey you—what are you up to?*

Anabelle: *Rearranging some IKEA furniture I just bought and put together.*

Elliot: *Oh yeah? Like what?*

[Anabelle Donnelly sent an attachment]

Elliot: *You put that shelf together yourself???*

Anabelle: *Why are you saying it like that?! With all those questions marks? YE OF LITTLE FAITH.*

Elliot: *That thing is huge!*

Anabelle: *I love them. My friend said white bookshelves are hard to decorate, but I'm in love with these. I need more room because my mom just sent some books I had at her house.*

Elliot: *Don't get too comfortable. You're only there for two more semesters. You're going to have to move all that shit out.*

Anabelle: *That's what dads and friends with pickup trucks are for.*

Elliot: *You have a friend with a pickup truck?*

Anabelle: *Not yet, but I'm determined to find one.*

Anabelle: *Where are you now?*

Elliot: *I stopped in Indiana last night, so I'm somewhere near the Great Lakes. Have you ever seen Lake Michigan in the summer?*

Anabelle: *No, what's it like?*

Elliot: *Like being on the ocean, along the east coast. Really fucking pretty. You'd love it.*

Anabelle: *Send me a picture before you get back in your car and keep driving.*

[Elliot St. Charles sent an attachment]

Anabelle: *Wow. You're right, that does look like the ocean.*

Elliot: *That's not what I'd really like to be looking at right now.*

Anabelle: *What would you rather be looking at right now?*

Elliot: *Your sleeping face on the pillow next to mine.*

Anabelle: *Don't say things like that anymore.*

Elliot: *Sorry, I won't.*

Two weeks later

Elliot: *This apartment sucks.*

Anabelle: *How so?*

Elliot: *It always sounds like the tenant in the unit upstairs is rearranging furniture in the middle of the night. I think he's a med student working second shift at the hospital.*

Anabelle: *At least it's not yelling and screaming. I once lived in a house with someone living in the basement, and she'd fight with her boyfriends all the time. Yeah, that's right, I said boyfriends, as in multiple.*

Elliot: *I appreciate you trying to make me feel better, but the dude is still soooo fucking loud.*

Anabelle: *I can gladly say my new roommate is NOT. I can barely tell she's here because, well, she's barely ever here.*

It's kind of a bummer—I thought Madison would be better company, thought we'd watch movies and crap.

Elliot: *So a replacement Elliot?*

Anabelle: *Without the benefits, LOL*

Elliot: *Maybe she'll come around more when school starts. Everyone is MIA in the summer because there's nothing to do in town.*

Anabelle: *She was with me at the party last semester. You know the one...*

Elliot: *That party will be etched into my brain forever.*

Anabelle: *Because I humiliated myself???*

Elliot: *No, because you let me be there for you.*

Anabelle: *What do you mean?*

Elliot: *I didn't realize it at the time, but I'd never felt so protective over anyone. That night was a first.*

Anabelle: *Seriously? But I was so drunk.*

Elliot: *Maybe, but I knew the reason why, and you looked so fucking pretty.*

Anabelle: *Despite being drunk?*

Elliot: *Yeah, despite you being drunk. And the morning after? Man, I thought you were so cute.*

Anabelle: *I was HUNG-OVER AF. The morning after was a train wreck. I wore the same clothes home.*

Elliot: *You did seem pretty embarrassed, but man were you cute.*

Anabelle: *Humiliated.*

Elliot: *Thank God there was no repeat performance.*

Anabelle: *OH! Changing gears! Did Dev tell you I'm still playing soccer with those guys? They've started playing once a week, so I go to the gym less.*

Elliot: *You guys are playing once a week? Damn, now you're making me jealous. I could never get their lazy asses onto the field more than once a month.*

Anabelle: *I found a few more girls to join the team so I'm no longer outnumbered. **brushes dust off shoulders** The field is full of Devin's drool. Plus, I think he likes me.*

Elliot: *Oh I bet he likes you.*

Anabelle: *Not like THAT, LOL. We're bros.*

Elliot: *Bros my ass. He's probably so fucking glad I'm gone.*

Anabelle: *Probably, LOL. I do catch him staring at my ass a lot.*

Elliot: *Tell him to knock that shit off.*

Anabelle: *Why? He's not GRABBING it. He tries to hide it, but subtlety is not his forte, the poor guy. I bent over twice last night just to test the theory.*

Elliot: *Sometimes you're a real fucking brat, do you know that, Donnelly?*

Anabelle: *You love it.*

Elliot: *I do.*

Elliot: *And I miss you.*

Anabelle: *I miss you, too.*

Six weeks later

Friday, August 22nd

Dear Elliot,

I thought I'd email you instead of text because I told myself I'd stay off my phone until this midterm paper is done. So, I'm doing this the old-fashioned way, modern day snail mail...or maybe I'm sending you this letter because I've had a glass of wine tonight and am slightly buzzed and missing you more than I probably should or have any right to. Who knows, by the time I get to the end, I might delete it instead of hitting send.

Madison has been great to live with. She has a few friends who come hang out at our place, and I'm starting to consider them friends, too. She's been waitressing all summer at Mad Dog Jacks, which I didn't know served food. She says the tips are awesome, mostly because during the day, it's barflies that come in, over-tipping because they're drunk. I don't know, maybe I'll apply there. I have some nights free and could use the extra cash.

I finally met your old roommate Zeke at the fundraiser for the Big Brothers mentoring program—they moved up the date this year or I would have invited you to come along as my date. Zeke was with his girlfriend, Violet, and I sat next to her. She's so sweet, I think I'm half in love with her myself. Zeke is so dark and broody and she's so kind. They dote on each other—he bought her a purple sapphire necklace on a gold chain and hung it around her neck as they were walking out. Stopped her in the doorway, pulling her blonde hair back and kissing her on the neck before clasping it. It was almost painful to watch and made me miss you.

If you were here, I would have taken you. I wore a dark burgundy cocktail dress and heels. Lips were red. Madison put my hair in an up-do, so it was all very ooh-la-la, so fancy.

I don't know what else to say without spilling my guts and making this awkward, and we're both about to start school, but I will tell you this. If I close my eyes, I can see you standing shirtless in the kitchen, your skin tan from playing soccer with no shirt on.

Of course, this is the wine talking.

In the light of day, I'm strong and moving on, just like all the greatest love songs say to do.

It's too bad I've taken them all off of repeat.

Love,

Anabelle.

Saturday, August 23rd

Anabelle,

Stop talking about me like I'm a ghost. I'm not dead, I'm in Michigan. I've read and reread your notes at least thirty times and decided to level the sobriety playing field, I'd do a few Jagerbombs before typing this message.

If you think Iowa is boring, you should come to Michigan. I hear they get buried in snow in winter, and the population here is a bustling 120k. It's not even September and I'm already freezing my balls off.

I texted Dev and told him to stop staring at your ass and find someone new to lust after. He didn't seem fazed and I know he enjoys riling me up, the fucking dickhead. He said you went and or-

dered a new pair of socks to cover your shin guards, yellow and blue stripes. Bet they're adorable—you have the sexiest legs.

Dev was bragging about you, said they switched your position and tried playing you at forward. Why didn't you tell me you scored two goals?

Class officially begins on the 25ᵗʰ—two more days—but I've got the syllabus for my classes printed out and have been prepping for the course load. Such a fucking nerd, I swear.

My internship is great. As you know, I'm working with the football players and their team of trainers and therapists. If everything goes well, I'm hoping they'll offer me a permanent position once I get my degree. Then again, it's Michigan and it's fucking cold, so we'll see if I can hack it in winter.

I love you, Anabelle. You are undoubtedly one of my best friends, and I think about you every second of every damn day.

"Getting into a relationship
seemed like a good idea.
But so did the Titanic,
and look what happened."

Anabelle

I stare at my reflection in the bathroom mirror, angling my head from left to right, studying myself. My cheeks are flushed and my eyes are bright, but something isn't quite right. *Hmm.*

I lean forward, pulling down on my lower lids with my forefingers, checking my irises. Pat at my cheeks. Run a hand down the front column of my throat, poking at my collarbone. *Hmm.*

"Hey, you almost done in here? I was going to freshen up my face." Madison sticks her head through the bathroom door, giving me a thorough once-over. She's done up and downright adorable. "You look pale—are you feeling all right?"

I frown at my reflection. "I look pale? Really? I thought I looked rather flushed." I suck in my cheeks, grimacing at my fish face.

"Nope, you're definitely pale." Our eyes connect in the mirror and I can see that she's raised her brows. "You don't think you're getting sick, do you? Three people in my econ class had the flu last week."

"No...maybe? I'm just off. Everything is...off lately."

"Do you think it's depression? I know you miss Elliot, but it's not like you were in love with him."

She's wrong; I *was* in love with him, and I want to point out that sometimes suffering through a love you never had is worse than suffering through one you did. Everything with Elliot and me was left unfulfilled.

"Anabelle, you had the entire summer to get over him and move on. It's been more than two months."

Three.

It's been almost three months of summer break and I still miss him like crazy. Our letters back and forth mean *nothing* if he's not here. They're a weak replacement.

"I know, Madison, but it's just not the same."

"It doesn't help that you're sleeping in his damn bedroom." She's mentioned this a few times as cause for my melancholy.

"You wanna switch?"

"Please, I wasn't born yesterday," I tease. "You just want the queen-sized bed."

"True. The twin bed *sucks*—I can't bring anyone home because it's way too small to get laid in safely. Last weekend when you were having dinner at your dad's, I brought a random home and he fell off the side while he was going down on me. It was so embarrassing."

The visual of that makes me giggle. "I mean, he was already down on the floor, on his knees—couldn't he just have kept going?"

She rights herself against the doorframe. "Dammit, you're right! He totally could have!" Crosses her arms. "Shit, now I feel robbed of an orgasm."

"He didn't get you off after that?"

"No. He kept complaining about the bed."

"Did he invite you back to his place?"

Madison makes a face. "For real? Like I'd screw him at the fraternity house. Gross, no. Nothing against those guys, but the Pi house is disgusting—no one cleans it."

"It's definitely not like the other houses on Greek Row."

"Hell no it's not—those houses are gorgeous."

"Even the houses on Jock Row are fifty times better than the Pi house."

We chatter, bantering back and forth until she has to leave, and I go back to scrutinizing myself in the mirror. There are dull purple bags under my eyes from fatigue, and my hair looks dull.

Something isn't right.

Hmm.

Elliot: *How you holding up without me now that you're back in class? Haha.*

Anabelle: *It's a struggle—this female roommate business is overrated **winks** She always wants to talk about feelings.*

Elliot: *Guess it depends on the female—I never had any complaints.*

Anabelle: *Flattery will get you everywhere.*

Elliot: *Not really—not from way over here.*

Anabelle: *Why is Michigan so far?!*

Elliot: *The car ride sucks—I don't know if I told you that. Six hours in the car with nothing to do but think.*

Anabelle: *I've never driven any farther than my dad's cabin in the woods, and that's only a two-hour drive, tops. I should make you a playlist so you can listen to it when you come home for break.*

Elliot: *What would you put on it?*

Anabelle: *I'm not sure...probably all the songs I listened to after you left.*

Elliot: *You listened to sad songs after I left?*

Anabelle: *I never said they were SAD, weirdo. LOLOL.*

Elliot: *I just assumed they were.*

Anabelle: *Oh please, don't act like you're not missing me too.*

Elliot: *I'd be lying if I said I wasn't.*

Anabelle: *Then I guess we're even.*

Anabelle: *Also, maybe some of the songs were sad...*

"Sorry fellas, but I already have my sights set on a guy that's not interested."

Anabelle

"Anabelle, what brings you in today?"

I've driven myself to the health clinic across town after some convincing from Madison and a new insurance card from my dad. The nurse on duty flutters around the exam room, pulling up a chair for me and adjusting the reading glasses perched on her nose.

Rolling to the computer on the small desk inside the room, she peers down her spectacles at me, smiling.

"We'll briefly go over your health history, then I'll take your vitals." The wheels on the chair squeak. "Are you feeling okay?"

"I figured I'm overdue for a pap. I haven't had an exam since I moved here and I'm not feeling the greatest. My roommate thought I should come get checked out."

She stares at the monitor, reading out loud from my chart. "It lists your primary reason for getting the pill was help with menstrual cramping and moodiness associated with PMS. Is that still correct?"

I nod. "Correct."

Tap tap tap on the keys.

"This may take a little longer to complete than usual since this is your first visit to this clinic. Even though this isn't your first medical exam within our network, we do consider you a new patient."

"Okay, sure. That's fine."

Her fingers click away, entering all my information into their database. "Still taking a daily multivitamin?"

She waits for me to reply, hands hovering over the keyboard.

"Uh, not really." More like, *never, not at all*.

Click click click.

Next, she takes my blood pressure and checks my temperature. Takes my heart rate, entering that information into the computer, too.

"I see you're currently prescribed the birth control pill. Is that still working out for you?"

"Yes."

I shift in the chair, straining to see my chart.

The nurse glances at the computer, confirming. "I'm going by what's in the file your last physician sent over."

"Sure. Right, sorry." Nervously, I tuck a stray hair behind my ear.

She's all business, plowing ahead with her pre-exam questions. "Any other forms of birth control? Condoms?"

I smile. "I'm not currently sexually active."

"Any pregnancies?"

"No."

Click click. "No spotting, bleeding, abdominal pain, or side effects normally associated with the pill?"

"Nope, but let me grab my phone to see the last time I had my period—I track all that in an app." I pull the smartphone out of my purse, tapping the Aunt Flo app, swiping on my period tracker.

Stare.

Frown. "I had some spotting within the past two weeks and a fever on the twelfth. I haven't added any cycles, though. Sorry, is that okay?"

"That's fine. I'll just make those quick notes." Her fingers fly over the keys. "Any chance you could currently be pregnant?"

I laugh. "No."

"Okay, great, I think that covers the basics." She pulls her hands away from the computer. Stands and goes to the blue cabinet, pulling out a blue hospital gown, laying it on the exam table. "Remove everything and put this on, open to the back. You can cover your legs with this." She lays out a paper square moonlighting as a blanket.

Her smile is motherly. "Sit tight and I'll let the doctor know you're here. We'll both be in shortly."

"Thanks."

I make quick work of getting changed then hop onto the table, legs dangling over the side when there's a short knock at the door. It opens, my new gynecologist sticking his head through.

"Knock knock." He enters the room, nurse trailing along behind him. Extends his hand. "Hello, Anabelle, I'm Doctor Pritchard."

We make idle chitchat while he and his nurse prepare for the physical, and a moment later, I have my legs spread in the stirrups, exam underway.

Dr. Pritchard rolls back in his chair, staring up at me over the tops of his black-rimmed glasses. "Anabelle, are you sure there is no chance you could be pregnant?"

I frown. "Yes, I'm sure. Why?"

"Your cervix appears to be softening and slightly enlarged. Because you're a first-time patient, with your permission, I'm going to go ahead and order a pregnancy test, just to be certain."

"Are you sure that's necessary?"

He nods, standing, peeling off his gloves and tossing them in the trash. Smiles. "Fairly certain."

Five minutes later, I'm dressed and peeing in a cup.

Twenty minutes later, I'm pregnant.

Pregnant.

Pregnant.

Holy shit.

No matter how many times I say it, it's not real.

"Do you have time for an ultrasound?" the doctor is asking. Dazed, I shake my head, doing my best to focus on the words coming out of his mouth. "I can send an order down and get you in today, within the next two hours if you have time to wait around, or we should be able to schedule one later in the week. I'd like to get a better idea of how far along you are."

How far along I am.

I'm pregnant.

The doctor drops his head, scribbling on a notepad. "This is the name of a prenatal you should grab on your way out, or just stop at the drug store. Folic acid should also be taken with food, every morning."

I give a barely perceivable nod.

Folic acid. Prenatal.

"I have time to stick around."

The wait feels like an eternity, the waiting room a beige, cold cube devoid of personality. Sterile. Head down, I occasionally glance at the patients surrounding me: two older couples waiting for their weekly blood draws and a young expectant mother with her hands securely wrapped around her stomach.

I stare at that stomach, palms sliding to my own, over the waistband of my black yoga pants.

It's flat.

For now.

Sleepwalking through the rest of my appointment, numb, I lie on the table in the ultrasound room, arms at my sides, holding back tears as the oblivious technician rolls the wand around my stomach.

"According to this ultrasound, you're measuring roughly twelve weeks along." She smiles cheerfully.

"What?" I practically shout, trying to sit up, the flimsy paper blanket falling halfway to the exam room floor. "Twelve weeks? How is that possible?"

"Oh, how cute are you going to be when you start showing?" She chirps pleasantly, all smiles, wand gliding across my stomach, below my belly button, the clear gel a cold reminder of why I'm here.

"You're one of those lucky first-time moms who doesn't show any pregnancy symptoms until she's rather far along, I would imagine. So lucky—I was as big as a house with my first one," she says, teasing.

I muster up a feeble smile, bottom lip threatening to tremble. "No signs whatsoever."

"Not even morning sickness?"

I shake my head. "Not even morning sickness."

"That's great. With every one of my kids, I threw up so much I could barely make it to work. I think I called in sick most of my entire first trimester."

Eventually, I stop listening, and when the technician prints out the ultrasound pictures and hands them to me, I stare dazedly at the blurry black and white image.

A baby.

"It's about the size of a sweet little strawberry. Imagine that." She winks, washing her hands in the sink. "Now you have an excuse to go home and take a nap."

"A strawberry."

"Yes, ma'am!"

Why is she so cheery? It's throwing me off, postponing the panic that will surely come by the time I hit the parking lot.

Elliot: *Hey, I haven't heard from you all day.*

I almost don't have the heart to answer him, but I don't have the heart to avoid him, either.

Me: *I know. Sorry, I was…preoccupied.*

Elliot: *Rough day?*

Me: *You could say that.*

Elliot: *Want to talk about it?*

Me: *Not right now.*

Elliot: *Anabelle, is everything all right?*

Me: *It'll be fine. I just need to think.*

Elliot: *Okay...*

Me: *Tell me about your day, it had to have been better than mine.*

Elliot: *The usual—research and writing. Spent most of the day in the library.*

Me: *That is one of your favorite spots.*

Elliot: *I have a few of them.*

Me: *Oh yeah, where else?*

Elliot: *You know that smooth skin along your collarbone...*

I don't reply.

Elliot: *You still there?*

Me: *Yeah—sorry, I have a lot on my mind.*

Elliot: *I get it, getting into the swing of things when the school year starts sucks.*

Me: *I'm just having a crappy day.*

Elliot: *What about this weekend? Are you going out? I know Madison has been dragging you out into public.*

Me: *She has been, but nothing exciting. The usual crowd. She gets irritated with me because I'm boring, LOL. I just never want a repeat of the night you had to carry me home.*

And now that I'm an unwed, single, expectant mother, it's never going to happen. Ever.

Elliot: *But that turned out okay, didn't it?*
Me: *Sure it did. Look at us now—friends and all that.*

I change the subject; my hormones cannot handle where this conversation could possibly be headed, talking about how we've remained close during the past weeks, though he's all the way across Lake Michigan.

Me: *What about you—are you doing anything this weekend?*
Elliot: *Probably. I've actually been hanging out with a few people from the medical program. We grab beer a few nights a week.*
Me: *Yeah?*
Elliot: *Yeah. There's this one girl who reminds me of you. Her dad is actually a professor here. I posted a picture on IG when we went out last night.*

My stomach drops, the thought of him getting emotionally involved with someone new making me ill. I'm queasier than I've felt all day.

My hands fly to my stomach.

Me: *I haven't looked.*
Elliot: *I hope you're doing well, Anabelle.*

Doing well.

Me: *I am. Same to you.*

Elliot: *I should shut my phone off. This term paper isn't going to write itself.*

Me: *Talk to you later. Good luck with your paper.*

In the bathroom, I strip down and remove all my clothes, standing in front of the mirror for the second time today, eyes trailing down my naked body, looking for any signs that there's a baby growing inside me.

I cup my boobs, but they aren't tender and don't appear—or feel—any bigger. My hips look the same—slender.

Still…

A baby.

Elliot and I made a baby.

The harder I stare at my body, the more impactful the word *baby* becomes. I'm alone, standing in a cold bathroom, barefoot and pregnant.

I lift a hand to cover my mouth, muffling the sob rising from my throat. Then, the other palm covers my eyes, my face.

Wracking sobs of guilt taking over my entire tired body. Wet tears coming by the bucket-full, streaming down my face.

"What am I going to do?" I whisper, crying into my hands.

What am I going to tell him? What am I going to say?

He's nearly a seven-hour car ride away with two years of schooling to go, paid for by hard work and long dedicated hours.

A flutter in my stomach has me pausing.

There it goes again.

I should be showing by now, the ultrasound technician said. I should have a baby bump.

Pulling Madison's pink robe off the hook on the back of the door, I slide into its fuzzy comfort, tying the belt before opening the door. Padding to my bedroom and crawling into my big, empty bed.

Elliot's bed.

His.

Then *mine*.

I close my weary eyes, imagining what I'll say when I see him—it has to be in person. This cannot be done over the phone, and he's not likely to be home before the holidays.

Three more months.

An eternity.

25

#DOUCHEBAG

"There is nothing classy about being the pregnant girl at a frat party."

Anabelle

"Sup Anabelle Donnelly. No offense, but you look like shit."

I recognize that voice.

Glance up to see Rex Gunderson walking up the aisle toward me and groan—he is the last person I want walking into my class, the last person I want to spend another entire semester with.

Thanks, karma, for piling more crap onto my already shitty day.

"What are you doing in this class, Rex? I thought I'd gotten rid of you."

His grin is mischievous. "I'm like a fungus—that's why they call me a *fun guy*."

"I would bet no one has ever called you that."

He laughs good-naturedly, gesturing toward the seat beside me. "Mind if I sit here?"

"You really want to?" Is this guy a sadist? "There are plenty of open seats."

We haven't spoken since that night in the stadium, the night where I humiliated him in front of the entire wrestling team, my father, and the coaching staff, when I was the driving force behind him getting fired from his management position.

"We social pariahs can't be too choosy these days," he jokes, plunking his bag down.

It's on the tip of my tongue to apologize—my knee-jerk reaction as a kind and caring human being—but I stop myself because I'm not sorry.

He didn't deserve to have the position he held when he abused it, and it was about time he was removed.

"How's life treating you otherwise?" I ask, genuinely curious, sincerely wanting to know how someone moves on after spending three years of their life committed to the same team.

"Boring as fuck."

"What about Johnson?"

"He's gone. Went back home, transferred to a community college."

"Why?"

"He was here on a partial athletic scholarship and out-of-state tuition is fucking expensive, so when he got suspended, his parents made him move home." Rex shrugs.

"Sure. Makes sense."

"You're stone cold, do you realize that?"

"I am? How so?"

"Most girls would be embarrassed to be sitting with me, and they sure as shit wouldn't want to be talking about it. You humiliated me."

"You had it coming."

"You're right."

I stare. "Did you have a *come to Jesus* moment this summer?"

"Something like that." He laughs, stretching his legs out in front of him, slouching in the desk.

I eyeball his jeans and raise my brows. "No more khakis?"

"No more khakis," he confirms.

"Wow, Gunderson, you really have changed."

"That's pitiful."

"What is?"

"That the main thing you've noticed about me is that I'm not wearing beige-colored pants anymore."

He sounds so disgruntled.

It has me laughing all over again. "Sorry, but they were kind of your trademark."

"Guess I'm giving up a lot of shit I used to be down with."

"Has it been a rough few months?"

"At first. I was getting paid to be the team manager, and since basically being fired, I had to get a job off campus, which—whatever, it's not a big deal. Then obviously this summer I had to break the news to my parents. They were real proud of my position, you know?"

"I'm sure they were."

"Summer was hell, if you want to know the truth, not that I expect you to care since that whole bet thing exploded in my face." He studies me anew, studies my face and eyes, the set of my mouth. "Don't take this the wrong way, Anabelle, but you don't look good."

"I...have a lot on my mind. It's been a really rough week."

"Looks like it. What a pair we make."

I smile because he's right. We really do make an odd pair: a wrestling team reject and the knocked-up coach's daughter. It's almost like a friendship with Rex Gunderson was destined.

"Did you hear?

"Hear what?"

"That dickhead Zeke Daniels is getting engaged."

"How did you hear that?"

"I heard the buzz before getting kicked off the team. Elliot had to have told you."

"Elliot is gone."

"Where'd he go?"

"Grad school. Michigan."

"Oh. Well. I won't complain if I have you to myself without him wanting to punch my lights out." When I blanch, he reaches an arm around me with a laugh. "Relax, I'm kidding. At least you weren't dating him or anything—long distance sucks."

If that wasn't the understatement of the year, I don't know what is.

"Wait, rewind." I gape at him. "When did Elliot threaten to punch your lights out?"

"That night we went on our date. You left to go to the bathroom and he got all up in my face and told me to keep my hands off you. I thought it was extremely over the top considering you were just roommates."

"*You* thought he was being over the top?"

"He was definitely acting jealous, that's for sure."

"I'm sure he was."

"Were the two of you dating before he left?"

I feel a blush creeping up my chest, splotchy on my neck and staining my cheeks. "You could say that."

"Ahh, okay. Now I see how it is."

Somehow, after class, I let Gunderson take me to the university's small coffee shop, huddle in a corner booth. I'm just not ready to go home yet and instead drown my sorrows in a hot chocolate with extra whipped cream.

Laugh at all Rex's stupid jokes (and they're all stupid), letting him make me forget all my troubles, even if just for a little while.

"I have a confession to make," he's saying now over his iced coffee or latte, or whatever drink it was he ordered. "I'm shocked as hell you came here with me. I thought for sure you'd shoot me down when I suggested it."

"As weird as it sounds, I actually don't mind your company."

"That sounds oddly like a compliment."

Laughing, I snort. "It was...I think. Do you not get those much?"

"Not very often." He grins, biting down on his straw, a big toothy smile that has me smiling, too. "I've spent the last year getting my ass handed to me."

In another life, under better circumstances, Rex Gunderson might have been someone redeemable enough to date.

But they're not better circumstances; they're worse than they were yesterday.

I am pregnant.

I am single.

I am a broke college student.

My small circle of friends in Iowa includes Madison, who is barely around and only wants to party, Elliot, who moved to Michigan, and Rex Gunderson, who had a bounty on my vagina last semester.

Still…

I have a lot on my mind and no one to talk to, and he's right here, sitting in front of me, watching me intently, like he knows what's going on inside my head.

For all I know, he does.

I worry my bottom lip, suddenly thinking about my parents and what's going to happen when I tell them about…

Oh God.

I almost said, *about the baby.*

What am I going to tell my parents?

My dad is going to lose his mind and my mother is going to blame my father, and the entire thing is going to be an utter disaster.

And I'll have to do it alone.

"Earth to Anabelle."

I look up, not realizing I've just been staring into space, into my half-empty mug.

"Huh?"

"You looked lost there for a second."

"That's because I am."

Rex sits back in the booth, reclining back on the navy blue seat, crossing his arms. "What's going on with you? I don't remember you being like this last year."

"Like what?"

He waves a hand around in front of him, at me. "You're so preoccupied. I know you hate my guts, but—"

"I don't hate your guts, Rex. I'm just…" I inhale, taking a deep breath. "I found out some news this week that I'm preoccupied with. Sorry, it's nothing personal."

One of his sandy brown brows goes up. "What kind of news?"

"I'd rather…it's private."

Shit, why did I say that?

"Why?" He laughs. "Are you pregnant?"

I don't laugh.

And I don't answer.

I stare back at him, wide-eyed, worst poker face in the history of trying to keep secrets.

"Holy shit, Anabelle." He breathes heavily. "Are you?"

I have nothing to say.

Which is enough.

"Jesus. I don't know what to say," he says. "I was just joking."

I toy with the handle of my mug, scoffing. "Yeah, well."

We sit silently in that booth for the next ten minutes, only the sounds of the café keeping us company. Waitresses collecting mugs and saucers, the door opening and closing. The music. The chatter. Even the clanking of the dishes piling up in the kitchen can be heard. The sound of the coffee grinder.

"I can't believe you came out in public."

"Excuse me?"

"I just meant, if I was a chick, I'd be balled up in the corner of my room, crying."

"Believe me, I've had that pity party already."

"When did you find out?"

"This week."

"Wow." He takes another sip of his drink. "Does the father know?"

"No. Not yet."

He nods slowly, accepting this answer and not probing for a name.

"What are you going to do?"

"I don't know yet."

"Shit, and here I was blabbing away about engagement parties and how shitty my summer was. At least I haven't knocked anyone up."

His crude honesty puts a goofy smile on my face. "It's okay. Your babble takes my mind off it."

"Well, it's not the *worst* thing to happen."

I gape at him. "What do you mean?"

"I mean, a fucking baby? Babies are the shit, dude. I can't wait to have one."

My brow goes up. "You wouldn't be upset if you found out some girl you were sleeping with was pregnant?"

He shakes his head. "I doubt it. Maybe at first I'd be like *What the fuck, dude!* because I'd be shocked, but after I thought about it, I'd probably be chill. It's not like we're in high school anymore, Anabelle. We're old enough to procreate and successfully keep a human alive."

That's true.

I'm twenty-one years old and a senior in college, and Elliot is...

How old *is* Elliot? I don't think we've ever talked about it.

I quietly do the math.

If he graduated at eighteen, spent four years doing undergrad, that would make him...*holy crap*, Elliot is almost twenty-three? Can that be right?

"What are you so worried about?"

"Everything," I answer honestly.

How is Rex Gunderson not absolutely appalled by discussing this?

"Are you more worried about how people are going to react, or are you worried about actually *having* a baby?"

I'm deafened by my own silence.

His hands fold on the tabletop. "Okay, let me ask you this: are you worried the baby's dad is going to freak out and disappear on you?"

I consider the question: am I concerned Elliot is going to ghost me when he finds out I'm expecting a child?

"Not really."

"Are you worried your parents are going to disown you?"

I snort. "They'd never do that."

"Are you scared you're going to be cast out into the street, cold and alone, and you and your baby are going to starve?"

"Okay, now you're just being ridiculous."

"No I'm not, Anabelle—these are legitimate concerns people have."

"How would you know?"

"Haven't you ever watched *Teen Mom*?"

"I'm not a teen mom!" I shout indignantly.

"My point exactly." He pops a stick of gum, chomping down on it. "So what the hell are you freaking out about?"

"I never said I was freaking out."

"Maybe not, but when I saw you in class today, you looked like you were about to barf all over my shoes."

"I did not!"

"No lie. Pale as Casper the Friendly Ghost." He's back to leaning back in the booth. "You hungry? You should try eating."

"I'm not hungry."

"You're eating for two now." He is such a know-it-all.

"Haha, very funny."

"Have you been sick at all? My friend Adam knocked up his girlfriend our freshman year, and she tossed her cookies every morning like clockwork."

Seriously? His questions and concern are making me want to cry. He's being so sweet—so freaking sweet—and the fact that he isn't judging me is an enormous relief.

271

It gives me hope that my other friends will be as support-ive…my other friends from back home, who will have mixed re-views on my unexpected pregnancy.

It also gives me hope that I can do this, with or without Elliot in my life.

"I haven't been sick—that's why I didn't know until now that I'm…" The word gets lodged in my throat. "Pregnant."

"How far along are you, anyway?"

"Twelve weeks."

He lets out a low whistle. "Damn Anabelle, pretty soon you'll be able to find out if it's a girl or a boy." Pause. "Are you going to find out? I would." He laughs.

"I don't know."

I don't know anything.

"If you need me to come to any of your doctor's appoint-ments, let me know. I have so much fucking spare time these days, it's stupid."

"You do not want to come to my appointments." I laugh, the thought of the whole thing making me almost hysterical.

"I'll hold the diaper bag."

"I don't have a diaper bag." I'm grinning like a fool though, imagining it—imagining Rex Gunderson trailing along beside me with a pink diaper bag strapped to his body.

Pink.

Girl.

I shake my head, banishing the thought.

"Not yet you don't." He winks at me, flipping his phone to check the time. "Shit, I have to go—I work in an hour."

"Thanks for the hot chocolate, Rex."

"Hey, no problem. You look like you needed it."

"I did. It was just what I needed."

"I probably needed it, too."

I smile and it feels…

Good.

I can't actually share my thoughts with Elliot.

Can't call him on the phone and break the news. Doing it over the phone feels wrong. He deserves to find out in person.

I have so much on my mind, so many things to tell him—but if I do, will that weigh him down?

I sit down at the kitchen table with a journal, one I've had for ages that has never been completely filled, used to record my thoughts.

I crack it open, glancing through a few pages I haven't looked at in months, the last entry from two years ago. I was dating this guy, Will, from college. We were in the same town, at different universities—and I scan a passage about him that I wrote after we broke up. *"Will is someone I will definitely get over...not worth the tears, Anabelle. Chin up and move on."*

My mouth curves at the memory of those weeks following. I did more soul searching than crying, and I realized I wouldn't ever need a guy to fulfill me. Dating and falling in love were great, but they wouldn't make me whole.

Only I could do that.

Just like I could have and raise this baby on my own, without Elliot's involvement, but at some point, I would have to tell him, just like I'll have to tell my parents and other friends.

I grab a pen, hovering the tip over a clean page in my journal. Press down, hesitating.

I'll never send this letter I'm writing, but there is far too much to get off my chest. If I don't, I'll break inside. Burst.

I write:

Dear Elliot,

This is one letter I'm never going to send you, but I'm going to write it anyway, locked away in a diary no one but me will read or see. I have so much on my mind that's been keeping me awake the past few days.

There is no good way to tell you this. I'm just going to say it. I'm pregnant.

God, I thought it would be easier to write the words, but it's not, because now they're in ink, forever, scrolled across these pages for me to read anytime I open this notebook.

I'm pregnant. Pregnant.

I have a really small baby bump that people are going to start noticing at some point, but thank goodness for yoga pants and sweatshirts. I wonder what you'd think about the bump. Would you freak out, or would you be as levelheaded as I think you would?

Want to hear something crazy? I'm not as upset as I thought I'd be. I'm getting used to the idea of being a mom. A mom. I'm staring at that sentence, reading it over and over again. Crazy. Life is crazy, don't you think?

What's even crazier than us being parents is Rex Gunderson. We've been spending all kinds of time together, believe it or not. He's been great, considering he's the first person who found out— not because I told him, but because he guessed. I always figured he was smarter than he let on, and he is.

He's also turning into an amazing friend, Elliot. We talk all the time and go to the café a lot. Last week we went for pedicures—he said it was practice for when my feet start to swell up. He's such a nag, always on me about eating healthy. In a way, I think he needs a project now that he's been fired from the team and could only find part-time work, but he genuinely likes me, too, and we've put the past behind us.

You would absolutely hate it, LOL.

My dad certainly does.

I finally broke the news to Dad a few days ago about befriending Gunderson, and he was so mad, but I know he'll come around. He's going to have to. Madison has been really support-

ive, but Rex...I think I'm going to take him with me when I tell Dad and Linda about the baby. Our baby.

I wish you were here.

You were so easy to fall in love with, do you realize that?

It's killing me not telling you my news—our news—but I refuse to do it over the phone. You deserve to hear it in person, but now is not the time, and I cannot come there.

I love you, and I'm proud of you.

Love, Anabelle.

AKA Your baby mama.

Kidding, omg. But I have always wanted to say that. Haha.

Elliot

It's been a shitty week, and the only thing getting me through is the countdown to winter break.

I think about Anabelle nonstop, wondering if she thinks about me as much as I think about her. Today in class, I caught myself staring off at the wall twice, daydreaming instead of taking notes.

Doodling on a loose-leaf sheet of paper, then finally, hand writing her a note in small, tidy penmanship.

Ana. Annie. Anabelle.

Guess what? I'm coming home for a family event soon, a banquet for my dad. Remember I told you about him? He's a law- yer and every year, his firm hosts a big to-do. So, I'm coming home!

I'm not going to tell you, I want it to be a surprise—I want to see the look on your face when I show up on your doorstep Friday night. I'm flying and get in late, so my ass will be seriously drag- ging.

Dead on my feet will never have been more worth it.

If it weren't for you, I wouldn't be coming back at all. I would skip the awards dinner altogether and give my parents an excuse about being busy, but they're buying me a plane ticket and I'd be stupid to pass up the chance to see you.

Michigan isn't the same without my friends here, without you. Jesus, I lie in bed every night, staring at the ceiling, wondering if I made the right decision. Logically, I know it is—my professors are incredible, and this internship is going to set me up after I gradu- ate.

Still, I have my doubts.

That's why I can't wait to see you. I'm going to spoon the shit out of you in that big bed—I didn't book a hotel, so I hope you don't mind me crashing at your place. I just want to hold you.

I hope you'll let me.

I miss the smell of your skin and the taste of your lips, and the way you back up into me in bed when you're sleeping.

Not to sound like a total pussy, but whoever said absence makes the heart grow fonder wasn't fucking around.

I miss you like crazy.

I love you.

When class is over, I rise from the desk, crushing the letter I just wrote in the palm of my hand, wadding it into a ball. Toss it in the trash can in the corner.

It goes in easy, the perfect basket.

Score!

26

#DOUCHEBAG

"To do list:
don't get anyone pregnant."

Elliot

I'm back.

It's been months since I've been back or seen anyone, if you don't count social media—which I do not since I'm not active on it. No one knows I'm here; no one knows I've safely landed but my mother.

My father is being honored by the state bar association for his pro bono work and dedication to developing innovative ways to deliver volunteer legal services to those who can't afford them, and naturally, I'm expected to attend the ceremony in Iowa.

Home.

I didn't hesitate to book my flight, not wanting to waste any time driving the distance in my car.

My cab pulls up to the curb, stalling while I grab my carry-on and laptop bag, sliding out of his backseat. Feet hitting the ground, I stand, heart racing, staring down the sidewalk of that tiny college rental.

Anabelle is inside.

The kitchen light is on, the small one above the sink I always kept on when Anabelle was out and I didn't want her coming home to a dark house.

Slamming the door of my ride, I heft up my bags, staring up the walkway. Raise my hand to the door and knock.

Step back off the stoop, waiting.

Did I mention my heart is jackhammering right out of my fucking chest? So hard I can hear it and feel it beating in my throat.

The door cracks a few inches and a familiar face appears. Opens farther.

Anabelle stands there, shell-shocked.

Jesus, she looks good.

She's practically glowing.

It only takes us seconds to recover and launch our bodies at one another; my arms wrap around her waist, lifting her off the ground until her feet dangle. Spin her around, desperate to put my lips on her.

"I fucking missed you." I plant kisses on her mouth, cheek, and hairline.

"Oh my God." Her voice is muffled, face buried in the crook of my neck.

"Are you crying?"

"No." She sniffs, definitely crying. "I can't believe you're here." She pulls back, swiping at a stray tear. "Why *are* you here? Did someone say something?"

"Say something about what?"

She pales, wiping back a stray tear. "Nothing. I'm just— you're here. I can't believe it."

I'm beaming, arms still wrapped around her waist.

"The bar association is honoring my dad tomorrow for thirty years of service, and it was a perfect excuse to hop on a plane and come see everyone." To see her.

"I see."

"Anyway, I know it's late and I just showed up on your doorstep, but I was hoping I could stay here."

"With *me*?"

"Is that all right?"

"Yes. Yes, I... we have so much to catch up on." The door opens all the way and Anabelle steps aside, giving me room to enter the house. "Come in."

I step up, stealing another kiss along the way, planting it on her surprised mouth. "Mind if I take this to your room? I'm so fucking tired—would it be weird if we called it a night early?"

I'm babbling but too tired to care.

"No! No, go ahead. I'll just...I'll..." God, she's cute, stumbling over her words, bottom lip trembling. "I'll just..."

I close the front door, locking it behind us, and reach for her. Wrap her in another hug, resting my chin on top of her head. She's visibly shaken; whatever reaction I thought she'd have when she saw me again, this isn't it. By now, I thought we'd be laughing in the kitchen, possibly ripping off our clothes and going at it hard on the table.

"I really didn't think I'd see you again until Christmas."

"I didn't either," I respond honestly because I had no plans to come to Iowa until the holiday calendar demanded I did. "Are you sure you're okay with me being here? I can go stay with Zeke and Violet, or check into a hotel."

"It's okay, I'm just freaking out a little. Well, a lot." Her laugh is coupled with nerves. "Sorry, I'm being awkward."

Anabelle squirms to be released, so I give her space, picking up my two bags and following her to the bedroom I once called my own. Set my bags on the floor, next to the dresser, peeling off my socks.

"Mind if I jump in the shower? I'd love to wash the travel off."

"Yeah, sure—just let me grab you a towel. Madison gets weird about sharing things like that."

When she's gone, I take a few seconds to survey the room, to see what she's done with it now that I'm not living here anymore.

Same bed, different bedspread. Hers is white, with ruffles, fluffy and inviting. Same TV and TV stand. Same dresser.

She's added a nightstand and a lamp, and I run my fingers along the books piled on top. The top one is a parenting book, which is weird since she's a law student, but I move on to the dresser, thinking it must be for a friend. Remove my watch and set it down, cuffing my wrist with my fingers and massaging it.

"All set." Her voice rings out from across the hall.

The shower is running when I hit the bathroom, and I shuck my clothes, ducking into the warm spray. God, it feels good; this whole trip was such a great fucking idea.

I stand for a solid five minutes, then spend another five washing my hair, lathering my pits, cock, and ass. Rinse. Shut off the water and dry off. I wrap the towel around my waist, grabbing up my dirty clothes by the armful.

Anabelle is on the bed, already lying down when I return, arms behind her head, watching me.

Close the door.

Toss my dirty clothes into a pile I'll deal with later.

Bending, I dig in my bag for clean boxers and pajama pants before I drop the towel, letting it fall to the floor in a heap. I glance over my shoulder to see if she's watching, and note her eyes fastened on my ass with satisfaction.

Sliding into bed with her is oddly exhilarating, and I roll toward her, propping my chin in my hand. She does the same.

Smiles.

"Hi."

"Hi."

She looks tired, like she hasn't slept, so I reach out to stroke my thumb over the smooth skin beneath her eyes. "You look exhausted."

Her smile is wobbly. "I am."

"How are you? Really."

I know she misses me and took my leaving hard, probably harder than she let on, always presenting me with a brave face in our messages and emails. At first, I was thankful for it—her fake smile made it easier to drive away from the house that day. Her shoving me off the porch toward my car allowed me to freely walk toward it, climb inside, and actually start the engine.

But the truth is, I secretly prayed it would break down before I was out of town that day. It didn't. Everything went according to plan, and I was in Michigan before bed the next night.

"How am I." It's a statement, not a question, and she seems to consider it. "I'm..." Lets out a loud puff of air, tears welling up.

Anabelle rolls to her back, eyes trained on the ceiling. Reaches for my hand and places it on her pelvis, just below the waistband of her shorts, lifting the hem of her loose T-shirt.

Naturally, my hand begins a slow glide north, gliding over the warm skin I've dreamed about for days. Weeks.

Months, even.

I pause when my palm slopes upward.

My eyes meet her watering eyes.

"Anabelle?" I whisper, unsure.

She bites her trembling bottom lip, chin quivering when I pull my hand away, shocked.

Hesitate.

Set my hand back on her stomach.

Her belly.

Her fucking *baby* bump.

"Are you…" I can't even say the words.

Instead of answering, she swallows, wet tears streaking down her beautiful face.

"Anabelle, is this…i-is it…"

Mine?

She nods.

I lean back, silent, not having a single clue what to do with myself. My hands, my body, my thoughts.

Mine.

Holy fuck.

Holy shit.

Holy fucking shit.

I'm not going to panic, I'm not going to panic, I'm not going to panic.

"How far along?" My voice is barely recognizable.

"Sixteen weeks."

I damn near jump off the bed. "Sixteen weeks!"

Then I do jump off the bed, climbing off, burying my fingers into the hair that could probably use a trim while Anabelle sobs on the bed—and now I'm on the verge of sobbing myself.

"I'm s-sor...s-sorry," she cries.

Oh my God.

She's pregnant.

My apartment. My friends. My mom, my dad, my family. Everything important in my life flashes before me in a time lapse. The grades. The degree. The master's.

The parenting book on the bedside table.

I reach for it, raise it from the table, study the cover. *What to Expect When You're*—I set it down like it's on fire, and it falls to the floor with a thud.

Sitting on the edge of the bed with my back to Anabelle, the sound of her sobs, muffled by the sound of the blood rushing to my brain, has the analytical part of me piecing together our entire relationship, one fast, orgasmic fuck at a time.

We didn't use a condom because she's on birth control.

Stupid, stupid, stupid.

Despite all this, the unhappy noises coming from Anabelle draw me to her. Crawling under the covers, I scoot up next to her, pulling her into my front side. "Shh, don't cry."

She nods feebly but doesn't stop—*can't* stop.

"Anabelle," I ask cautiously, "how long have you known?"

"A few weeks."

A few weeks? *Jesus Christ!* She's been dealing with this information by herself for weeks?

Guilt settles in the pit of my stomach.

"How many is a *few*?"

"I don't know, I was afraid to keep track," she croaks out her confession, throat raw. "Four? Three? Five?"

Gathering my courage, I run my hand down her hip, gently nudging her to her back. Gently lift the hem of her shirt, folding it back so it's out of my way.

Study her stomach.

Her skin is still satin smooth, but now it's beginning to stretch taut. It couldn't be more obvious that she's pregnant.

"Can I feel it?"

"Yes."

My palm touches just below her belly button as she watches breathlessly. I run my hand over the bump, back and forth, fingers skimming over the baby growing inside.

"Say something," she whispers. "Please."

"I don't know what to say. I'm…"

Freaking out.

Stunned. Shocked. Dismayed.

Fascinated.

"Speechless."

"I know. Me too." She nods. "Do you hate me?"

"No." I'm not sure how to bring this up. "But I thought you were on birth control."

"I am. I was." She's on the verge of tears again. "It obviously wasn't effective."

Obviously.

"What the fuck are we going to do?" I feel like such a dumbass asking, but Jesus, I'm twenty-one years old—what the hell do I know about raising a kid? My mom still makes my doctor's appointments. I'm still on my parents' fucking health insurance, for God's sake.

Speaking of parents…

"Have you told your dad?"

"Yes."

"What did he say?"

Anabelle laughs, though it's the least appropriate time to giggle. "What do you *think* he said?"

"Dumb question, sorry. When did you tell him?"

"Last week. I wasn't alone, if you're worried about that."

"Who went with you?" Absentmindedly, without even realizing I'm doing it, my hand caresses her belly, insatiably curious about the small bump.

"Don't be mad when I tell you, okay?"

I roll my eyes, a gesture I'm normally not prone to. "Anabelle, nothing you say right now could surprise me more than the fact that you're pregnant."

Nothing.

Not a single, goddamn thing.

A fucking elephant could break through the wall right now and I wouldn't flinch. Steady as a rock.

"I probably should have mentioned it sooner, but at the beginning of the year, I reconnected with Rex."

"Say again?" I pause, needing clarification, as if I didn't hear her clearly. "Gunderson?"

"One and the same." She chuckles beside me, red eyes finally drying.

"I don't understand."

"We've become friends."

I pull back, hand frozen on the swell of her stomach. "I'm not following."

"We have a class together like we did last year, and he invited me to coffee so we could talk…and I went, and it was nice."

"Nice."

"Yeah, it was nice. I'm sorry if it upsets you, but he really isn't as terrible as he's been in the past."

"Why do I find that hard to believe?"

"Because you don't like him."

"You're right, I don't."

"I don't know what to tell you, Elliot. He's been really supportive." She chooses her next words carefully. "Anyway, he came with me to my dad's—who knows Rex and I are friends, by the way—and sat there while I told them. Linda cried, of course, and my dad blew up and kicked Rex out."

"Why'd he do that?"

"He assumed the baby was Rex's."

"Awesome." Just *great*.

As if the fucking situation wasn't fucked up *enough*, people are going to think this baby—*my* baby—is Rex motherfucking Gunderson's, the biggest dipshit on campus?

Over my dead body.

I've never been jealous of a single soul before meeting that moron, but I'm jealous now—insanely so.

I can't believe Anabelle is naïve enough to fall for his nice-guy routine after being shit on by him once before.

Jesus H. Christ.

"Don't get mad, Elliot." Her voice is cajoling, low and soft. "I didn't want to tell you over the phone, and I was afraid I wouldn't see you until December, because by then I'll be huge and oh my God, this is so bad. First I'm fine, then I'm crying, then I'm fine. I'm a mess—I never would have known I was pregnant if I hadn't gone to the doctor, and since I hadn't been to a doctor in Iowa before, I was required to have a physical." She's crying and babbling at the same time. "And the doctor started asking me all these questions about being pregnant, and I thought there was no way I could be, no way, but the pill isn't one hundred percent and I was devastated when I found out.

"And so scared. I couldn't sleep and I looked like shit, but I had to go to class. I couldn't stay in bed crying forever—that wouldn't be doing anyone any good. So, I showed up to the lecture hall, and who walks in but Rex. There he was, said I looked tired and did I want some coffee? He made an offhanded comment about the way I looked then a wisecrack about me being pregnant, and what could I say? I couldn't lie. Because I am.

"One time we went to Target and walked through the baby aisle looking at all the tiny clothes." She laughs. "He thought it would cheer me up."

I want to be sick, want to puke all over this white bedspread at the thought of Gunderson taking her to the fucking baby department at goddamn Target. *What the actual fuck?*

It's like I went to bed last night and woke up in a parallel universe where Rex Gunderson has taken over my life and is filling my shoes.

You moved to Michigan, remember?

She doesn't say it, but we're both thinking it.

I shut my mouth and save my comments for myself. Run my hand over her abs, up toward her breasts, not daring to actually touch them. "Have these gotten any bigger?" I blurt out rudely.

"Oh my God, seriously?" Anabelle groans. "You just found out I'm pregnant and you're asking if my boobs are bigger."

"Well, yeah."

"Well they aren't, not yet, but they probably will be."

"Huh."

She yawns.

"Anabelle?"

"Yeah?"

"I just want you to know I'm…sorry, for this, for everything I missed."

"You don't have to apologize, we're both responsible."

"I know, but I should have known better."

She tilts her head, trying to get a better look at me. "What do you mean?"

"Until you're in a committed relationship, you should always wear a condom. That's like, textbook common sense—Oz and Zeke lectured me about it all the fucking time."

"I was committed to you, Elliot, in my own way, whether you wanted me to be or not."

"I didn't mean it as an insult."

"What did you mean, then?"

"Unless two people are planning a future together, they should be careful."

"You know what, Elliot? I've been living like this for weeks with nothing to do but lie here, by myself, and think about this baby inside me over and over and over again. I lie in the dark, dwelling on it, on what we could have done differently and how my life is going to change. How disappointed my parents are. My mother barely speaks to me, blames this whole thing on my dad." She yawns. "Can we just sleep? This second trimester is kicking my ass." Her hand reaches for mine, pulling it around her waist. "I'm glad you're here."

The lights are shut off and after Anabelle dozes off, I'm still lying in the dark, hands behind my head, staring at the ceiling.

I'm going to be a father at the age of twenty-two.

A dad.

Because I got a girl I'm not in a relationship with pregnant.

Knocking a girl up is something I would have expected my old roommates to have done before they found love and settled. *They're* the ones who used to sleep around, not me.

What the hell am I going to do?

27

#DOUCHEBAG

"Maybe we were meant to be…
but we did it wrong."

Anabelle

"So how did it go at your dad's thing?"

He's been gone for *hours*, having left the house late morning, looking dapper in black dress pants and a button-down shirt. I helped him with his tie, a periwinkle blue and bright pink paisley, my trembling hands so embarrassingly unknowledgeable on the task, I had to redo it four times.

Elliot stood patiently, smelling like a fresh shower while I fumbled. Then, with a self-conscious backward glance—as if he almost couldn't make himself go—his black leather dress shoes carried him out the door and down the steps. Headed to some fancy hotel downtown when between us, there were so many things left unsaid.

But he's back now, sitting in my kitchen, able to rationally discuss "the situation."

The situation—is that what I'm calling it now?

"How did it go? I honestly have no idea—I could barely concentrate on anything my father or his colleagues were saying during their speeches. This baby thing is all I could fucking think about. I sleepwalked through the entire day."

This baby thing...

I know he didn't mean to say it like *that*, but still, a knot forms in the pit of my stomach and I resist the urge to put my hands on my belly protectively. I've been doing that a lot lately—touching my small bump, rubbing it and gazing at it in the mirror, watching it grow.

Gunderson calls it AnaBean, convinced that it's a girl.

That thought puts a smile on my face.

"I'm sorry. I know it's...I know I gave you the shock of a lifetime last night." I fiddle with the straw in my water glass. "Rex thinks I should have told you sooner."

"Oh?" His inflection is sarcastic, lip uncharacteristically curled. "Rex thinks so, huh? What else does he say?"

I sigh, frustrated, knowing Elliot can't stand Gunderson, but still determined to make him accept the fact that Rex is in my life. I bite back a moody reply that would probably only serve to piss him off even further. The tension at this table is already palpable; no need for me to make it worse.

"When do you leave?"

"In the morning."

Tomorrow.

That knot in my belly tightens; he's leaving.

Again.

"I don't know what else to do here, Anabelle. I have to go back and finish the semester. My hands are tied—I can't stay, you have to know that."

I do know it.

"I felt like a dickhead leaving before. This is going to kill me." He reaches across the table, grasping for my hands. "I'll be back for the holidays, and we can figure out what we're going to do then."

"What do you mean?"

"I want...I want to be here for you, dammit—I don't want you relying on that fuckstick Gunderson."

"Because you care or because you're jealous?"

"Both! Jesus, both. That kid drives me fucking nuts—he shouldn't be the one walking you around the baby aisle."

Relief floods my body. "When did you decide this?"

"Last night. I couldn't sleep for shit. And today, all fucking morning while I let my sisters race me around town to buy a gift for our dad, I wanted to pull my hair out."

I've had a lot of sleepless nights myself, full of fear and worry and paranoia. "Are you saying you want to leave your master's program?"

"That's exactly what I'm saying. It's not fair that you're doing this alone, and if the next words out of your mouth are 'But I'm not doing it alone, I'm doing it with Rex,' I swear to you Anabelle, I'll lose my mind."

"I am made of sterner stuff than that, Elliot. My father is the coach for one of the best college wrestling teams in the United States. He did not raise me to rely on any man. I can do this on my own. I can. I promise you, I'm strong enough."

I've given it a lot of thought, day in and day out, until it was the only thing getting me through the week, the idea of having and raising this baby on my own while still going to school.

After this semester, I'll only have one more to single-parent my way through.

"Anabelle…" Elliot hedges.

"Stop. We are not discussing it." I squeeze my eyes shut, rather immaturely. "The best thing for your future—for this baby's future"—I place my hand on my stomach—"is for you to get your master's from Michigan. Make something of yourself—that's what I want. You hate it in Iowa."

"Is that what you think? That I hate it here?"

"I don't think you hate it, but I don't think it's where you want to be. Before you left, you said there was nothing here for you."

"I was an idiot," he sputters. "I didn't mean you."

"Elliot," I say patiently, "I like you too much to ask you to leave school, and I know you're still getting over the shock of all this, but if you want to support this child, you'll stay where you are and get your degree." I pause. "We both know it's the right thing to do."

Elliot is quiet and I know he's considering my words, thinking through their logic.

He knows I'm right.

The place for him is where he's at, not here with me.

"Are you pushing me away on purpose?"

"I'm not pushing you away, I'm trying not to be selfish so we can do what's *right*."

Why does doing what's right hurt so much?

"You need some time just like I did. You're going to go back home, to Michigan, and it's going to hit you all over again that I am pregnant. I'm *pregnant*, Elliot, and I'm having this baby and it took me an entire month to get used to the idea, an entire month until I stopped ugly crying." I'm watching him carefully, eyes perilously close to welling up. "You've known less than thirty-six hours—you haven't experienced the whole range of emotions."

"I just feel…" He's holding back, I can feel it.

"Tell me. Be honest."

His head shakes. "I can't say it without sounding like a fucking douchebag, but I'm relieved that I get to leave, okay? I also feel *guilty* that I'm going. Disgusted with myself. Ashamed. Jesus, I feel it all, and it feels like shit."

My lips part wordlessly.

I wanted him to be honest, yes, but the kind of truth tormenting him is the hardest to bear. It's raw and real and complicated.

Elliot runs his fingers through his hair, tugging at the strands, and I can tell without even feeling it that his heart is beating fast.

"Your flight leaves at seven in the morning, and when it takes off, we both know you'll be on it."

Elliot

"**A**nabelle? Are you sleeping?"
        "No."
        "Me either."

Obviously.

I feel the mattress dip as she rolls toward me. With the bright full moon shining, there's enough light to make out the delicate features of her face, the slope of her nose and the curved jawline. The bow of her lips. The faint arch of her brows.

"I don't know what to do, Anabelle."

The room is silent as she gathers her thoughts.

"Me either, but…that's okay."

"How the hell are you so calm about this?"

"I'm not calm, I've just had more time to get used to the idea."

I want to reach out and pull her close, touch her and kiss her and feel the warm press of her body against mine. Am I allowed to now that I've gone and gotten her pregnant? Would she let me hold her, or would she tell me to go fuck myself?

"Kind of wish you would have met my roommate this weekend."

"Where has she been?"

"She doesn't usually go home much, but this weekend her grandpa turned one hundred. Her family is only a few hours away, so…"

"Does she think I'm an asshole?"

"No. She knows the situation."

The situation—is that what we're calling it now?

"Good. I mean, you don't need the added stress of having friends who think you're irresponsible for getting…"

I can't say the word *pregnant* out loud. Cannot.

"Madison hasn't said anything judgmental, not that I know of, and definitely not to my face. A few of my friends back home in Mass...that's a different story. You remember that I went to a Catholic college, right?"

I nod in the dark, mentally counting all the times I've used the Lord's name in vain, just in the past few months—hundreds.

Thousands, and counting.

"I'd be lying if I said I hadn't lost a few friends over this. It's been rough. My freshman roommate Savannah won't speak to me. She called me a charlatan."

"What!"

Her voice is composed. "That's how she was raised, Elliot, with the belief that we save ourselves for marriage. Touching and fooling around are for committed relationships. I miss her, but I don't blame her." Anabelle's voice is the epitome of patience and understanding, and it occurs to me that this is how she'll be with her child.

Our child.

The thought is rather mollifying.

She changes the subject, enquiring quietly, "When are you going to tell your parents?"

"Eventually. As shitty as it sounds, I might just call and tell my mom over the phone."

"Elliot! Are you serious?"

"Look, Anabelle, I have to live with the idea a little while first. Plus, without sounding callous, I don't think they're going to melt down about it, not like your dad. I'm pretty sure they'll be understanding."

"How can you be sure?"

"I'm not, but I have older sisters and one of them—Jill—had a baby in high school. I don't remember my mom ever yelling or crying about it. I remember her being super chill, considering." My mom is the most caring and quiet woman I've ever met, the calming force in my father's stressful life, and in mine and my sisters'.

Growing up, my mother would be standing at the kitchen counter when I walked through the door after school, always with a snack prepared and dinner in the oven.

Always.

Nauseatingly idyllic, my childhood was a goddamn Norman Rockwell painting of home-cooked dinners, perfect grades, and playing outside on our manicured lawn.

Anabelle hums in her throat. "What's it like having parents who are relaxed and sympathetic? Mine are both so intense and intimidating. I was petrified to tell them."

"Tell me about it—what happened?"

"Well, when I told my dad, the season hadn't started and I picked a time I assumed he'd be less stressed out. I hadn't been sleeping a lot, so I looked like complete shit when I went over there."

Pfft. "I find that hard to believe."

"That's sweet of you to say." Her hand finds mine in the dark, giving it a gentle pat. "In any case, Dad noticed the differences in me right away, right? It's his job to be observant, and he started asking me all these questions. I'm convinced he thought I was on drugs."

"Why?"

"All the sudden changes. I was slightly depressed at the beginning and wanted to be alone. Lost some weight from not eating. I got no sleep—it was tearing me up inside. And now…I know what I have to do to graduate and I'm not a fool. I know it's going to be hard, but how am I supposed to do an internship with an infant? Who's going to hire me? It's depressing just thinking about it."

"You'll get an internship, Anabelle—who wouldn't want to hire you?"

"If you're trying to flatter me, it's working. Not to sound like a drag, but I needed someone to make me feel better." In the dim light of her bedroom, I see her white teeth peeking through a grin.

"Is it too soon for me to put my hand on your stomach again?" I ask softly, determined to take advantage of the lightened mood.

"Sure, that's fine. She's not kicking or anything."

"She?"

"AnaBean." She laughs. "I don't know that it's a girl—we can't find out until twenty weeks—but it's the nickname Rex gave the baby."

I stiffen, trying to ignore the fact that she used Gunderson's name in reference to my baby, and smile because the name is so damn cute.

"AnaBean," I repeat, somewhat amazed—*amazed* that being with her here like this isn't freaking me out. Me, lying in the dark with my pregnant old roommate. Me, lying in the dark with a girl I left behind in pursuit of better things.

I'm almost twenty-three years old.

I thought I had my life mapped out.

Instead, I lay my hand on Anabelle's stomach, letting her guide me over her skin, flesh different but the same. In the short amount of time I lived with her, I learned a few things I knew I'd never forget, like the fact that she smells good all the time, even without showering.

Her skin is always smooth.

She doesn't hold a grudge and forgives easily—almost *too* easily. Case in point: Rex Gunderson, who, oddly enough, she let into her life.

I consider these factoids as my big palm caresses her stomach, basking in the memories we've shared in this bed. The late nights watching television, arguing over which show to watch…whether or not to eat in bed…who was going to turn the light off…whether there were too many blankets.

And the sex.

Sweaty and sweet and fucking fantastic.

Anabelle isn't shy or self-conscious, which made it good—so goddamn good. I'm getting excited remembering all the times we screwed. Against the wall by the front door. She came home from an afternoon class wearing a yellow sundress and Converse, and I met her at the door, hands sliding down her waist, up the back of her flower-covered skirt.

She dropped her bag to the floor, wrapping her arms around me, tiptoeing to meet my lips, and we made out like two desperate teenagers with only three minutes of unsupervised gum swapping. Sucking face. Frenching.

Whatever you want to call it, it gave me a raging hard-on she wanted to play with. My fingers groped her ass and cupped her tits over the fabric of her pretty dress as she toyed with the zipper of my jeans. Then we fucked, hard and fast, standing up against the wall by the door, lips locked together.

God, it was good.

I've never behaved like that with a girl before. Never in my four years at Iowa have I ever brought a girl home. I lived like a monk, sticking to myself and minding my own business, never meddling in others' affairs. Didn't date, certainly didn't sleep around.

Never had a girlfriend.

What does it say about me as a person that when I finally lived with a female, I couldn't keep my fucking dick to myself? Am I just a horny bastard, or do I genuinely love Anabelle like a man should? Not just as a friend.

Will I ever know the difference?

As my hand grazes her stomach, sliding over that swollen slope of her body, I wonder if our last time together was the exact moment her birth control decided to stop being effective.

"When are you due?"

"Second week of March."

Five more months.

I do the math in my head, going back in time, counting back the weeks. December, November, October…July…

June.

It had to have been one of the last times we had sex.

"How are you feeling?" I don't know why I haven't asked her before now.

"Tired. Nervous." She pauses, chuckling. "Horny."

One word and she has my full attention, dick twitching. "Yeah?"

Anabelle's hips shift against the mattress, under my hand.

"Yeah."

Shit. What would she do if I moved my hand lower? Or higher? If I put it between her legs?

It stays firmly planted on her abdomen.

"That's a thing, you know—the increased sex drive from all the raging hormones," she says it with authority. Confidently.

"I, uh, didn't know that."

"It's an entire chapter in the baby book I'm reading, and at first I didn't think it would apply to me…" her voice trails off suggestively.

"But it does?"

Her hips shift again and when her thighs rub together, our eyes meet in the shadows, the tension becoming palpable. Expectant.

Unbearable.

Would it be weird to screw her while she's pregnant? Is it weird that I want to get her naked and touch her entire body, view it in the soft glimmer of moonlight? Instead of fantasizing about Anabelle, my dirty mind should crawl out of the gutter and be supportive, not mentally strip her clothes off, not mentally be feeling up her tits.

Tits I've daydreamed about.

Jesus, why am I thinking about this right now! *Because you haven't fucked her in months, moron, and you miss her like fucking crazy. You think about her every goddamn day, picturing her in your mind every time you whack off.*

"Yes, it applies to me."

Am I losing my mind right now, or has her voice gone a little breathless?

"How?"

"I can't believe we're even talking about this."

"We've passed the point where we have to be self-conscious, wouldn't you say?"

"Definitely."

"Then tell me, how does it apply to you?" I'm entering dangerous territory here and don't give one fuck.

"According to the books, I have rising levels of estrogen and progesterone and extra blood flow in my vagina." She laughs quietly. "Sorry, that sounded terrible."

"I've taken several medical courses—I can handle the clinical terms."

"Vagina is a clinical term?"

"Sure."

"Huh." Anabelle goes quiet, body humming in the dark. "I think about sex *all* the time. I dream about it in my sleep. I think about it during class and when I'm eating."

What a coincidence, so do I.

She goes on, speaking in a low murmur. "I've learned to be creative in the past few months to take my mind off it."

My fingers itch, forefinger beginning a leisurely trace around her belly button. "What do you mean?"

"You're a guy, you tell me."

Is she talking about masturbating? *Holy hell, girls do that?*

"Well, like I said, I'm here to help."

A giggle bubbles in her throat. "You never said that."

"I'm saying it now."

"What a good Samaritan you are, always ready to lend a hand." She croons seductively, arms behind her head, hair fanned out on the pillow. Anabelle lets one fall, reaching across her body to tussle my hair, twirling the strands aimlessly, carelessly, like she used to. All those hours we spent in this bed, laughing and talking and rolling around on the mattress.

"Anabelle, I don't want to hurt you."

"You won't." Not any more than she has been.

I know enough about the human body to *know* sex won't hurt the baby; that's the last of my worries. So what am I worried about?

How having sex will affect us? Will we be more fucked in the heads than we were before?

Is it worth an orgasm or two to have our hearts ripped out all over again, knowing I have a flight to catch?

"How do you know I won't hurt you?" I'm so fucking insecure, needing this reassurance. "How?"

"I don't." There's a long pause. "But I'm willing to find out if you are."

"Please don't make this my decision."

Anabelle rolls from her back to her side, facing me, all of our sentiments blanketed by shadows and moonlight. Along with the fears and doubts gripping us tightly, we have expectations of each other that remain largely unspoken.

I have no idea what Anabelle wants or expects of me, no idea what to offer her at this point. I have no real job, no real home, no fucking health insurance of my own, and there weren't nearly enough hours this weekend to discuss what needed discussing with eighteen long years of uncertain future ahead of us to plan.

"It's not that I don't want to have sex with you," I rationalize. "I just don't think it's fair."

"Fair to whom?" I catch her rueful smile, even though it's dark. "Besides, it's a little late for *fair*, don't you think?"

She's right—of course she is. The damage has already been done.

"Forget I mentioned it, okay? It's the raging hormones talking."

I won't forget it, and if I leave tomorrow without having acted on what we both want so goddamn bad, I'll regret it until the day I set eyes on her again, which could be weeks from now.

I'll be gone her entire third trimester if I continue school in Michigan. She'll be alone, with only her friends and parents and Rex *fucking* Gunderson swooping in to support her in his tinfoil suit of armor.

I owe her this one night, don't I? Don't I owe us *both*? We love and care for each other; we're friends.

I don't have to lean in that far to kiss the side of her face, pulling away when I find it stained with salt.

"Are you crying?" It's too dark for me to tell, and I'm not about to start feeling up her cheeks.

"No."

Liar.

She inches into my body, seeking my warmth, face buried in the crook of my neck. I bunch up her hair, kissing the column of her throat, in the tender spot behind her ear. Close my eyes and inhale her. The lotion and shampoo I used in the bathroom without telling her. The clean sheets that smell like her perfume.

Every nuance and sound from this girl—from the young woman having my child—I catalog, committing to memory.

For those nights when I'm alone in my apartment, listening *not* to the sounds of Anabelle's quiet sighs, but to the loud asshole upstairs who keeps me awake. Doing what's best for both of us by being at that school, in that shithole apartment.

God, why am I hesitating to touch her?

I love her.

When my hand grazes her hip, she sucks in a breath. When she doesn't tell me to go fuck myself, I let it run the length of her leg, up the curve of her waist, and ribcage. Brushing the long hair off her shoulder, I let the silky strands lace through my fingers; it's been forever since I've felt it.

"Do you remember," I ask slowly, "that time you had me give you a backrub and you took your shirt off?" I'm still futzing with her hair.

"Yes." I can hear her smiling. "Of course I remember."

"You do know that ninety-five percent of all girl-guy massages lead to sex? That's an actual statistic—I looked it up after that night."

"Is that so?"

"Don't act like you didn't know what you were doing when you took your shirt off."

She makes a humming sound, low in her throat. "Maybe, but it didn't work on you, did it? You're such a gentleman."

"Trust me, I wanted you so bad—I remember exactly what you looked like lying on the bed, face down while I rubbed your back."

"Yeah?" she whispers. "How did I look?"

"Your cheeks were flushed and your skin was so fucking smooth, and every time I got close to your ass your eyes would close and your mouth would fall open a little."

"It felt good. I wanted you to go lower."

"You kept wiggling your hips."

"I was turned on."

"And I was content to just look at you." I take her jawline in my palm, caressing with the pads of my fingers. "I'm always content to just look at you."

I see her in my dreams, and I'll continue seeing her there.

"I was so excited to come home," I intone quietly. "I couldn't wait to see you. It was like a rush."

"Do you regret coming home?"

"No." *I just wish I'd done it sooner.*

"Elliot, I wouldn't blame you for being pissed at me...for getting pregnant."

"You didn't get yourself pregnant, Anabelle. You had some help."

"I know, but—"

I silence her with a kiss, pressing my mouth over her parted lips. They're warm, fuller than I remember, and quickly intake a breath when I finally give in, giving my hand permission to travel south. Down the porcelain column of her slim neck. Across her clavicle.

Cup her breast.

Weigh it in my palm before plucking at the nipple. Stroke it with my thumb before moving on.

No more words are spoken, not when she leans into me, melting into my arms. Not when we peel off our clothes, one piece at a time, throwing them to the cold floor. Not when I'm sliding into her, long and hard and throbbing with fucking need.

I need her.

We need each other desperately after the last twenty-four emotional hours we've had after she gave me the shock of my goddamn life. Pretty face and crying eyes, soft lips and smooth hands.

I need her.

She needs me.

I slide between her spread legs, wanton. More wanton than I've been in an age, horny and hallow and scared. There are so many unknowns and impending choices I have no control over.

But I have control over this moment; I have control over how I make Anabelle feel.

Our mouths fuse, dragging drunkenly open, tongues get reacquainted. Hips rolling, pelvis unhurriedly thrusting. Leisurely in and out.

My fingers plant themselves in her long hair, stroking the silky locks as I stroke inside her. Kiss her forehead and temples.

Kiss away a tear, pumping my hips.

Her hands grip my ass, digging. Arches her back. Crying.

Kissing.

Anabelle buries her face in my neck. "I love you."

I love you, too.

I love you.

More than you'll know.

Dear Elliot,

I'm back to writing in my diary.

Since I'm not going to see you until your winter break, I thought I would keep you in the loop by journaling. You're busy and the last thing you need is me burdening you every day with baby updates.

So I will write them here.

Someday, when you're ready, I'll share these letters with you. Until then, they will go here where only my eyes can see them.

It's Monday and getting cold. I stopped for hot chocolate on my way to class this morning and added extra whipped cream because I haven't really taken advantage of the "eating for two" philosophy yet. Pretty sure this baby will come out being addicted to cocoa, whipped cream, and marshmallows.

I felt my first flutters of life today, Elliot. Don't worry, I was alone when I felt it—no Rex to swoop in and steal your thunder. Not today anyway, but he does love having a "knocked-up friend," as he calls me. He is so weird sometimes, LOL.

Tonight I'm going to my dad's for dinner. It's been a rough road, but we're finally getting there. I think mostly he's embarrassed he has this respectable position at the university, and my first year here, I got pregnant. Linda thinks he's angry because he couldn't prevent me getting hurt, but I'm not so sure. He stomps around the house, slamming drawers and grunting.

As for my mom? She isn't ignoring my phone calls anymore like she did for three weeks after finding out, and she has stopped calling my dad to scream at him. Talk about dysfunctional.

You know, everyone thinks they have the family with the most problems, but when you look further, you see all the cracks.

For the sake of my sanity, I'm hopeful we can all look back and laugh about it.

Hope you're well. I'm tired and ready for another nap.

Anabelle

Elliot,

I was thinking about the conversation we had in my room about my dad, and I realized I haven't told you the story—any of it—about when I told Dad about the baby.

So I will tell you now, the memory turning my stomach a little.

I dragged Rex along for moral support, which I had mixed feelings about to begin with. Dad is warming up to Rex but not at the rate I was hoping, and I knew having them in the house together would be touchy. But, I didn't want to go alone. I wanted someone's hand to hold, just in case, so he was my guy.

I could barely eat the dinner Linda had prepared, and I heard none of the conversation (mostly wrestling talk). Then, when we'd cleaned the kitchen and went to sit in the living room, I told him.

I just blurted it out because WHAT ELSE DO YOU SAY? There is no easy way to give this news.

He stood up in his chair, stared at me. Then walked from the room, stormed outside. He stood outside, in the cold for a good ten minutes, Elliot, stewing. Swearing. Lots of swearing—I cannot imagine what the neighbors thought.

Dad wouldn't look at me when he finally came back inside. He asked one thing: "Who did this?" If looks could kill, Rex Gunderson would have been a dead man.

"Not him," I said.

"Not me! Don't hurt me!" Rex had his hands up in the surrender position, and if it wasn't so sad, I would have laughed so hard.

"It's that roommate of yours, isn't it?"

I nodded. "Yes, but I love him."

"Love." He snorted. "How is that working out for you? Didn't that boy move out?"

He was being mean, but I don't blame him. This is not what he had planned for me. I think if he had known this is how me moving here was going to turn out, he never would have had me come. Never in a million years...

"Obviously you're going to move back home."

"I'm not. Right now, I can make it on my own."

"Because I'm paying your rent."

"Dad..."

"You have no job, no degree, and your roommate got you pregnant. You are moving home."

At that moment there was no arguing with him, but for now, I'm still in your house. My house.

We'll see what happens in a few more months.

I miss you,

Anabelle

Dear Elliot,

It was great hearing your voice on the phone last night. Sorry I sounded so tired—that's happening a lot lately. I know you bought your own copy of What to Expect When You're Expecting. Did you know they have websites where you can track your pregnancy progress and read forums? Don't know if there are any dads lurking among them, but if you're ever curious, take a peek.

I go on them a lot, mainly to find other young women in my situation, always searching for...something. Normalcy, I guess. I wonder if my life will ever be normal after this.

After the baby is born.

I wonder every day what I'm going to do in the spring— probably get a job and put the baby in daycare. I would rather date that douchebag Eric Johnson than ask Linda to babysit.

It's important that I do this myself.

It might have been harsh when my mom told me I had to deal with the consequences myself, but she was right. I'll worry about my plan tomorrow though, I'm so so tired. **yawn** Madison and I have been watching movies together at night, just like you and I would. She crawls into bed with me sometimes, and we watch our shows. I like not being alone—that big bed is lonely.

She and I have been talking about it, and while she really loves me, I don't think she wants to stay living with me once this baby comes. She likes sleep, LOL. I feel bad but totally understand. Who could blame her?

Anabelle

Elliot,

Well, it's finally happened. I'm up to two cups of steaming hot chocolate a day. I'm officially addicted! Guess there are worst things to crave, like McDonald's in the middle of the night, or ice cream. I read that lots of women crave apples—why can't I want fruit?! It's so much healthier, but I suppose cocoa is harmless enough, yeah?

Only ONE time this week did I ask Rex to run and fetch me potato chips. Fine, and French onion dip. Seriously though, you can't eat one without the other, and I was craving it so bad. He must think I'm so gross, I ate almost that entire bag myself—don't know if that's something I should be putting in this diary, but I'm trying to be honest.

Nothing says honesty like getting drunk on chips and dip.

My dad and Rex have had a reckoning of sorts, and they're finally getting along, better than they did when Rex was working for the team as the manager. He and I went over again this weekend, and he helped my dad rake the yard then we all had dinner, mashed potatoes and gravy and OH MY GOD, IT WAS SO GOOD. Did you know Rex is from Iowa, too? He grew up not too far away, and his mom sent me a few bags of really good hot chocolate mix and marshmallows last time he went home. It was so sweet and it is SO GOOD.

Crap, I just realized this entire letter has been about food.

Promise that's not all I do, LOL. It's just the only thing I talk about.

I'm not even that big yet. You still can't tell I'm pregnant, at least not from the back. Maybe from the side, if you're looking for the bump. I'll attach a picture.

Love,

Miss you.

Anabelle

Dear Elliot,

I had to break down and buy a new, long puffy coat. My one from last year no longer fits. Thank God I've been saving money, because holy cow staying warm is expensive. I've been searching for a part-time job, on campus if I can manage it, for some extra spending money. Storing it away like a squirrel.

There is one job that sounds perfect. It's in the registrar's office and carries some actual responsibility, which would be nice.

Yesterday I finally had someone ask if I was pregnant, so I guess you CAN tell, LOL. I was taking off my jacket in a contract law class and one of my classmates (a guy) was sort of checking me out from head to toe. When he got to my stomach his whole expression changed. He goes, "Whoa. You're not knocked up, are you?"

I don't think I was embarrassed, exactly, more caught off guard because I wasn't ready for it. I should probably start preparing myself for more of those reactions. Of course he was horrified; we're in college—who the hell wants to be pregnant? I was his walking, talking, living nightmare. Bet he went home and thanked Jesus he'd never slept with me.

Rex said I should forget about it and that the guy is an idiot, but I thought about it all night, and here I am writing about it, so it must have really bothered me, right? Rex was just being sweet, as usual, trying to take my mind off it.

Last night I caved and let him rub my feet. It felt so good I almost fell asleep while it was happening. I went to his place and instead of going to the movies like we'd planned, we ended up taking it old school and renting a few. Nothing like the early 2000s to bring back a flash of old memories...not to mention that foot rub.

I should totally angle for another one soon—it was bliss.

Have a great weekend. I won't be around—Madison is springing for a hotel room in the city and we're going to do some holiday shopping. My goal is to stay off my phone.

Talk soon,
Anabelle

Dear Elliot,

You know, I haven't wanted to bring this up but it's been weighing on me. When a woman is twenty weeks pregnant, they can find out if their baby is a girl or a boy, and my obstetrician asked if I wanted to find out. I don't want to tell you because I know you wouldn't want me finding out without you, and I know you wouldn't want Rex to come to the appointment with me.

Madison is no help anymore. She is all over the place, freaking out about final exams, which I should be doing, too, but for whatever reason, I'm retaining EVERYTHING. I swear, this baby is giving me superpowers—I'm soaking up information like a sponge, retaining everything they're teaching in class. I could recite legal terms blindfolded—next time you call, let's see if I can actually do it. I'm going to be the best friggin' lawyer.

If I ever have time to become one. Haha.

It's freezing here, but I won't talk to you about that. I saw on the news last night Michigan is getting slammed with bad weather. Eight inches of snow in one night?! That's crazy. Do you ski? You're in the perfect state for it. I used to go when I was a teenager, but never when it was below twenty degrees. Probably because one year, I stayed out in the cold too long and one of my big toes got frostbite. Was that too much information?? LOL, it seemed relevant to the conversation.

Back to the point, I'm dying to know if it's a girl or a boy. How do you feel about that? How do you feel about not being here?

Rex said you probably wouldn't care since you're not here anyway, but I have no desire to add that to the list of things I already feel guilty about.

Anabelle

HOW TO DATE A DOUCHEBAG

Elliot,

I felt it kick yesterday for the first time.
A real kick, not a flutter. It startled me. I was in class, taking notes (remember my superpowers?), focused on the professor's lecture when it happened. My hand flew to my stomach and I held my breath. I know it sounds dramatic, but it kind of was. It's all becoming so real now that I'm showing and can feel movement. It's surreal. I feel big as a house even though I know I'm not, not like I will be in January or February.

Did I tell you your mom reached out to me? You should have warned me! Not that I mind because I don't—of course not. She called and was so sweet it made me cry (everything does lately, so that's nothing new, haha). She asked a bunch of questions about myself, how I felt, and wanted to know when she could meet me. I've never been so relieved after a phone call in my entire life, Elliot, I almost passed out, holding my breath when I heard the sound of her voice. She introduced herself as Baby Gramma, LOL. Seriously, she was so funny and nice. So, thank you for giving her my number. I'd hug you right now if I could.

When do you come home? I hope the weather cooperates.
I worry about you each and every day.
Miss you so much (and that's not just the hormones talking),
Your baby mama

Elliot,

I had lunch with your mom and sister, Beth, today. Did they tell you? God, I was so nervous. I may or may not have been sick in the bathroom before leaving the house (Spoiler alert: I vomited). Why do you suppose I was more panicked meeting your family than I was telling my dad? I wasn't even as scared to tell you, but I

*freaked out when I arrived at the restaurant and it took forever for
me to walk inside.*

That's weird, isn't it?

*We met halfway between your hometown and Iowa City, at a
cute little diner. Your mom held me and we both cried before we
sat down at the table. I ordered breakfast for lunch and a white
soda to calm my stomach then just picked at my food—I WAS SO
NERVOUS!!!!*

*Your sister rubbed my stomach a million times and must have
called me 'adorable Anabelle' at least a dozen. Your mom tried to
take a few selfies and I wonder if she sent them to you.*

*They brought me a couple gifts, which made me all emotional.
A pretty cream-colored baby blanket and a onesie with little yellow
ducks. It was so sweet, Elliot, and I think your mom would like to
come with me to a few doctor's appointments. They feel horrible
that you're so far away, but we all agree it's the best place for you.
It was reassuring to know they're going to be in my life from now
on, too.*

*The more pregnant I become, the more sentimental I am,
wanting to be surrounded by people I love and care about. I crave
it more than I crave hot chocolate with whipped cream! Madison
and Rex and my parents, and now your mother and sister, too.*

*Speaking of my dad—he's calling practice early tonight and
coming jogging with Rex and me around campus, which we've
been doing so I can stay in shape. Don't worry, my doctor said
exercise is the best thing for me. **wink** Anyway, Dad found out
I've been going and offered to come along. I don't know how far
he'll be able to jog without passing out, but he's going to try.*

*He has a newfound respect for Rex and as odd as it is, they've
become friends. I think he likes having another guy around the
house when we drop by.*

I'm counting down the days until your Christmas break.

Anabelle

"He's a total cuddler.
Every time I attempted
to pull away to get clothes on,
he'd pull me back in. I think
I'm going to be here awhile."

Anabelle

"Thanks for coming over tonight and fixing this leak. Madison and I really appreciate it. You know how I hate calling my dad—he hates that I'm living here, and I don't need him thinking it's such a dump he makes me move home."

Rex's feet stick out from under our sink, handing me the wrench he used to tighten the pipes in the kitchen before hauling himself out and to his feet.

He has a black smudge on his face and I reach out to wipe it away with my thumb.

"How did you get so messy? That's where we keep all the cleaning supplies—how can it be dirty under there?"

His fingers gently grab hold of my wrist, kissing at the sensitive skin there before releasing it. "Don't worry about the mess, Donnelly. The sink is fixed and you can run the faucet without it leaking."

Whoa. That's the first time Rex has shown any type of physical affection for me, always keeping a safe, respectable distance.

"The plumbing shouldn't give you any more problems, but if it does, I'm not leaving to head home for Christmas until tomorrow. You need me to do anything else, you call, okay? Change a light bulb or something? I'm your guy."

I laugh. "That we can do ourselves. Normally I would have tightened that bolt, too, but with this bump getting bigger, I wasn't taking any chances under the sink. I probably would have had to call the fire department to have them come save me."

"You're so fucking cute pregnant." Gunderson surveys me while running the water, scrubbing his hands clean.

"You think so?" My long, dark hair is shiny from the prenatal vitamins, thick and lush, falling over my breasts in silky waves. Skin? Flawless.

"Yes, Anabelle." He glances at me, absentmindedly wiping his hands dry on a towel. "You're definitely one of those women who can pull off the sexy *preggo* look."

Women.

Not *girl*. Not *chick*.

He sees me as a *woman*.

It's been ages since anyone has told me I look sexy or complimented me on my appearance, and I miss it. It feels wonderful.

"Hey, Anabelle?"

I glance up at Rex, who's leaning against my kitchen counter in jeans and an Iowa wrestling hoodie, head cocked to the side, looking young and hopeful. Adorkable, if I'm being honest.

"Yeah?"

"Have you ever thought about, you know...*me*."

"You? I think about you all the time, you goof."

His head shakes. "No, Anabelle, have you thought about what it would be like *being* with me?"

"Why? Have you thought about what it would be like to be with me?"

His big, brown eyes are intense. Sweet. "*All* the time."

All the time? How did I not know that?

"I don't know. I haven't thought much about relationships lately. Truthfully, who would want to be with me, Rex? I'm not exactly a *catch* at the moment."

I'm roughly six months pregnant and getting bigger every day. My hormones are out of whack and I cry all the time. Sure, my hair and skin look amazing, and I haven't gained much pregnancy weight, but...

He straightens to his full height, inching toward me, reaching for my hands.

"I consider you a catch, Anabelle Donnelly. You and your neon pink poster board were probably the best thing that happened to me this year. Without you, I'd be acting like a dumbass somewhere, wasting my fucking education."

Oh God, he is too, too sweet.

"You *can* do better than me, Rex," I chastise quietly, letting him lace our fingers. "And your mother would drop dead from a heart attack if you started dating me."

I would know because I've *met* his mother. She's one of those high-maintenance suburban housewife socialites with regular Botox injections and pouting lips. She loves me as his friend but would have a conniption fit if we were romantically involved.

He shrugs. "Maybe she would, maybe she wouldn't."

"Rex…"

"Will you at least let me kiss you before I go?"

Yes. Yes, I'll let him kiss me. I'm single and lonely, and the father of my child hasn't made any declarations. And I'm curious.

I tip my chin up as his hands slide along my shoulders and up my neck, cupping my face as Elliot has done dozens of times in the past. God, the contact feels good.

His lips are timid, like butterfly kisses, soft and gentle and exploratory, gradually gaining confidence. He kisses me tenderly and I'm curious enough to open my mouth, to let his tongue slip inside.

Our breaths mingle. Tongues roll.

He tastes good, like gum and the cologne I bought for his birthday to replace the terrible scent he always wore before.

The kiss doesn't last long, but it's nice.

Definitely *nice.*

My toes aren't curling inside my socks like they did with Elliot, but as far as first kisses go, I've had worse, with guys who didn't care about me like Gunderson does.

Still, is nice enough?

As scared as I am to be alone, is it fair to give Rex hope? I nibble my bottom lip, thinking.

"I never thought I would actually get the chance to kiss you— never in a million fucking years."

"Why?"

"Because you're…you."

"What does that mean?"

"Well, for one, you're Coach Donnelly's daughter. He fired me and hated my guts, like, forever. Two, that stupid, fucking bet. Three, you're beautiful and smart and should know better than to be friends with someone like me."

I place a hand on his shoulder, squeezing it tenderly.

"You're more than dumb pranks and tasteless jokes. That's why I'm friends with you, Rex. I see the good in you. You're one of my best friends."

"I can live with that assessment." He pauses, hand blazing a trail down my arm. "Can I ask you something?"

"Sure."

"Are you waiting for Elliot?"

I avoid his inquisitive gaze. "Define *wait*."

"Anabelle, you know he's not coming back, right?" He asks quietly enough that my shoulders sag.

Why is he saying this? I don't need him pointing out the obvious—it makes me feel like shit. "I know he's not coming back, I'm not a fool. I watched him leave—twice."

Backing away, he crosses his arms and leans back against the counter. "You have to be realistic. He is *gone*. He's moved on with his life. You video chat and email for Christ's sake—what kind of a relationship is that? What kind of involvement do you want for the baby? An absentee dad or one that's right here? I'm right fucking here, Anabelle."

"Rex, don't do this now." *Please don't*, I silently beg.

I'm already so confused. Rex is baring his soul when mine isn't nearly ready for him, not just yet.

"I'm sorry, Anabelle. That's how I feel, and I've done a lot of growing up this past semester. I just wanted you to acknowledge that, and maybe, when you're ready, give me a chance. I'm going to be an engineer," he boasts.

I close the distance between us, raising my palm to his cheek, stroking it softly. "You are so good to me, and I haven't done anything to deserve it."

"Are you kidding me? You're the best friend I have right now—everyone else abandoned me when I fucked up. You're the only one who has my back, and now I have yours."

"God, you're so…"

"Marvelous?" He flashes me a cocky grin. "I know."

I pat his face. "The ego on you."

"It gets me through the day, Donnelly. Days like this where I pour my heart out and it gets stomped on."

My hands fly to my hips now, affronted. "I am not stomping on your heart, you brat!"

"But you're never going to fall in love with me, are you?"

"I don't…" *I don't think so.* "I don't know."

We stare each other down, the kitchen silent, clock above the window ticking loudly. *Tick, tock. Tick, tock.*

Then, from the front of the house, a knock on the door. Three short raps, followed by more deafening silence.

"Guess that's my cue to leave." Rex gathers the black winter parka draped over one of my kitchen chairs, sliding his arms into the sleeves. Zips it up the front.

I flirtatiously bump him with my hip. "I'll walk you out."

"Let me go first. It's dark out, you shouldn't be answering the door. You have no peephole." Passing the couch on his way to the entryway, he snatches a blanket from the back, unfolding it. Drapes it across my shoulders. "Here, wrap up. It's cold out."

My heart leaps at his gesture, wishing the circumstances were different, wishing my heart wasn't aching for someone hundreds of miles away.

"Thank you."

We're still grinning at each other like fools when Rex unlocks and pulls open my front door, smiles dropping when we both catch an eyeful of the man standing on my front stoop.

My breath catches.

"Elliot?"

Those soulful eyes I love so much gaze up at mine, flickering between Rex and me, flashing a mix of curiosity and anger. Jealousy.

"Well, well, well, look who decided to show up." Rex's laugh is slightly maniacal and my brows shoot up, surprised. "Hey, baby daddy. Long time no see."

"Rex!" I gasp, mortified and uncomfortable. "*Stop.*"

Elliot shifts on his heels. "It's okay, Anabelle. He's right."

"Damn right I am." Rex's nostrils flare.

I drag my gaze off my friend, fixating on the guy I haven't laid eyes on in far too long. "Elliot, what are you doing here?"

"Yeah, Elliot," Rex parrots, "what are you doing here?"

"Please, Rex." I turn to face him, laying my palms in the middle of his chest, over his puffy winter coat. "Maybe it's best if you left. I can handle this on my own."

I can't describe the change in his expression—couldn't if I tried—and I want to beg him to forgive me for sending him away when he's just trying to protect me from myself, from getting hurt when it's obviously inevitable.

Hurt and devastation. Love and devotion.

That's what I see reflected in Gunderson's half-hooded eyes as he looks down at me, debating.

"Fine." His lips purse. He leans in and presses a kiss to my cheek, speaking low into my ear. "Text if you want me to come back."

"I will."

"Night, Anabelle." He yanks a knit cap out of his pockets, pulling it down on his head. Snarls at Elliot, bumping his broad shoulder as he passes, stepping down onto the sidewalk. "Deuces, douchebag."

I give him an embarrassed, feeble wave. "Bye."

He walks backward down the sidewalk, facing the house, calling out to me in the frigid cold. "I'll be back in two weeks. I'll message you while I'm gone."

Another wave. "Drive safe."

It's freezing and our warm breaths mingle with the frigid air, tension-filled puffs wafting into the night. I can't stop my chest from rising and falling, breathing hard from the shock of seeing Elliot on the concrete steps of the house.

I drag my eyes off the road, off the taillights of Rex Gunderson's retreating vehicle to Elliot's, afraid of what I'll see there.

"I know it's not my place to ask, but what the hell was *that*?"

He's right—it really is not his place. Not anymore, not after he left without any declarations or commitments toward me.

"That was Rex." I'm deliberately being obtuse.

"Clearly." He pauses, tone laced with irritation. "What was he doing here?"

"We're just friends."

"*Just* friends. You expect me to buy that bullshit?"

I throw my hands up, too tired to argue, too excited to see him. He's big and strapping and finally—FINALLY—standing on my doorstep, just as I've dreamed about hundreds of times.

"Elliot, I'm really glad to see you, but if all you want to do is argue about my friendship with Gunderson, then you've come to the wrong place." I swallow the lump in my throat before tears threaten to spill. "Besides, I thought you'd go home to your parents when you came back."

"No. I came straight here." He swallows a lump, too. "This was where I wanted to be."

At his feet sit two huge duffel bags I don't recognize, large, full duffels that look nothing like overnight bags. They're big, overstuffed, made for travel.

"What is all this? You're only home for a few weeks, this seems…excessive."

"I left school, Anabelle. I packed up my shit and left."

"What do you mean?" I swear my breath hitches, breathlessly anticipating what he's about to say. Hopeful but wary. Excited but cautious. Guilty.

"I quit. Done. Dropped out—whatever words you want to assign to it. I withdrew."

"Elliot, we talked about this." I cannot keep the nerves out of my voice. Why would he drop out of school and come back to Iowa when he hates it here? When he was so sure Michigan was the best school for him? For his future?

"I wanted to Anabelle. This has been eating me up inside. You have no fucking idea—none. I missed you like crazy before I even moved there, and there was no fucking way I was going to stay in Michigan knowing you're here doing this pregnancy thing on your own. No fucking way."

"I don't know what to say."

"Can I come in?" He bounces on the balls of his feet, blowing on his hands though they're covered with big, black mittens. "It's cold as balls out here."

Elliot

A
s soon as Anabelle closes the door behind me, drops the blanket wrapped around her shoulders, and I see that baby bump...

I drop to my knees, coming face to face with her pregnant belly. Place my hands on either side of it, smoothing my palms over the stretched cotton of her long-sleeved navy T-shirt.

"Oh my God, look at you." I don't know what to say next; the sight of her isn't what I was expecting. This Anabelle is ethereal and gorgeous—not that she wasn't before—and glowing. Everything about her is calming and serene, and it's no wonder Rex Gunderson is sniffing around.

She's never looked more beautiful than she does now.

She's sent me photos of herself and I follow her on Instagram, but photographs and the reality of it are two completely different things.

It's surreal.

It's beautiful.

"I'm huge." She reddens, dipping her face to hide the blush creeping across her cheeks and down her neck. "It's embarrassing going to class now if you want to know the truth."

I rise to my feet.

"My mom said you looked great." She wasn't kidding. "She gushes about you—my sisters call you Baby Mama, but it's just to give me shit about not being married and having a kid out of wedlock."

"I love your sisters."

"They're pretty fucking cool." And now that they've officially met the girl I knocked up, have discovered Anabelle is not a grasping, irresponsible, sleazy party girl, they're actually pretty damn excited to have a new niece or nephew. *Thank fucking God* because my sisters can be assholes when they're not happy or don't like someone. Together, when presenting a united front, they have made grown men cry; I can't imagine what they'd do with a female they loathed, especially one who made me a father at the age of twenty-two.

"Is your roommate home?"

"No, she went home. She actually packed up and is coming back for her boxes when she gets back from break."

Good.

"What do you mean, good?"

"Shit—did I say that out loud?"

She laughs, and it's the first time I've heard the sound since one of our FaceTime chats—and we haven't done one of those in weeks.

"Why would you say that?"

"Because we're going to need that room."

"Elliot…" Her pale hands cover the expanse of her stomach, delicate fingers spanning over her belly button protectively.

"I know what you're thinking—you don't want to get your hopes up. I've left twice already. I get that, okay? I understand why you're scared, but I'm not going anywhere this time, and if you want, I'll sleep in your old room until you're comfortable having me back—or forever, I don't care. I just want to be here for you."

"How? You need to be in school."

"After I left last time and told my parents, the three of us talked. I don't know if my mom told you, but we worked out a plan. I applied here, just in case—and just got my acceptance. One semester at Michigan in the bag. Packed my shit. Kissed my loud neighbor's ass goodbye, and here I am."

"Here."

"Here to stay. For good."

Her twinkly little laugh cannot disguise her nerves. "God Elliot, how much have I cost you in furniture in the past year?"

"It doesn't matter. What matters is that I'm here—I'm just sorry it took so long."

"I wouldn't have blamed you for not coming back—I really wouldn't have. I understand why you need Michigan, and I can't ask you to give up the best program for kinesiology for me. I can't and won't."

My head goes back and forth, and I choose my words carefully.

"You know…every night I was alone in the miserable apartment. Every night I came home and sat there alone. Ate alone. Did homework alone. Ran alone. It sucked. And do you know why?"

She shakes her head no, feebly, eyes wide.

"Yes, you do. Even surrounded by people, I was alone because I wasn't with you. I would haven't lasted a year, with or without this baby, Anabelle. I would have been back for you regardless."

"Stop it." Her nose sniffs.

"Why?"

"Because you're going to make me cry."

"Anabelle. I don't know what to say to you. If you—" I gulp. "If you want me to step aside so you can see other people, I'll do that because I love you. I want you to be happy and I've put you through enough already this year, but I also want you to know I want to try."

"Elliot—"

"Would you let me finish? I've had almost seven hours in the car with nothing to do but think this through, think about you and this baby. It's a fucking miracle I was able to finish this last semester, Anabelle. I have no idea how to be a dad, but mine is pretty fucking great, and so is yours—that right there is an automatic win for us."

I babble on, driven by nerves. "I'm excited. I want to barf sometimes, but who doesn't? I'm scared shitless, but so are you, and we're old enough to make this work."

She's worrying her bottom lip, nibbling, and I'm not sure if that's good or bad, so I do the only thing I can do. I ask.

"I'm freaking the fuck out, Anabelle. Would you please say something?" You could cut the thick silence in the room with a dull knife.

"Rex is…just my friend."

Seriously? She's going to start the conversation by bringing that douche canoe into it? I bristle.

"He is just my friend and he's been amazing. I love him, and it's important you know that because he's not going anywhere. He's rubbed my back and kept me company, and shoveled my sidewalk in the freezing cold. Rex has done all the things a good friend does to be supportive."

"Is he in love with you?"

Anabelle bites her lip again. Nods. "I think he might be."

Unrequited love sucks dick.

I've never felt it, never been in it, but I imagine loving someone who doesn't love me back would gut me. Poor bastard.

"Did he say as much?"

"No, but he kissed me."

"When?"

Why am I asking her these questions when the answer will only serve to piss me off? Glutton for punishment.

"Tonight. Before you got here."

"And you let him?" My voice raises a notch, heart racing.

"I did."

"And?" The suspense is killing me.

"It was nice."

It was nice?

What the hell does that mean? I'm not sure what to do with that information or how to react, so I stand there, gazing down at her, baffled. Patient but confused as shit.

Then, "You're just friends, but the kiss was nice?"

"Yes."

Sort of how she and I were "just friends," but the sex was fantastic? We were "just friends," but are having a baby?

Shit.

"He knows he's not the one for me."

"Does he though?"

"Yes. We talk about you all the time."

Oh, awesome! I can imagine how those conversations go if we're basing it on his behavior on the porch. He called me a douche and "baby daddy", and neither came out his mouth sounding like compliments.

I roll my eyes. "He didn't seem thrilled to see me."

"No, he wasn't, but put yourself in his shoes. We have a class together, we have fun together, and he didn't judge me when he found out I was pregnant—in fact, he loves babies. Weird, right?"

Yeah. Weird.

I scowl.

"He's introduced me to his parents and really cares, Elliot. He's changed in the past few months. I think getting kicked off the team was the best thing that's happened to him, strange as that sounds."

"Okay, can we please stop talking about Rex Gunderson and start talking about us?"

I'm so irritated.

"But don't you see? He's a part of my life and he'll have to be part of yours too if we're going to make this work, if we're going to be together. That's what you want, right? To be together?"

Yes. "Hell yes."

"Then you'll figure out a way to tolerate each other, for my sake. I'm not abandoning a friend because the two of you can't act mature. Suck it up."

Jealousy is a powerful sentiment, elevated when the situation is already fucked up.

"That's something a mom would say," I murmur.

Anabelle grins, beaming. "Is it?"

"Yeah." I glance down two overflowing bags dumped by the door. "You're going to be an awesome mom, Anabelle. I'm sorry it's sooner than you planned."

I can't meet her eyes, can't do anything but stare at that stomach, nestled beneath that navy cotton T-shirt, bump proudly on display. Long hair down, falling around her left shoulder, thick and shiny.

My eyes drift to her breasts.

Her narrow waist, despite the expanding bump, and I would wager if she turned around, I wouldn't be able to tell she was pregnant.

She's checking me out, too, gaze skimming across my broad shoulders like she's done a hundred times before, but this feels different.

"The semester has been good to you. You look good."

"Do I? I feel like shit."

"Do you?"

"Yes. I've done nothing but worry since I went back to Michigan. I didn't know what you'd say when you saw me tonight, didn't know if you'd tell me to go fuck myself or let me through the door. It's been horrible."

I wasn't kidding when I said I almost threw up.

I had to stop a few times en route and dry heave out my driver's side window. The closer I got to the house, the tighter the knots in my stomach pulled, a jumbled fucking mess.

"I will admit, when I opened the door tonight, it was like seeing a ghost."

"You did look pretty pale."

"I'm always pale," she jokes.

And laughs, smiling, so big and wide it makes my fucking heart...race.

Jump. Leap. Skip.

"Anabelle."

A grin. "Elliot."

"I *love* you."

Say you love me, too. Say it so my palms stop sweating and my heart stops palpitating, and I can catch my breath. Put me out of my goddamn misery, because I've been miserable the past few weeks without you.

Say it, I silently plead.

Please.

Finally, she does.

"I...I think I've loved you since you brought me home and I looked up from your bed and saw you standing in the doorway—that had to have been the moment. I was embarrassed, but I also knew you had a beautiful soul, and I looked like such shit."

"You didn't look like shit—you looked gorgeous."

She rolls her big blue eyes. "You're just saying that now because you love me."

Maybe, or maybe she was thrown in my damn path so many goddamn times for a reason, which sounds crazy, but...

There it is.

The story of us.

"Do you want to take off your coat?" She interrupts my musing and I glance down at my puffy coat, brows raised. I hadn't realized I was wearing my jacket because I was engrossed by one thing. Her.

"You're okay with me staying?"

"I've been waiting to hear you say that for months, Elliot. Months."

"Then I'm staying."

"Say that again." Her sweet voice is a whisper.

"I'm staying," I whisper back, reaching for her. "I love you and we are *doing* this."

"We're really doing this."

Elliot

Nine months later

Once upon a time, I would have thought I was suffering a loss—the loss of my youth and social life and career. I didn't realize how much I would be gaining—how could I possibly have? I was young and foolish and vulnerable after leaving Iowa, leaving Anabelle. I didn't leave because I wanted to, but because that was my plan.

Education, career, social life—in that order.

In that order, always sticking to the plan.

But if everything went according to plan, Rex Gunderson wouldn't be prancing around an engagement party, holding *my* daughter, and he sure as shit wouldn't—

"I still cannot *believe* Gunderson is the godfather of my freaking child."

Next to me on the lawn, Anabelle smacks my arm, a gentle warning. "Would you stop complaining so loud, someone will hear you." To mollify me, she grabs my hand, lacing our fingers together. "He loves the baby almost as much as we do."

"I know," I grumble. "And it's really fucking annoying."

I had to draw the line when Anabelle wanted to use Regina as Lilly's middle name. Rex. Reginald. Regina.

No.

Hell fucking *no*.

My lip curls at the thought, earning me another nudge.

"Babe, wipe that disgusted look off your face! This is a happy occasion—and look how cute they are!"

Rex the Moron, AKA my baby's godfather, is holding my daughter, parading her around the party like *The Lion King*, stopping every time a hot girl croons in their direction. "He's using Lilly to pick up women. How are you okay with this?"

My girlfriend snorts. "Pfft, it's harmless, and you have to admit, it's working. He already has a date for Saturday night."

She says that like it's a good thing.

"Would you please go take the baby from him? She's not a pimp."

Anabelle gives me a sidelong glance. "Did you just compare our precious daughter to a street pimp?"

"Babies and puppies are the best marketing ploys. He obviously knows this." I nod absentmindedly, staring off toward Gunderson and Lilly. "Give it a few weeks, he'll find a way to get ahold of a puppy, too."

"Probably." Anabelle shrugs with a laugh. "But he is an amazing babysitter."

"No comment."

But the little fucker is. I hate acknowledging it, but it's true. Gunderson is always there when we need him, especially if I can't be home to help. Like a slowly thawing iceberg, I'm warming up to him.

Slowly.

Like the berg that dropped the Titanic—really, really fucking slowly.

"Just look how cute she is in her pretty little dress."

She *does* look cute, and Lilly is a tiny, pink spitting-image replica of *me*, which pisses Rex off, so I guess that makes things even between him and I.

"I should go grab her anyway. I bet she's getting hungry."

Eye roll from Anabelle. "Lilly is *not* hungry—I fed her right before we got here."

"But she's sucking on his shirt sleeve." Even I know that's a stretch.

"Would you relax? She's teething. Stop dreaming up reasons to take her away from Rex."

"But…"

Anabelle slides up to me, stepping into my arms, pulling them around her waist. My hands slide over her hips, and I stand ramrod straight, letting her tease me.

"Know what would make you less crabby?"

"What?" My ears perk up.

"If we *watch television* tonight."

"Television?" We're always watching TV, how does that make—

Oohhhhh. Now I get it. *Television* television.

Sex.

"How soon can we leave?"

She kisses the tip of my nose. "We can't. Zeke and Violet haven't gotten here yet."

"So?" I pout. "We've been decorating for this party an entire three days. I did my time."

"Elliot, we can't leave their engagement party before they arrive because you're horny and can't wait to get laid!"

"Why? Zeke won't give a shit."

"Trust me, he'll notice if you're not here."

Dammit, she's right. He will notice. That dude notices *everything*. He might be broody and quiet, but my old roommate is freakishly observant.

And this is his engagement party, the one *he* is throwing for his fiancée, Violet. He enlisted our help, and we've been planning for the past few months so he could surprise her.

Romantic bastard.

He makes us all look bad.

"If you think this party is elaborate, just wait until their wedding," Anabelle gushes. "He told me he wants her to have the best of everything."

"Yeah, yeah. It's nauseating."

"You talk so smart." She kisses the underside of my chin. "But you'd do the same thing for me."

I would.

I would give her the world if I could.

And I'm going to spend the rest of my life protecting my girls from douchebags, or die trying.

"Now can we go grab Lilly?"

Anabelle glances over at our group of friends, grinning from ear to ear. Rex holds Lilly in her frilly party dress, and they're dancing to the music the small band is playing, spinning in little circles. Both of them giggle as everyone coos and awws at the cute baby.

And Rex.

For fuck's sake.

Fortunately, my girlfriend is immune to his antics. "You want to go dance with your daughter, don't you?"

"Yes," I admit begrudgingly.

"Then why are we still standing here? Let's go get her."

And we do, together. Hand in hand, we cross the yard, my long stride confident as I scoop Lilly out of Gunderson's arms.

Planting a kiss on her rosy cheeks, I swing her around. Pull Anabelle in by the waist and kiss her, too.

"I love you," I croon into her ear, right below the spot that drives her crazy for me.

I love her. When we're done with school, I'm going to propose and make her my wife.

And I can't fucking wait.

Acknowledgements

A re these the final hours?

I *think* so. Yes **nods firmly**

It takes a village to write a novel; lots of hard work and pounding away at the keyboard. The hours I spend at Starbucks, toiling, are actually hours sacrificed away from my family. So I'd like to thank them first and foremost for being supportive (especially my sister, who keeps begging me to use her as research).

The crew at Starbucks.

My friends (they know who they are **wink, wink**)

The members of *Neys Little Liars*, for loving my books enough to join my group and listen to me ramble.

Thank you to my assistant, Christine Kuttnauer. My Beta readers, Laurie Darter, Aly Hyne and Sarah Sawyer, who I rely on for honest feedback. My publicist Dani Sanchez with Inkslinger, PR. My cover designer, Sarah Hansen, at Okay Creations, who always kills it... Elisabeth Rossman, for the marketing, and Gel Ytayz for my gorgeous graphics.

And to the people who make it all pretty:

My Editors, C Marie and Ellie McLove (is that even your name, Eelie?)—thank you for being patient; I *vow* never to be late again. The proofreader who polished, Jennifer VanWyk. Julie Titus at JT Formatting for making everything beautiful.

And last but not least: my agent Kimberly Brower, with Brower Literary Agency, for representing me with such class.

Now.

On to the next one....

Sara Ney is the USA Today Bestselling Author of the How to Date a Douchebag series, and is best known for her sexy, laugh-out-loud New Adult romances. Among her favorite vices, she includes: iced latte's, historical architecture and well-placed sarcasm. She lives colorfully, collects vintage books, art, loves flea markets, and fancies herself British.

For more information about Sara Ney and her books, visit:

Facebook
https://www.facebook.com/saraneyauthor/

Twitter
https://twitter.com/saraney

Website
http://www.authorsaraney.com/

Instagram
https://www.instagram.com/saraneyauthor/?hl=en

Books + Main
http://subscribepage.com/saraney

Subscribe to Sara's Newsletter
http://subscribepage.com/saraney

Facebook Reader Group: **Ney's Little Liars**
https://www.facebook.com/groups/1065756456778840/

Other Titles by Sara

The Kiss and Make Up Series

Kissing in Cars
He Kissed Me First
A Kiss Like This

#ThreeLittleLies Series

Things Liars Say
Things Liars Hide
Things Liars Fake

How to Date a Douchebag Series

The Studying Hours
The Failing Hours
The Learning Hours
The Coaching Hours

CPSIA information can be obtained
at www.ICGtesting.com
Printed in the USA
LVOW10s2111160218
566878LV00005B/525/P